ARTHUR MORRISON
MARTIN HEWITT
INVESTIGATOR

FLAME TREE

COLLECTABLE CRIME CLASSICS
Complete & Unabridged

FLAME TREE PUBLISHING
6 Melbray Mews, Fulham,
London SW6 3NS, United Kingdom
www.flametreepublishing.com

First published and copyright © 2020
Flame Tree Publishing Ltd

This edition is based on the original publication in parts 1894 by *Strand
Magazine* and as a novel by Ward, Lock & Bowden, Limited (London)

20 22 24 23 21
1 3 5 7 9 10 8 6 4 2

ISBN: 978-1-83964-154-1

Cover and pattern art was created by Flame Tree Studio.

Special thanks to Rosemary Herbert for the biography of Arthur Morrison

Judith John (Glossary) is a writer and editor specializing in literature
and history. A former secondary school English Language and Literature
teacher, she has subsequently worked as an editor on major educational
projects, including *English A: Literature* for the Pearson International
Baccalaureate series. Judith's major research interests include Romantic
and Gothic literature, and Renaissance drama.

A copy of the CIP data for this book is available
from the British Library.

Designed and created in the UK | Printed and bound in China

ARTHUR MORRISON
MARTIN HEWITT
INVESTIGATOR

With a new Glossary of
Crime, Mystery & Literary Terms
by Judith John

FLAME
TREE

COLLECTABLE
CRIME CLASSICS
Complete & Unabridged

CONTENTS

ARTHUR MORRISON
MARTIN HEWITT
INVESTIGATOR

I. THE LENTON
CROFT ROBBERIES

THOSE WHO RETAIN any memory of the great law cases of fifteen or twenty years back will remember, at least, the title of that extraordinary will case, "Bartley *v.* Bartley and others," which occupied the Probate Court for some weeks on end, and caused an amount of public interest rarely accorded to any but the cases considered in the other division of the same court. The case itself was noted for the large quantity of remarkable and unusual evidence presented by the plaintiff's side—evidence that took the other party completely by surprise, and overthrew their case like a house of cards. The affair will, perhaps, be more readily recalled as the occasion of the sudden rise to eminence in their profession of Messrs. Crellan, Hunt & Crellan, solicitors for the plaintiff—a result due entirely to the wonderful ability shown in this case of building up, apparently out of nothing, a smashing weight of irresistible evidence. That the firm has since maintained—indeed enhanced—the position it then won for itself need scarcely be said here; its name is familiar to everybody. But there are not many of the outside public who know that the credit of the whole performance was primarily due to a young clerk in the employ of Messrs. Crellan, who had been given charge of the seemingly desperate task of collecting evidence in the case.

This Mr. Martin Hewitt had, however, full credit and reward for his exploit from his firm and from their client, and more than one other firm of lawyers engaged in contentious work made good offers to entice Hewitt to change his employers. Instead of this, however, he determined to work independently for the future, having conceived the idea of making a regular business of doing, on behalf of such clients as might retain him, similar work to that he had just done with such conspicuous success for Messrs. Crellan, Hunt & Crellan. This was the beginning of the private detective business of Martin Hewitt, and his action at that time has been completely justified by the brilliant professional successes he has since achieved.

His business has always been conducted in the most private manner, and he has always declined the help of professional assistants, preferring to carry out himself such of the many investigations offered him as he could manage. He has always maintained that he has never lost by this policy, since the chance of his refusing a case begets competition for his services, and his fees rise by a natural process. At the same time, no man could know better how to employ casual assistance at the right time.

Some curiosity has been expressed as to Mr. Martin Hewitt's system, and, as he himself always consistently maintains that he has no system beyond a judicious use of ordinary faculties, I intend setting forth in detail a few of the more interesting of his cases in order that the public may judge for itself if I am right in estimating Mr. Hewitt's "ordinary faculties" as faculties very extraordinary indeed. He is not a man who has made many friendships (this, probably, for professional reasons), notwithstanding his genial and companionable manners. I myself first made his acquaintance as a result of an accident resulting in a fire at the old house in which Hewitt's office was situated, and in an upper floor of which I occupied bachelor chambers. I was able to help in saving a quantity of extremely important papers relating to his business, and, while repairs were being made, allowed him to lock them in an old wall-safe in one of my rooms which the fire had scarcely damaged.

The acquaintance thus begun has lasted many years, and has become a rather close friendship. I have even accompanied Hewitt on some of his expeditions, and, in a humble way, helped him. Such of the cases, however, as I personally saw nothing of I have put into narrative form from the particulars given me.

"I consider you, Brett," he said, addressing me, "the most remarkable journalist alive. Not because you're particularly clever, you know, because, between ourselves, I hope you'll admit you're not; but because you have known something of me and my doings for some years, and have never yet been guilty of giving away any of my little business secrets you may have become acquainted with. I'm afraid you're not so enterprising a journalist as some, Brett. But now, since you ask, you shall write something—if you think it worth while."

This he said, as he said most things, with a cheery, chaffing good-nature that would have been, perhaps, surprising to a stranger who thought of him only as a grim and mysterious discoverer of secrets and crimes.

Indeed, the man had always as little of the aspect of the conventional detective as may be imagined. Nobody could appear more cordial or less observant in manner, although there was to be seen a certain sharpness of the eye—which might, after all, only be the twinkle of good humor.

I *did* think it worth while to write something of Martin Hewitt's investigations, and a description of one of his adventures follows.

At the head of the first flight of a dingy staircase leading up from an ever-open portal in a street by the Strand stood a door, the dusty ground-glass upper panel of which carried in its center the single word "Hewitt," while at its right-hand lower corner, in smaller letters, "Clerk's Office" appeared. On a morning when the clerks in the ground-floor offices had barely hung up their hats, a short, well-dressed young man, wearing spectacles, hastening to open the dusty door, ran into the arms of another man who suddenly issued from it.

"I beg pardon," the first said. "Is this Hewitt's Detective Agency Office?"

"Yes, I believe you will find it so," the other replied. He was a stoutish, clean-shaven man, of middle height, and of a cheerful, round countenance. "You'd better speak to the clerk."

In the little outer office the visitor was met by a sharp lad with inky fingers, who presented him with a pen and a printed slip. The printed slip having been filled with the visitor's name and present business, and conveyed through an inner door, the lad reappeared with an invitation to the private office. There, behind a writing-table, sat the stoutish man himself, who had only just advised an appeal to the clerk.

"Good-morning, Mr. Lloyd—Mr. Vernon Lloyd," he said, affably, looking again at the slip. "You'll excuse my care to start even with my visitors—I must, you know. You come from Sir James Norris, I see."

"Yes; I am his secretary. I have only to ask you to go straight to Lenton Croft at once, if you can, on very important business. Sir James would have wired, but had not your precise address. Can you go by the next train? Eleven-thirty is the first available from Paddington."

"Quite possibly. Do you know any thing of the business?"

"It is a case of a robbery in the house, or, rather, I fancy, of several robberies. Jewelry has been stolen from rooms occupied by visitors to the Croft. The first case occurred some months ago—nearly a year ago, in fact. Last night there was another. But I think you had better get the details on the spot. Sir James has told me to telegraph if you are coming, so that he may meet you himself at the station; and I must hurry, as his drive to the station will be rather a long one. Then I take it you will go, Mr. Hewitt? Twyford is the station."

"Yes, I shall come, and by the 11.30. Are you going by that train yourself?"

"No, I have several things to attend to now I am in town. Good-morning; I shall wire at once."

Mr. Martin Hewitt locked the drawer of his table and sent his clerk for a cab.

At Twyford Station Sir James Norris was waiting with a dog-cart. Sir James was a tall, florid man of fifty or thereabout, known away from home as something of a county historian, and nearer his own parts as a great supporter of the hunt, and a gentleman much troubled with poachers. As soon as he and Hewitt had found one another the baronet hurried the detective into his dog-cart. "We've something over seven miles to drive," he said, "and I can tell you all about this wretched business as we go. That is why I came for you myself, and alone."

Hewitt nodded.

"I have sent for you, as Lloyd probably told you, because of a robbery at my place last evening. It appears, as far as I can guess, to be one of three by the same hand, or by the same gang. Late yesterday afternoon—"

"Pardon me, Sir James," Hewitt interrupted, "but I think I must ask you to begin at the first robbery and tell me the whole tale in proper order. It makes things clearer, and sets them in their proper shape."

"Very well! Eleven months ago, or thereabout, I had rather a large party of visitors, and among them Colonel Heath and Mrs. Heath—the lady being a relative of my own late wife. Colonel Heath has not been long retired, you know—used to be political resident in an Indian native state. Mrs. Heath had rather a good stock of jewelry of one sort and another, about the most valuable piece being a bracelet set with a particularly fine pearl—quite an exceptional pearl, in fact—that had been one of a heap of presents from the maharajah of his state when Heath left India.

"It was a very noticeable bracelet, the gold setting being a mere feather-weight piece of native filigree work—almost too fragile to trust on the wrist—and the pearl being, as I have said, of a size and quality not often seen. Well, Heath and his wife arrived late one evening, and after lunch the following day, most of the men being off by themselves—shooting, I think—my daughter, my sister (who is very often down here), and Mrs. Heath took it into their heads to go walking—fern-hunting, and so on. My sister was rather long dressing, and, while they waited, my daughter went into Mrs. Heath's room, where Mrs. Heath turned over all her treasures to show her, as women do, you know. When my sister was at last ready, they came straight away, leaving the things littering about the room rather than stay longer to pack them up. The bracelet, with other things, was on the dressing-table then."

"One moment. As to the door?"

"They locked it. As they came away my daughter suggested turning the key, as we had one or two new servants about."

"And the window?"

"That they left open, as I was going to tell you. Well, they went on their walk and came back, with Lloyd (whom they had met somewhere) carrying their ferns for them. It was dusk and almost dinner-time. Mrs. Heath went straight to her room, and—the bracelet was gone."

"Was the room disturbed?"

"Not a bit. Everything was precisely where it had been left, except the bracelet. The door hadn't been tampered with, but of course the window was open, as I have told you."

"You called the police, of course?"

"Yes, and had a man from Scotland Yard down in the morning. He seemed a pretty smart fellow, and the first thing he noticed on the dressing-table, within an inch or two of where the bracelet had been, was a match, which had been lit and thrown down. Now nobody about the house had had occasion to use a match in that room that day, and, if they had, certainly wouldn't have thrown it on the cover of the dressing-table. So that, presuming the thief to have used that match, the robbery must have been committed when the room was getting dark—immediately before Mrs. Heath returned, in fact. The thief had evidently struck the match, passed it hurriedly over the various trinkets lying about, and taken the most valuable."

"Nothing else was even moved?"

"Nothing at all. Then the thief must have escaped by the window, although it was not quite clear how. The walking party approached the house with a full view of the window, but saw nothing, although the robbery must have been actually taking place a moment or two before they turned up.

"There was no water-pipe within any practicable distance of the window, but a ladder usually kept in the stable-yard was found lying along the edge of the lawn. The gardener explained, however, that he had put the ladder there after using it himself early in the afternoon."

"Of course it might easily have been used again after that and put back."

"Just what the Scotland Yard man said. He was pretty sharp, too, on the gardener, but very soon decided that he knew nothing of it. No stranger had been seen in the neighborhood, nor had passed the lodge gates. Besides, as the detective said, it scarcely seemed the work of a stranger. A stranger could scarcely have known enough to go straight to the room where a lady—only arrived the day before—had left a valuable jewel, and away again without being seen. So all the people about the house were suspected in turn. The servants offered, in a body, to have their boxes searched, and this was done; everything was turned over, from the butler's to the new kitchen-maid's. I don't know that I should have had this carried quite so far if I had been the loser myself, but it was my guest, and I was in such a horrible position. Well, there's little more to be said about that, unfortunately. Nothing came of it all, and the thing's as great a mystery now as ever. I believe the Scotland Yard man got as far as suspecting *me* before he gave it up altogether, but give it up he did in the end. I think that's all I know about the first robbery. Is it clear?"

"Oh, yes; I shall probably want to ask a few questions when I have seen the place, but they can wait. What next?"

"Well," Sir James pursued, "the next was a very trumpery affair, that I should have forgotten all about, probably, if it hadn't been for one circumstance. Even now I hardly think it could have been the work of the same hand. Four months or thereabout after Mrs. Heath's disaster—in February of this year, in fact—Mrs. Armitage, a young widow, who had been a school-fellow of my daughter's, stayed with us for a week or so. The girls don't trouble about the London season, you know, and I have no town house, so they were glad to have their old friend here for a little in the dull time. Mrs. Armitage is a very active young lady, and was scarcely in the house half an hour before she arranged a drive in a pony-cart with Eva—my daughter—to look up old people in the village that she used to know before she was married. So they set off in the afternoon, and made such a round of it that they were late for dinner. Mrs. Armitage had a small plain gold brooch—not at all valuable, you know; two or three pounds, I suppose—which she used to pin up a cloak or anything of that sort. Before she went out she stuck this in the pin-cushion on her dressing-table, and left a ring—rather a good one, I believe—lying close by."

"This," asked Hewitt, "was not in the room that Mrs. Heath had occupied, I take it?"

"No; this was in another part of the building. Well, the brooch went—taken, evidently, by some one in a deuce of a hurry, for, when Mrs. Armitage got back to her room, there was the pin-cushion with a little tear in it, where the brooch had been simply snatched off. But the curious thing was that the ring—worth a dozen of the brooch—was left where it had been put. Mrs. Armitage didn't remember whether or not she had locked the door herself, although she found it locked when she returned; but my niece, who was indoors all the time, went and tried it once—because she remembered that a gas-fitter was at work on the landing near by—and found it safely locked. The gas-fitter, whom we didn't know at the time, but who since seems to be quite an honest fellow, was ready to swear that nobody but my niece had been to the door while he was in sight of it—which was almost all the time. As to the window, the sash-line had broken that very morning, and Mrs. Armitage had propped open the bottom half about eight or ten inches with a brush; and, when she returned, that brush, sash, and all were exactly as she had left them. Now I scarcely need tell *you* what an awkward job it must have been for anybody to get noiselessly in at that unsupported window; and how unlikely he would have been to replace it, with the brush, exactly as he found it."

"Just so. I suppose the brooch, was really gone? I mean, there was no chance of Mrs. Armitage having mislaid it?"

"Oh, none at all! There was a most careful search."

"Then, as to getting in at the window, would it have been easy?"

"Well, yes," Sir James replied; "yes, perhaps it would. It was a first-floor window, and it looks over the roof and skylight of the billiard-room. I built the billiard-room myself—built it out from a smoking-room just at this corner. It would be easy enough to get at the window from the billiard-room roof. But, then," he added, "that couldn't have been the way. Somebody or other was in the billiard-room the whole time, and nobody could have got over the roof (which is nearly all skylight) without being seen and heard. I was there myself for an hour or two, taking a little practice."

"Well, was anything done?"

"Strict inquiry was made among the servants, of course, but nothing came of it. It was such a small matter that Mrs. Armitage wouldn't hear of my calling in the police or anything of that sort, although I felt pretty certain that there must be a dishonest servant about somewhere. A servant might take a plain brooch, you know, who would feel afraid of a valuable ring, the loss of which would be made a greater matter of."

"Well, yes, perhaps so, in the case of an inexperienced thief, who also would be likely to snatch up whatever she took in a hurry. But I'm doubtful. What made you connect these two robberies together?"

"Nothing whatever—for some months. They seemed quite of a different sort. But scarcely more than a month ago I met Mrs. Armitage at Brighton, and we talked, among other things, of the previous robbery—that of Mrs. Heath's bracelet. I described the circumstances pretty minutely, and, when I mentioned the match found on the table, she said: 'How strange! Why, *my* thief left a match on the dressing-table when he took my poor little brooch!'"

Hewitt nodded. "Yes," he said. "A spent match, of course?"

"Yes, of course, a spent match. She noticed it lying close by the pin-cushion, but threw it away without mentioning the circumstance. Still, it seemed rather curious to me that a match should be lit and dropped, in each case, on the dressing-cover an inch from where the article was taken. I mentioned it to Lloyd when I got back, and he agreed that it seemed significant."

"Scarcely," said Hewitt, shaking his head. "Scarcely, so far, to be called significant, although worth following up. Everybody uses matches in the dark, you know."

"Well, at any rate, the coincidence appealed to me so far that it struck me it might be worth while to describe the brooch to the police in order that they could trace it if it had been pawned. They had tried that, of course, over the bracelet without any result, but I fancied the shot might be worth making, and might possibly lead us on the track of the more serious robbery."

"Quite so. It was the right thing to do. Well?"

"Well, they found it. A woman had pawned it in London—at a shop in Chelsea. But that was some time before, and the pawnbroker had clean forgotten all about the woman's appearance. The name and address she gave were false. So that was the end of that business."

"Had any of the servants left you between the time
the brooch was lost and the date of the pawn ticket?"

"No."

"Were all your servants at home on the day the brooch
was pawned?"

"Oh, yes! I made that inquiry myself."

"Very good! What next?"

"Yesterday—and this is what made me send for you.
My late wife's sister came here last Tuesday, and we gave
her the room from which Mrs. Heath lost her bracelet.
She had with her a very old-fashioned brooch, containing
a miniature of her father, and set in front with three very
fine brilliants and a few smaller stones. Here we are,
though, at the Croft. I'll tell you the rest indoors."

Hewitt laid his hand on the baronet's arm. "Don't pull
up, Sir James," he said. "Drive a little farther. I should like
to have a general idea of the whole case before we go in."

"Very good!" Sir James Norris straightened the horse's
head again and went on. "Late yesterday afternoon, as my
sister-in-law was changing her dress, she left her room for
a moment to speak to my daughter in her room, almost
adjoining. She was gone no more than three minutes,
or five at most, but on her return the brooch, which had
been left on the table, had gone. Now the window was
shut fast, and had not been tampered with. Of course the
door was open, but so was my daughter's, and anybody
walking near must have been heard. But the strangest
circumstance, and one that almost makes me wonder
whether I have been awake to-day or not, was that there
lay *a used match* on the very spot, as nearly as possible,
where the brooch had been—and it was broad daylight!"

Hewitt rubbed his nose and looked thoughtfully

before him. "Um—curious, certainly," he said, "Anything else?"

"Nothing more than you shall see for yourself. I have had the room locked and watched till you could examine it. My sister-in-law had heard of your name, and suggested that you should be called in; so, of course, I did exactly as she wanted. That she should have lost that brooch, of all things, in my house is most unfortunate; you see, there was some small difference about the thing between my late wife and her sister when their mother died and left it. It's almost worse than the Heaths' bracelet business, and altogether I'm not pleased with things, I can assure you. See what a position it is for me! Here are three ladies, in the space of one year, robbed one after another in this mysterious fashion in my house, and I can't find the thief! It's horrible! People will be afraid to come near the place. And I can do nothing!"

"Ah, well, we'll see. Perhaps we had better turn back now. By the by, were you thinking of having any alterations or additions made to your house?"

"No. What makes you ask?"

"I think you might at least consider the question of painting and decorating, Sir James—or, say, putting up another coach-house, or something. Because I should like to be (to the servants) the architect—or the builder, if you please—come to look around. You haven't told any of them about this business?"

"Not a word. Nobody knows but my relatives and Lloyd. I took every precaution myself, at once. As to your little disguise, be the architect by all means, and do as you please. If you can only find this thief and put an end to this horrible state of affairs, you'll do me the greatest service I've ever asked for—and as to your fee, I'll gladly make it whatever is usual, and three hundred in addition."

Martin Hewitt bowed. "You're very generous, Sir James, and you may be sure I'll do what I can. As a professional man, of course, a good fee always stimulates my interest, although this case of yours certainly seems interesting enough by itself."

"Most extraordinary! Don't you think so? Here are three persons, all ladies, all in my house, two even in the same room, each successively robbed of a piece of jewelry, each from a dressing-table, and a used match left behind in every case. All in the most difficult—one would say impossible—circumstances for a thief, and yet there is no clue!"

"Well, we won't say that just yet, Sir James; we must see. And we must guard against any undue predisposition to consider the robberies in a lump. Here we are at the lodge gate again. Is that your gardener—the man who left the ladder by the lawn on the first occasion you spoke of?"

Mr. Hewitt nodded in the direction of a man who was clipping a box border.

"Yes; will you ask him anything?"

"No, no; at any rate, not now. Remember the building alterations. I think, if there is no objection, I will look first at the room that the lady—Mrs.—" Hewitt looked up, inquiringly.

"My sister-in-law? Mrs. Cazenove. Oh, yes! you shall come to her room at once."

"Thank you. And I think Mrs. Cazenove had better be there."

They alighted, and a boy from the lodge led the horse and dog-cart away.

Mrs. Cazenove was a thin and faded, but quick and energetic, lady of middle age. She bent her head very slightly on learning Martin Hewitt's name, and said: "I must thank you, Mr. Hewitt, for your very prompt attention. I need scarcely say that any help you can afford in tracing the thief who has my property—whoever it may be—will make me most grateful. My room is quite ready for you to examine."

The room was on the second floor—the top floor at that part of the building. Some slight confusion of small articles of dress was observable in parts of the room.

"This, I take it," inquired Hewitt, "is exactly as it was at the time the brooch was missed?"

"Precisely," Mrs. Cazenove answered. "I have used another room, and put myself to some other inconveniences, to avoid any disturbance."

Hewitt stood before the dressing-table. "Then this is the used match," he observed, "exactly where it was found?"

"Yes."

"Where was the brooch?"

"I should say almost on the very same spot. Certainly no more than a very few inches away."

Hewitt examined the match closely. "It is burned very little," he remarked. "It would appear to have gone out at once. Could you hear it struck?"

"I heard nothing whatever; absolutely nothing."

"If you will step into Miss Norris' room now for a moment," Hewitt suggested, "we will try an experiment. Tell me if you hear matches struck, and how many. Where is the match-stand?"

The match-stand proved to be empty, but matches were found in Miss Norris' room, and the test was made. Each striking could be heard distinctly, even with one of the doors pushed to.

"Both your own door and Miss Norris' were open, I understand; the window shut and fastened inside as it is now, and nothing but the brooch was disturbed?"

"Yes, that was so."

"Thank you, Mrs. Cazenove. I don't think I need trouble you any further just at present. I think, Sir James," Hewitt added, turning to the baronet, who was standing by the door—"I think we will see the other room and take a walk outside the house, if you please. I suppose, by the by, that there is no getting at the matches left behind on the first and second occasions?"

"No," Sir James answered. "Certainly not here. The Scotland Yard man may have kept his."

The room that Mrs. Armitage had occupied presented no peculiar feature. A few feet below the window the roof of the billiard-room was visible, consisting largely of skylight. Hewitt glanced casually about the walls, ascertained that the furniture and hangings had not been materially changed since the second robbery, and expressed his desire to see the windows from the outside. Before leaving the room, however, he wished to know the names of any persons who were known to have been about the house on the occasions of all three robberies.

"Just carry your mind back, Sir James," he said. "Begin with yourself, for instance. Where were you at these times?"

"When Mrs. Heath lost her bracelet, I was in Tagley Wood all the afternoon. When Mrs. Armitage was robbed,

I believe I was somewhere about the place most of the
time she was out. Yesterday I was down at the farm." Sir
James' face broadened. "I don't know whether you call
those suspicious movements," he added, and laughed.

"Not at all; I only asked you so that, remembering
your own movements, you might the better recall
those of the rest of the household. Was anybody, to
your knowledge—*anybody*, mind—in the house on all
three occasions?"

"Well, you know, it's quite impossible to answer for all
the servants. You'll only get that by direct questioning—I
can't possibly remember things of that sort. As to the
family and visitors—why, you don't suspect any of them,
do you?"

"I don't suspect a soul, Sir James," Hewitt answered,
beaming genially, "not a soul. You see, I can't suspect
people till I know something about where they were.
It's quite possible there will be independent evidence
enough as it is, but you must help me if you can. The
visitors, now. Was there any visitor here each time—or
even on the first and last occasions only?"

"No, not one. And my own sister, perhaps you will
be pleased to know, was only there at the time of the
first robbery."

"Just so! And your daughter, as I have gathered, was
clearly absent from the spot each time—indeed, was in
company with the party robbed. Your niece, now?"

"Why hang it all, Mr. Hewitt, I can't talk of my niece
as a suspected criminal! The poor girl's under my
protection, and I really can't allow—"

Hewitt raised his hand, and shook his
head deprecatingly.

"My dear sir, haven't I said that I don't suspect a soul? *Do* let me know how the people were distributed, as nearly as possible. Let me see. It was your, niece, I think, who found that Mrs. Armitage's door was locked—this door, in fact—on the day she lost her brooch?"

"Yes, it was."

"Just so—at the time when Mrs. Armitage herself had forgotten whether she locked it or not. And yesterday— was she out then?"

"No, I think not. Indeed, she goes out very little—her health is usually bad. She was indoors, too, at the time of the Heath robbery, since you ask. But come, now, I don't like this. It's ridiculous to suppose that *she* knows anything of it."

"I don't suppose it, as I have said. I am only asking for information. That is all your resident family, I take it, and you know nothing of anybody else's movements— except, perhaps, Mr. Lloyd's?"

"Lloyd? Well, you know yourself that he was out with the ladies when the first robbery took place. As to the others, I don't remember. Yesterday he was probably in his room, writing. I think that acquits *him*, eh?" Sir James looked quizzically into the broad face of the affable detective, who smiled and replied:

"Oh, of course nobody can be in two places at once, else what would become of the *alibi* as an institution? But, as I have said, I am only setting my facts in order. Now, you see, we get down to the servants— unless some stranger is the party wanted. Shall we go outside now?"

Lenton Croft was a large, desultory sort of house, nowhere more than three floors high, and mostly only two. It had been added to bit by bit, till it zigzagged about its site, as Sir James Norris expressed it, "like a game of dominoes." Hewitt scrutinized its external features carefully as they strolled around, and stopped some little while before the windows of the two bed-rooms he had just seen from the inside. Presently they approached the stables and coach-house, where a groom was washing the wheels of the dog-cart.

"Do you mind my smoking?" Hewitt asked Sir James. "Perhaps you will take a cigar yourself—they are not so bad, I think. I will ask your man for a light."

Sir James felt for his own match-box, but Hewitt had gone, and was lighting his cigar with a match from a box handed him by the groom. A smart little terrier was trotting about by the coach-house, and Hewitt stooped to rub its head. Then he made some observation about the dog, which enlisted the groom's interest, and was soon absorbed in a chat with the man. Sir James, waiting a little way off, tapped the stones rather impatiently with his foot, and presently moved away.

For full a quarter of an hour Hewitt chatted with the groom, and, when at last he came away and overtook Sir James, that gentleman was about re-entering the house.

"I beg your pardon, Sir James," Hewitt said, "for leaving you in that unceremonious fashion to talk to your groom, but a dog, Sir James—a good dog—will draw me anywhere."

"Oh!" replied Sir James, shortly.

"There is one other thing," Hewitt went on, disregarding the other's curtness, "that I should like to know: There are two windows directly below that of the room occupied yesterday by Mrs. Cazenove—one on each floor. What rooms do they light?"

"That on the ground floor is the morning-room; the other is Mr. Lloyd's—my secretary. A sort of study or sitting-room."

"Now you will see at once, Sir James," Hewitt pursued, with an affable determination to win the baronet back to good-humor—"you will see at once that, if a ladder had been used in Mrs. Heath's case, anybody looking from either of these rooms would have seen it."

"Of course! The Scotland Yard man questioned everybody as to that, but nobody seemed to have been in either of the rooms when the thing occurred; at any rate, nobody saw anything."

"Still, I think I should like to look out of those windows myself; it will, at least, give me an idea of what *was* in view and what was not, if anybody had been there."

Sir James Norris led the way to the morning-room. As they reached the door a young lady, carrying a book and walking very languidly, came out. Hewitt stepped aside to let her pass, and afterward said interrogatively: "Miss Norris, your daughter, Sir James?"

"No, my niece. Do you want to ask her anything? Dora, my dear," Sir James added, following her in the corridor, "this is Mr. Hewitt, who is investigating these wretched robberies for me. I think he would like to hear if you remember anything happening at any of the three times."

The lady bowed slightly, and said in a plaintive drawl: "I, uncle? Really, I don't remember anything; nothing at all."

"You found Mrs. Armitage's door locked, I believe," asked Hewitt, "when you tried it, on the afternoon when she lost her brooch?"

"Oh, yes; I believe it was locked. Yes, it was."

"Had the key been left in?"

"The key? Oh, no! I think not; no."

"Do you remember anything out of the common happening—anything whatever, no matter how trivial—on the day Mrs. Heath lost her bracelet?"

"No, really, I don't. I can't remember at all."

"Nor yesterday?"

"No, nothing. I don't remember anything."

"Thank you," said Hewitt, hastily; "thank you. Now the morning-room, Sir James."

In the morning-room Hewitt stayed but a few seconds, doing little more than casually glance out of the windows. In the room above he took a little longer time. It was a comfortable room, but with rather effeminate indications about its contents. Little pieces of draped silk-work hung about the furniture, and Japanese silk fans decorated the mantel-piece. Near the window was a cage containing a gray parrot, and the writing-table was decorated with two vases of flowers.

"Lloyd makes himself pretty comfortable, eh?" Sir James observed. "But it isn't likely anybody would be here while he was out, at the time that bracelet went."

"No," replied Hewitt, meditatively. "No, I suppose not."

He stared thoughtfully out of the window, and then, still deep in thought, rattled at the wires of the cage with a quill toothpick and played a moment with the parrot. Then, looking up at the window again, he said: "That is Mr. Lloyd, isn't it, coming back in a fly?"

"Yes, I think so. Is there anything else you would care to see here?"

"No, thank you," Hewitt replied; "I don't think there is."

They went down to the smoking-room, and Sir James went away to speak to his secretary. When he returned, Hewitt said quietly: "I think, Sir James—I *think* that I shall be able to give you your thief presently."

"What! Have you a clue? Who do you think? I began to believe you were hopelessly stumped."

"Well, yes. I have rather a good clue, although I can't tell you much about it just yet. But it is so good a clue that I should like to know now whether you are determined to prosecute when you have the criminal?"

"Why, bless me, of course," Sir James replied, with surprise. "It doesn't rest with me, you know—the property belongs to my friends. And even if they were disposed to let the thing slide, I shouldn't allow it—I couldn't, after they had been robbed in my house."

"Of course, of course! Then, if I can, I should like to send a message to Twyford by somebody perfectly trustworthy— not a servant. Could anybody go?"

"Well, there's Lloyd, although he's only just back from his journey. But, if it's important, he'll go."

"It is important. The fact is we must have a policeman or two here this evening, and I'd like Mr. Lloyd to fetch them without telling anybody else."

Sir James rang, and, in response to his message, Mr. Lloyd appeared. While Sir James gave his secretary his instructions, Hewitt strolled to the door of the smoking-room, and intercepted the latter as he came out.

"I'm sorry to give you this trouble, Mr. Lloyd," he said, "but I must stay here myself for a little, and somebody who can be trusted must go. Will you just bring back a police-constable with you? or rather two—two would be better. That is all that is wanted. You won't let the servants know, will you? Of course there will be a female searcher at the Twyford police-station? Ah—of course. Well, you needn't bring her, you know. That sort of thing is done at the station." And, chatting thus confidentially, Martin Hewitt saw him off.

When Hewitt returned to the smoking-room, Sir James said, suddenly: "Why, bless my soul, Mr. Hewitt, we haven't fed you! I'm awfully sorry. We came in rather late for lunch, you know, and this business has bothered me so I clean forgot everything else. There's no dinner till seven, so you'd better let me give you something now. I'm really sorry. Come along."

"Thank you, Sir James," Hewitt replied; "I won't take much. A few biscuits, perhaps, or something of that sort. And, by the by, if you don't mind, I rather think I should like to take it alone. The fact is I want to go over this case thoroughly by myself. Can you put me in a room?"

"Any room you like. Where will you go? The dining-room's rather large, but there's my study, that's pretty snug, or—"

"Perhaps I can go into Mr. Lloyd's room for half an hour or so; I don't think he'll mind, and it's pretty comfortable."

"Certainly, if you'd like. I'll tell them to send you whatever they've got."

"Thank you very much. Perhaps they'll also send me a lump of sugar and a walnut; it's—it's a little fad of mine."

"A—what? A lump of sugar and a walnut?" Sir James stopped for a moment, with his hand on the bell-rope. "Oh, certainly, if you'd like it; certainly," he added, and stared after this detective with curious tastes as he left the room.

When the vehicle, bringing back the secretary and the policeman, drew up on the drive, Martin Hewitt left the room on the first floor and proceeded down-stairs. On the landing he met Sir James Norris and Mrs. Cazenove, who stared with astonishment on perceiving that the detective carried in his hand the parrot-cage.

"I think our business is about brought to a head now," Hewitt remarked, on the stairs. "Here are the police officers from Twyford." The men were standing in the hall with Mr. Lloyd, who, on catching sight of the cage in Hewitt's hand, paled suddenly.

"This is the person who will be charged, I think," Hewitt pursued, addressing the officers, and indicating Lloyd with his finger.

"What, Lloyd?" gasped Sir James, aghast. "No— not Lloyd—nonsense!"

"He doesn't seem to think it nonsense himself, does he?" Hewitt placidly observed. Lloyd had sank on a chair, and, gray of face, was staring blindly at the man he had run against at the office door that morning. His lips moved in spasms, but there was no sound. The wilted flower fell from his button-hole to the floor, but he did not move.

"This is his accomplice," Hewitt went on, placing the parrot and cage on the hall table, "though I doubt whether there will be any use in charging *him*. Eh, Polly?"

The parrot put his head aside and chuckled. "Hullo, Polly!" it quietly gurgled. "Come along!"

Sir James Norris was hopelessly bewildered. "Lloyd— Lloyd," he said, under his breath. "Lloyd—and that!"

"This was his little messenger, his useful Mercury," Hewitt explained, tapping the cage complacently; "in fact, the actual lifter. Hold him up!"

The last remark referred to the wretched Lloyd, who had fallen forward with something between a sob and a loud sigh. The policemen took him by the arms and propped him in his chair.

"System?" said Hewitt, with a shrug of the shoulders, an hour or two after in Sir James' study. "I can't say I have a system. I call it nothing but common-sense and a sharp pair of eyes. Nobody using these could help taking the right road in this case. I began at the match, just as the Scotland Yard man did, but I had the advantage of taking a line through three cases. To begin with, it was plain that that match, being left there in daylight, in Mrs. Cazenove's room, could not have been used to light the table-top, in the full glare of the window; therefore it had been used for some other purpose—*what* purpose I could not, at the moment, guess. Habitual thieves, you know, often have curious superstitions, and some will never take anything without leaving something behind—a pebble or a piece of coal, or something like that—in the premises they have been robbing. It seemed at first extremely likely that this was a case of that kind. The match had clearly been *brought in*—because, when I asked for matches, there were none in the stand, not even an empty box, and the room had not been disturbed. Also the match probably had not been struck there, nothing having been heard, although, of course, a mistake in this matter was just possible. This match, then, it was fair to assume, had been lit somewhere else and blown out immediately—I remarked at the time that it was very little burned. Plainly it could not have been treated thus for nothing, and the only possible object would have been to prevent it igniting accidentally. Following on this, it became obvious that the match was used, for whatever purpose, not *as* a match, but merely as a convenient splinter of wood.

"So far so good. But on examining the match very closely I observed, as you can see for yourself, certain rather sharp indentations in the wood. They are very small, you see, and scarcely visible, except upon narrow inspection; but there they are, and their positions are regular. See, there are two on each side, each opposite the corresponding mark of the other pair. The match, in fact, would seem to have been gripped in some fairly sharp instrument, holding it at two points above and two below—an instrument, as it may at once strike you, not unlike the beak of a bird.

"Now here was an idea. What living creature but a bird could possibly have entered Mrs. Heath's window without a ladder—supposing no ladder to have been used—or could have got into Mrs. Armitage's window without lifting the sash higher than the eight or ten inches it was already open? Plainly, nothing. Further, it is significant that only *one* article was stolen at a time, although others were about. A human being could have carried any reasonable number, but a bird could only take one at a time. But why should a bird carry a match in its beak? Certainly it must have been trained to do that for a purpose, and a little consideration made that purpose pretty clear. A noisy, chattering bird would probably betray itself at once. Therefore it must be trained to keep quiet both while going for and coming away with its plunder. What readier or more probably effectual way than, while teaching it to carry without dropping, to teach it also to keep quiet while carrying? The one thing would practically cover the other.

"I thought at once, of course, of a jackdaw or a magpie—these birds' thievish reputations made the guess natural. But the marks on the match were much too wide apart to have been made by the beak of either. I conjectured, therefore, that it must be a raven. So that, when we arrived near the coach-house, I seized the opportunity of a little chat with your groom on the subject of dogs and pets in general, and ascertained that there was no tame raven in the place. I also, incidentally, by getting a light from the coach-house box of matches, ascertained that the match found was of the sort generally used about the establishment—the large, thick, red-topped English match. But I further found that Mr. Lloyd had a parrot which was a most intelligent pet, and had been trained into comparative quietness—for a parrot. Also, I learned that more than once the groom had met Mr. Lloyd carrying his parrot under his coat, it having, as its owner explained, learned the trick of opening its cage-door and escaping.

"I said nothing, of course, to you of all this, because I had as yet nothing but a train of argument and no results. I got to Lloyd's room as soon as possible. My chief object in going there was achieved when I played with the parrot, and induced it to bite a quill toothpick.

"When you left me in the smoking-room, I compared the quill and the match very carefully, and found that the marks corresponded exactly. After this I felt very little doubt indeed. The fact of Lloyd having met the ladies walking before dark on the day of the first robbery proved nothing, because, since it was clear that the match had *not* been used to procure a light, the robbery might as easily have taken place in daylight as not—must have so taken place, in fact, if my conjectures were right. That they were right I felt no doubt. There could be no other explanation.

"When Mrs. Heath left her window open and her door shut, anybody climbing upon the open sash of Lloyd's high window could have put the bird upon the sill above. The match placed in the bird's beak for the purpose I have indicated, and struck first, in case by accident it should ignite by rubbing against something and startle the bird—this match would, of course, be dropped just where the object to be removed was taken up; as you know, in every case the match was found almost upon the spot where the missing article had been left—scarcely a likely triple coincidence had the match been used by a human thief. This would have been done as soon after the ladies had left as possible, and there would then have been plenty of time for Lloyd to hurry out and meet them before dark—especially plenty of time to meet them *coming back*, as they must have been, since they were carrying their ferns. The match was an article well chosen for its purpose, as being a not altogether unlikely thing to find on a dressing-table, and, if noticed, likely to lead to the wrong conclusions adopted by the official detective.

"In Mrs. Armitage's case the taking of an inferior brooch and the leaving of a more valuable ring pointed clearly either to the operator being a fool or unable to distinguish values, and certainly, from other indications, the thief seemed no fool. The door was locked, and the gas-fitter, so to speak, on guard, and the window was only eight or ten inches open and propped with a brush. A human thief entering the window would have disturbed this arrangement, and would scarcely risk discovery by attempting to replace it, especially a thief in so great a hurry as to snatch the brooch up without unfastening the pin. The bird could pass through the opening as it was, and *would have* to tear the pin-cushion to pull the brooch off, probably holding the cushion down with its claw the while.

"Now in yesterday's case we had an alteration of conditions. The window was shut and fastened, but the door was open—but only left for a few minutes, during which time no sound was heard either of coming or going. Was it not possible, then, that the thief was *already* in the room, in hiding, while Mrs. Cazenove was there, and seized its first opportunity on her temporary absence? The room is full of draperies, hangings, and what not, allowing of plenty of concealment for a bird, and a bird could leave the place noiselessly and quickly. That the whole scheme was strange mattered not at all. Robberies presenting such unaccountable features must have been effected by strange means of one sort or another. There was no improbability. Consider how many hundreds of examples of infinitely higher degrees of bird-training are exhibited in the London streets every week for coppers.

"So that, on the whole, I felt pretty sure of my ground. But before taking any definite steps I resolved to see if Polly could not be persuaded to exhibit his accomplishments to an indulgent stranger. For that purpose I contrived to send Lloyd away again and have a quiet hour alone with his bird. A piece of sugar, as everybody knows, is a good parrot bribe; but a walnut, split in half, is a better—especially if the bird be used to it; so I got you to furnish me with both. Polly was shy at first, but I generally get along very well with pets, and a little perseverance soon led to a complete private performance for my benefit. Polly would take the match, mute as wax, jump on the table, pick up the brightest thing he could see, in a great hurry, leave the match behind, and scuttle away round the room; but at first wouldn't give up the plunder to *me*. It was enough. I also took the liberty, as you know, of a general look round, and discovered that little collection of Brummagem rings and trinkets that you have just seen—used in Polly's education, no doubt. When we sent Lloyd away, it struck me that he might as well be usefully employed as not, so I got him to fetch the police, deluding him a little, I fear, by talking about the servants and a female searcher. There will be no trouble about evidence; he'll confess. Of that I'm sure. I know the sort of man. But I doubt if you'll get Mrs. Cazenove's brooch back. You see, he has been to London to-day, and by this time the swag is probably broken up."

Sir James listened to Hewitt's explanation with many expressions of assent and some of surprise. When it was over, he smoked a few whiffs and then said: "But Mrs. Armitage's brooch was pawned, and by a woman."

"Exactly. I expect our friend Lloyd was rather disgusted at his small luck—probably gave the brooch to some female connection in London, and she realized on it. Such persons don't always trouble to give a correct address."

The two smoked in silence for a few minutes, and then Hewitt continued: "I don't expect our friend has had an easy job altogether with that bird. His successes at most have only been three, and I suspect he had many failures and not a few anxious moments that we know nothing of. I should judge as much merely from what the groom told me of frequently meeting Lloyd with his parrot. But the plan was not a bad one—not at all. Even if the bird had been caught in the act, it would only have been 'That mischievous parrot!' you see. And his master would only have been looking for him."

II. THE LOSS OF
SAMMY CROCKETT

IT WAS, of course, always a part of Martin Hewitt's business to be thoroughly at home among any and every class of people, and to be able to interest himself intelligently, or to appear to do so, in their various pursuits. In one of the most important cases ever placed in his hands he could have gone but a short way toward success had he not displayed some knowledge of the more sordid aspects of professional sport, and a great interest in the undertakings of a certain dealer therein.

The great case itself had nothing to do with sport, and, indeed, from a narrative point of view, was somewhat uninteresting, but the man who alone held the one piece of information wanted was a keeper, backer, or "gaffer" of professional pedestrians, and it was through the medium of his pecuniary interest in such matters that Hewitt was enabled to strike a bargain with him.

The man was a publican on the outskirts of Padfield, a northern town, pretty famous for its sporting tastes, and to Padfield, therefore, Hewitt betook himself, and, arrayed in a way to indicate some inclination of his own toward sport, he began to frequent the bar of the Hare and Hounds. Kentish, the landlord, was a stout, bull-necked man, of no great communicativeness at first; but after a little acquaintance he opened out wonderfully, became quite a jolly (and rather intelligent) companion, and came out with innumerable anecdotes of his sporting adventures. He could put a very decent dinner on the table, too, at the Hare and Hounds, and Hewitt's frequent invitation to him to join therein and divide a bottle of the best in the cellar soon put the two on the very best of terms. Good terms with Mr. Kentish was Hewitt's great desire, for the information he wanted was of a sort that could never be extracted by casual questioning, but must be a matter of open communication by the publican, extracted in what way it might be.

"Look here," said Kentish one day, "I'll put you on to a good thing, my boy—a real good thing. Of course you know all about the Padfield 135 Yards Handicap being run off now?"

"Well, I haven't looked into it much," Hewitt replied. "Ran the first round of heats last Saturday and Monday, didn't they?"

"They did. Well"—Kentish spoke in a stage whisper as he leaned over and rapped the table—"I've got the final winner in this house." He nodded his head, took a puff at his cigar, and added, in his ordinary voice. "Don't say nothing."

"No, of course not. Got something on, of course?"

"Rather! What do you think? Got any price I liked. Been saving him up for this. Why, he's got twenty-one yards, and he can do even time all the way! Fact! Why, he could win runnin' back'ards. He won his heat on Monday like—like—like that!" The gaffer snapped his fingers, in default of a better illustration, and went on. "He might ha' took it a little easier, *I* think; it's shortened his price, of course, him jumpin' in by two yards. But you can get decent odds now, if you go about it right. You take my tip—back him for his heat next Saturday, in the second round, and for the final. You'll get a good price for the final, if you pop it down at once. But don't go makin' a song of it, will you, now? I'm givin' you a tip I wouldn't give anybody else."

"Thanks, very much; it's awfully good of you. I'll do what you advise. But isn't there a dark horse anywhere else?"

"Not dark to me, my boy, not dark to me. I know every man runnin' like a book. Old Taylor—him over at the Cop—he's got a very good lad at eighteen yards, a very good lad indeed; and he's a tryer this time, I know. But, bless you, my lad could give him ten, instead o' taking three, and beat him then! When I'm runnin' a real tryer, I'm generally runnin' something very near a winner, you bet; and this time, mind *this* time, I'm runnin' the certainest winner I *ever* run—and I don't often make a mistake. You back him."

"I shall, if you're as sure as that. But who is he?"

"Oh, Crockett's his name—Sammy Crockett. He's quite a new lad. I've got young Steggles looking after him—sticks to him like wax. Takes his little breathers in my bit o' ground at the back here. I've got a cinder-sprint path there, over behind the trees. I don't let him out o' sight much, I can tell you. He's a straight lad, and he knows it'll be worth his while to stick to me; but there's some 'ud poison him, if they thought he'd spoil their books."

Soon afterward the two strolled toward the taproom. "I expect Sammy'll be there," the landlord said, "with Steggles. I don't hide him too much—they'd think I'd got something extra on if I did."

In the tap-room sat a lean, wire-drawn-looking youth, with sloping shoulders and a thin face, and by his side was a rather short, thick-set man, who had an odd air, no matter what he did, of proprietorship and surveillance of the lean youth. Several other men sat about, and there was loud laughter, under which the lean youth looked sheepishly angry.

"'Tarn't no good, Sammy, lad," some one was saying, "you a-makin' after Nancy Webb—she'll ha' nowt to do with 'ee."

"Don' like 'em so thread-papery," added another. "No, Sammy, you aren't the lad for she. I see her—"

"What about Nancy Webb?" asked Kentish, pushing open the door. "Sammy's all right, any way. You keep fit, my lad, an' go on improving, and some day you'll have as good a house as me. Never mind the lasses. Had his glass o' beer, has he?" This to Raggy Steggles, who, answering in the affirmative, viewed his charge as though he were a post, and the beer a recent coat of paint.

"Has two glasses of mild a day," the landlord said to Hewitt. "Never puts on flesh, so he can stand it. Come out now." He nodded to Steggles, who rose and marched Sammy Crockett away for exercise.

On the following afternoon (it was Thursday), as Hewitt and Kentish chatted in the landlord's own snuggery, Steggles burst into the room in a great state of agitation and spluttered out: "He—he's bolted; gone away!"

"What?"

"Sammy—gone! Hooked it! *I* can't find him."

The landlord stared blankly at the trainer, who stood with a sweater dangling from his hand and stared blankly back. "What d'ye mean?" Kentish said, at last. "Don't be a fool! He's in the place somewhere. Find him!"

But this Steggles defied anybody to do. He had looked already. He had left Crockett at the cinder-path behind the trees in his running-gear, with the addition of the long overcoat and cap he used in going between the path and the house to guard against chill. "I was goin' to give him a bust or two with the pistol," the trainer explained, "but, when we got over t'other side, 'Raggy,' ses he, 'it's blowin' a bit chilly. I think I'll ha' a sweater. There's one on my box, ain't there?' So in I coomes for the sweater, and it weren't on his box, and, when I found it and got back—he weren't there. They'd seen nowt o' him in t' house, and he weren't nowhere."

Hewitt and the landlord, now thoroughly startled, searched everywhere, but to no purpose. "What should he go off the place for?" asked Kentish, in a sweat of apprehension. "'Tain't chilly a bit—it's warm. He didn't want no sweater; never wore one before. It was a piece of kid to be able to clear out. Nice thing, this is. I stand to win two years' takings over him. Here—you'll have to find him."

"Ah, but how?" exclaimed the disconcerted trainer, dancing about distractedly. "I've got all I could scrape on him myself. Where can I look?"

Here was Hewitt's opportunity. He took Kentish aside and whispered. What he said startled the landlord considerably. "Yes, I'll tell you all about that," he said, "if that's all you want. It's no good or harm to me whether I tell or no. But can you find him?"

"That I can't promise, of course. But you know who I am now, and what I'm here for. If you like to give me the information I want, I'll go into the case for you, and, of course, I shan't charge any fee. I may have luck, you know, but I can't promise, of course."

The landlord looked in Hewitt's face for a moment. Then he said: "Done! It's a deal."

"Very good," Hewitt replied; "get together the one or two papers you have, and we'll go into my business in the evening. As to Crockett, don't say a word to anybody. I'm afraid it must get out, since they all know about it in the house, but there's no use in making any unnecessary noise. Don't make hedging bets or do anything that will attract notice. Now we'll go over to the back and look at this cinder-path of yours."

Here Steggles, who was still standing near, was struck with an idea. "How about old Taylor, at the Cop, guv'nor, eh?" he said, meaningly. "His lad's good enough to win with Sammy out, and Taylor is backing him plenty. Think he knows any thing o' this?"

"That's likely," Hewitt observed, before Kentish could reply. "Yes. Look here—suppose Steggles goes and keeps his eye on the Cop for an hour or two, in case there's anything to be heard of? Don't show yourself, of course."

Kentish agreed, and the trainer went. When Hewitt and Kentish arrived at the path behind the trees, Hewitt at once began examining the ground. One or two rather large holes in the cinders were made, as the publican explained, by Crockett, in practicing getting off his mark. Behind these were several fresh tracks of spiked shoes. The tracks led up to within a couple of yards of the high fence bounding the ground, and there stopped abruptly and entirely. In the fence, a little to the right of where the tracks stopped, there was a stout door. This Hewitt tried, and found ajar.

"That's always kept bolted," Kentish said. "He's gone out that way—he couldn't have gone any other without comin' through the house."

"But he isn't in the habit of making a step three yards long, is he?" Hewitt asked, pointing at the last footmark and then at the door, which was quite that distance away from it. "Besides," he added, opening the door, "there's no footprint here nor outside."

The door opened on a lane, with another fence and a thick plantation of trees at the other side. Kentish looked at the footmarks, then at the door, then down the lane, and finally back toward the house. "That's a licker!" he said.

"This is a quiet sort of lane," was Hewitt's next remark. "No houses in sight. Where does it lead?"

"That way it goes to the Old Kilns—disused. This way down to a turning off the Padfield and Catton road."

Hewitt returned to the cinder-path again, and once more examined the footmarks. He traced them back over the grass toward the house. "Certainly," he said, "he hasn't gone back to the house. Here is the double line of tracks, side by side, from the house—Steggles' ordinary boots with iron tips, and Crockett's running pumps; thus they came out. Here is Steggles' track in the opposite direction alone, made when he went back for the sweater. Crockett remained; you see various prints in those loose cinders at the end of the path where he moved this way and that, and then two or three paces toward the fence—not directly toward the door, you notice—and there they stop dead, and there are no more, either back or forward. Now, if he had wings, I should be tempted to the opinion that he flew straight away in the air from that spot—unless the earth swallowed him and closed again without leaving a wrinkle on its face."

Kentish stared gloomily at the tracks and said nothing.

"However," Hewitt resumed, "I think I'll take a little walk now and think over it. You go into the house and show yourself at the bar. If anybody wants to know how Crockett is, he's pretty well, thank you. By the by, can I get to the Cop—this place of Taylor's—by this back lane?"

"Yes, down to the end leading to the Catton road, turn to the left and then first on the right. Any one'll show you the Cop," and Kentish shut the door behind the detective, who straightway walked—toward the Old Kilns.

In little more than an hour he was back. It was now becoming dusk, and the landlord looked out papers from a box near the side window of his snuggery, for the sake of the extra light. "I've got these papers together for you," he said, as Hewitt entered. "Any news?"

"Nothing very great. Here's a bit of handwriting I want you to recognize, if you can. Get a light."

Kentish lit a lamp, and Hewitt laid upon the table half a dozen small pieces of torn paper, evidently fragments of a letter which had been torn up, here reproduced in facsimile:

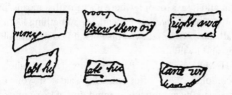

The landlord turned the scraps over, regarding them dubiously. "These aren't much to recognize, anyhow. *I* don't know the writing. Where did you find 'em?"

"They were lying in the lane at the back, a little way down. Plainly they are pieces of a note addressed to some one called Sammy or something very like it. See the first piece, with its 'mmy'? That is clearly from the beginning of the note, because there is no line between it and the smooth, straight edge of the paper above; also, nothing follows on the same line. Some one writes to Crockett—presuming it to be a letter addressed to him, as I do for other reasons—as Sammy. It is a pity that there is no more of the letter to be found than these pieces. I expect the person who tore it up put the rest in his pocket and dropped these by accident."

Kentish, who had been picking up and examining each piece in turn, now dolorously broke out:

"Oh, it's plain he's sold us—bolted and done us; me as took him out o' the gutter, too. Look here—'throw them over'; that's plain enough—can't mean anything else. Means throw *me* over, and my friends—me, after what I've done for him! Then 'right away'—go right away, I s'pose, as he has done. Then"—he was fiddling with the scraps and finally fitted two together—"why, look here, this one with 'lane' on it fits over the one about throwing over, and it says 'poor f' where it's torn; that means 'poor fool,' I s'pose—*me*, or 'fathead,' or something like that. That's nice. Why, I'd twist his neck if I could get hold of him; and I will!"

Hewitt smiled. "Perhaps it's not quite so uncomplimentary, after all," he said. "If you can't recognize the writing, never mind. But, if he's gone away to sell you, it isn't much use finding him, is it? He won't win if he doesn't want to."

"Why, he wouldn't dare to rope under my very eyes. I'd—I'd—"

"Well, well; perhaps we'll get him to run, after all, and as well as he can. One thing is certain—he left this place of his own will. Further, I think he is in Padfield now; he went toward the town, I believe. And I don't think he means to sell you."

"Well, he shouldn't. I've made it worth his while to stick to me. I've put a fifty on for him out of my own pocket, and told him so; and, if he won, that would bring him a lump more than he'd probably get by going crooked, besides the prize money and anything I might give him over. But it seems to me he's putting me in the cart altogether."

"That we shall see. Meantime, don't mention anything I've told you to any one—not even to Steggles. He can't help us, and he might blurt things out inadvertently. Don't say anything about these pieces of paper, which I shall keep myself. By the by, Steggles is indoors, isn't he? Very well, keep him in. Don't let him be seen hunting about this evening. I'll stay here to-night and we'll proceed with Crockett's business in the morning. And now we'll settle *my* business, please."

In the morning Hewitt took his breakfast in the snuggery, carefully listening to any conversation that might take place at the bar. Soon after nine o'clock a fast dog-cart stopped outside, and a red-faced, loud-voiced man swaggered in, greeting Kentish with boisterous cordiality. He had a drink with the landlord, and said: "How's things? Fancy any of 'em for the sprint handicap? Got a lad o' your own in, haven't you?"

"Oh, yes," Kentish replied. "Crockett. Only a young un not got to his proper mark yet, I reckon. I think old Taylor's got No. 1 this time."

"Capital lad," the other replied, with a confidential nod. "Shouldn't wonder at all. Want to do anything yourself over it?"

"No, I don't think so. I'm not on at present. Might have a little flutter on the grounds just for fun; nothing else."

There were a few more casual remarks, and then the red-faced man drove away.

"Who was that?" asked Hewitt, who had watched the visitor through the snuggery window.

"That's Danby—bookmaker. Cute chap. He's been told Crockett's missing, I'll bet anything, and come here to pump me. No good, though. As a matter of fact, I've worked Sammy Crockett into his books for about half I'm in for altogether—through third parties, of course."

Hewitt reached for his hat. "I'm going out for half an hour now," he said. "If Steggles wants to go out before I come back, don't let him. Let him go and smooth over all those tracks on the cinder-path, very carefully. And, by the by, could you manage to have your son about the place to-day, in case I happen to want a little help out of doors?"

"Certainly; I'll get him to stay in. But what do you want the cinders smoothed for?"

Hewitt smiled, and patted his host's shoulder. "I'll explain all my tricks when the job's done," he said, and went out.

On the lane from Padfield to Sedby village stood the Plough beer-house, wherein J. Webb was licensed to sell by retail beer to be consumed on the premises or off, as the thirsty list. Nancy Webb, with a very fine color, a very curly fringe, and a wide smiling mouth revealing a fine set of teeth, came to the bar at the summons of a stoutish old gentleman in spectacles who walked with a stick.

The stoutish old gentleman had a glass of bitter beer, and then said in the peculiarly quiet voice of a very deaf man: "Can you tell me, if you please, the way into the main Catton road?"

"Down the lane, turn to the right at the cross-roads, then first to the left."

The old gentleman waited with his hand to his ear for some few seconds after she had finished speaking, and then resumed in his whispering voice: "I'm afraid I'm very deaf this morning." He fumbled in his pocket and produced a note-book and pencil. "May I trouble you to write it down? I'm so very deaf at times that I— Thank you."

The girl wrote the direction, and the old gentleman bade her good-morning and left. All down the lane he walked slowly with his stick. At the cross-roads he turned, put the stick under his arm, thrust his spectacles into his pocket, and strode away in the ordinary guise of Martin Hewitt. He pulled out his note-book, examined Miss Webb's direction very carefully, and then went off another way altogether, toward the Hare and Hounds.

Kentish lounged moodily in his bar. "Well, my boy," said Hewitt, "has Steggles wiped out the tracks?"

"Not yet; I haven't told him. But he's somewhere about; I'll tell him now."

"No, don't. I don't think we'll have that done, after all. I expect he'll want to go out soon—at any rate, some time during the day. Let him go whenever he likes. I'll sit upstairs a bit in the club-room."

"Very well. But how do you know Steggles will be going out?"

"Well, he's pretty restless after his lost *protégé*, isn't he? I don't suppose he'll be able to remain idle long."

"And about Crockett. Do you give him up?"

"Oh, no! Don't you be impatient. I can't say I'm quite confident yet of laying hold of him—the time is so short, you see—but I think I shall at least have news for you by the evening."

Hewitt sat in the club-room until the afternoon, taking his lunch there. At length he saw, through the front window, Raggy Steggles walking down the road. In an instant Hewitt was down-stairs and at the door. The road bent eighty yards away, and as soon as Steggles passed the bend the detective hurried after him.

All the way to Padfield town and more than half through it Hewitt dogged the trainer. In the end Steggles stopped at a corner and gave a note to a small boy who was playing near. The boy ran with the note to a bright, well-kept house at the opposite corner. Martin Hewitt was interested to observe the legend, "H. Danby, Contractor," on a board over a gate in the side wall of the garden behind this house. In five minutes a door in the side gate opened, and the head and shoulders of the red-faced man emerged. Steggles immediately hurried across and disappeared through the gate.

This was both interesting and instructive. Hewitt took up a position in the side street and waited. In ten minutes the trainer reappeared and hurried off the way he had come, along the street Hewitt had considerately left clear for him. Then Hewitt strolled toward the smart house and took a good look at it. At one corner of the small piece of forecourt garden, near the railings, a small, baize-covered, glass-fronted notice-board stood on two posts. On its top edge appeared the words, "H. Danby. Houses to be Sold or Let." But the only notice pinned to the green baize within was an old and dusty one, inviting tenants for three shops, which were suitable for any business, and which would be fitted to suit tenants. Apply within.

Hewitt pushed open the front gate and rang the door-bell. "There are some shops to let, I see," he said, when a maid appeared. "I should like to see them, if you will let me have the key."

"Master's out, sir. You can't see the shops till Monday."

"Dear me, that's unfortunate, I'm afraid I can't wait till Monday. Didn't Mr. Danby leave any instructions, in case anybody should inquire?"

"Yes, sir—as I've told you. He said anybody who called about 'em must come again on Monday."

"Oh, very well, then; I suppose I must try. One of the shops is in High Street, isn't it?"

"No, sir; they're all in the new part—Granville Road."

"Ah, I'm afraid that will scarcely do. But I'll see. Good-day."

Martin Hewitt walked away a couple of streets' lengths before he inquired the way to Granville Road. When at last he found that thoroughfare, in a new and muddy suburb, crowded with brick-heaps and half-finished streets, he took a slow walk along its entire length. It was a melancholy example of baffled enterprise. A row of a dozen or more shops had been built before any population had arrived to demand goods. Would-be tradesmen had taken many of these shops, and failure and disappointment stared from the windows. Some were half covered by shutters, because the scanty stock scarce sufficed to fill the remaining half. Others were shut almost altogether, the inmates only keeping open the door for their own convenience, and, perhaps, keeping down a shutter for the sake of a little light. Others, again, had not yet fallen so low, but struggled bravely still to maintain a show of business and prosperity, with very little success. Opposite the shops there still remained a dusty, ill-treated hedge and a forlorn-looking field, which an old board offered on building leases. Altogether a most depressing spot.

There was little difficulty in identifying the three shops offered for letting by Mr. H. Danby. They were all together near the middle of the row, and were the only ones that appeared not yet to have been occupied. A dusty "To Let" bill hung in each window, with written directions to inquire of Mr. H. Danby or at No. 7. Now No. 7 was a melancholy baker's shop, with a stock of three loaves and a plate of stale buns. The disappointed baker assured Hewitt that he usually kept the keys of the shops, but that the landlord, Mr. Danby, had taken them away the day before to see how the ceilings were standing, and had not returned them. "But if you was thinking of taking a shop here," the poor baker added, with some hesitation, "I—I—if you'll excuse my advising you—I shouldn't recommend it. I've had a sickener of it myself."

Hewitt thanked the baker for his advice, wished him better luck in future, and left. To the Hare and Hounds his pace was brisk. "Come," he said, as he met Kentish's inquiring glance, "this has been a very good day, on the whole. I know where our man is now, and I think we can get him, by a little management."

"Where is he?"

"Oh, down in Padfield. As a matter of fact, he's being kept there against his will, we shall find. I see that your friend Mr. Danby is a builder as well as a bookmaker."

"Not a regular builder. He speculates in a street of new houses now and again, that's all. But is he in it?"

"He's as deep in it as anybody, I think. Now, don't fly into a passion. There are a few others in it as well, but you'll do harm if you don't keep quiet."

"But go and get the police; come and fetch him, if you know where they're keeping him. Why—"

"So we will, if we can't do it without them. But it's quite possible we can, and without all the disturbance and, perhaps, delay that calling in the police would involve. Consider, now, in reference to your own arrangements. Wouldn't it pay you better to get him back quietly, without a soul knowing—perhaps not even Danby knowing—till the heat is run to-morrow?"

"Well, yes, it would, of course."

"Very good, then, so be it. Remember what I have told you about keeping your mouth shut; say nothing to Steggles or anybody. Is there a cab or brougham your son and I can have for the evening?"

"There's an old hiring landau in the stables you can shut up into a cab, if that'll do."

"Excellent. We'll run down to the town in it as soon as it's ready. But, first, a word about Crockett. What sort of a lad is he? Likely to give them trouble, show fight, and make a disturbance?"

"No, I should say not. He's no plucked un, certainly; all his manhood's in his legs, I believe. You see, he ain't a big sort o' chap at best, and he'd be pretty easy put upon—at least, I guess so."

"Very good, so much the better, for then he won't have been damaged, and they will probably only have one man to guard him. Now the carriage, please."

Young Kentish was a six-foot sergeant of grenadiers home on furlough, and luxuriating in plain clothes. He and Hewitt walked a little way toward the town, allowing the landau to catch them up. They traveled in it to within a hundred yards of the empty shops and then alighted, bidding the driver wait.

"I shall show you three empty shops," Hewitt said, as he and young Kentish walked down Granville Road. "I am pretty sure that Sammy Crockett is in one of them, and I am pretty sure that that is the middle one. Take a look as we go past."

When the shops had been slowly passed, Hewitt resumed: "Now, did you see anything about those shops that told a tale of any sort?"

"No," Sergeant Kentish replied. "I can't say I noticed

anything beyond the fact that they were empty—and likely to stay so, I should think."

"We'll stroll back, and look in at the windows, if nobody's watching us," Hewitt said. "You see, it's reasonable to suppose they've put him in the middle one, because that would suit their purpose best. The shops at each side of the three are occupied, and, if the prisoner struggled, or shouted, or made an uproar, he might be heard if he were in one of the shops next those inhabited. So that the middle shop is the most likely. Now, see there," he went on, as they stopped before the window of the shop in question, "over at the back there's a staircase not yet partitioned off. It goes down below and up above. On the stairs and on the floor near them there are muddy footmarks. These must have been made to-day, else they would not be muddy, but dry and dusty, since there hasn't been a shower for a week till to-day. Move on again. Then you noticed that there were no other such marks in the shop. Consequently the man with the muddy feet did not come in by the front door, but by the back; otherwise he would have made a trail from the door. So we will go round to the back ourselves."

It was now growing dusk. The small pieces of ground behind the shops were bounded by a low fence, containing a door for each house.

"This door is bolted inside, of course," Hewitt said, "but there is no difficulty in climbing. I think we had better wait in the garden till dark. In the meantime, the jailer, whoever he is, may come out; in which case we shall pounce on him as soon as he opens the door. You have that few yards of cord in your pocket, I think? And my handkerchief, properly rolled, will make a very good gag. Now over."

They climbed the fence and quietly approached the house, placing themselves in the angle of an outhouse out of sight from the windows. There was no sound, and no light appeared. Just above the ground about a foot of window was visible, with a grating over it, apparently lighting a basement. Suddenly Hewitt touched his companion's arm and pointed toward the window. A faint rustling sound was perceptible, and, as nearly as could be discerned in the darkness, some white blind or covering was placed over the glass from the inside. Then came the sound of a striking match, and at the side edge of the window there was a faint streak of light.

"That's the place," Hewitt whispered. "Come, we'll make a push for it. You stand against the wall at one side of the door and I'll stand at the other, and we'll have him as he comes out. Quietly, now, and I'll startle them."

He took a stone from among the rubbish littering the garden and flung it crashing through the window. There was a loud exclamation from within, the blind fell, and somebody rushed to the back door and flung it open. Instantly Kentish let fly a heavy right-hander, and the man went over like a skittle. In a moment Hewitt was upon him and the gag in his mouth.

"Hold him," Hewitt whispered, hurriedly. "I'll see if there are others."

He peered down through the low window. Within Sammy Crockett, his bare legs dangling from beneath his long overcoat, sat on a packing-box, leaning with his head on his hand and his back toward the window. A guttering candle stood on the mantel-piece, and the newspaper which had been stretched across the window lay in scattered sheets on the floor. No other person besides Sammy was visible.

They led their prisoner indoors. Young Kentish recognized him as a public-house loafer and race-course ruffian, well known in the neighborhood.

"So it's you, is it, Browdie?" he said. "I've caught you one hard clump, and I've half a mind to make it a score more. But you'll get it pretty warm one way or another before this job's forgotten."

Sammy Crockett was overjoyed at his rescue. He had not been ill-treated, he explained, but had been thoroughly cowed by Browdie, who had from time to time threatened him savagely with an iron bar by way of persuading him to quietness and submission. He had been fed, and had taken no worse harm than a slight stiffness from his adventure, due to his light under-attire of jersey and knee-shorts.

Sergeant Kentish tied Browdie's elbows firmly together behind, and carried the line round the ankles, bracing all up tight. Then he ran a knot from one wrist to the other over the back of the neck, and left the prisoner, trussed and helpless, on the heap of straw that had been Sammy's bed.

"You won't be very jolly, I expect," Kentish said, "for some time. You can't shout and you can't walk, and I know you can't untie yourself. You'll get a bit hungry, too, perhaps, but that'll give you an appetite. I don't suppose you'll be disturbed till some time to-morrow, unless our friend Danby turns up in the meantime. But you can come along to jail instead, if you prefer it."

They left him where he lay, and took Sammy to the old landau. Sammy walked in slippers, carrying his spiked shoes, hanging by the lace, in his hand.

"Ah," said Hewitt, "I think I know the name of the young lady who gave you those slippers."

Crockett looked ashamed and indignant. "Yes," he said, "they've done me nicely between 'em. But I'll pay her—I'll—"

"Hush, hush!" Hewitt said; "you mustn't talk unkindly of a lady, you know. Get into this carriage, and we'll take you home. We'll see if I can tell you your adventures without making a mistake. First, you had a note from Miss Webb, telling you that you were mistaken in supposing she had slighted you, and that, as a matter of fact, she had quite done with somebody else—left him—of whom you were jealous. Isn't that so?"

"Well, yes," young Crockett answered, blushing deeply under the carriage-lamp; "but I don't see how you come to know that."

"Then she went on to ask you to get rid of Steggles on Thursday afternoon for a few minutes, and speak to her in the back lane. Now, your running pumps, with their thin soles, almost like paper, no heels and long spikes, hurt your feet horribly if you walk on hard ground, don't they?"

"Ay, that they do—enough to cripple you. I'd never go on much hard ground with 'em."

"They're not like cricket shoes, I see."

"Not a bit. Cricket shoes you can walk anywhere in!"

"Well, she knew this—I think I know who told her—and she promised to bring you a new pair of slippers, and to throw them over the fence for you to come out in."

"I s'pose she's been tellin' you all this?" Crockett said, mournfully. "You couldn't ha' seen the letter; I saw her tear it up and put the bits in her pocket. She asked me for it in the lane, in case Steggles saw it."

"Well, at any rate, you sent Steggles away, and the slippers did come over, and you went into the lane. You walked with her as far as the road at the end, and then you were seized and gagged, and put into a carriage."

"That was Browdie did that," said Crockett, "and another chap I don't know. But—why, this is Padfield High Street?" He looked through the window and regarded the familiar shops with astonishment.

"Of course it is. Where did you think it was?"

"Why, where was that place you found me in?"

"Granville Road, Padfield. I suppose they told you you were in another town?"

"Told me it was Newstead Hatch. They drove for about three or four hours, and kept me down on the floor between the seats so as I couldn't see where we was going."

"Done for two reasons," said Hewitt. "First, to mystify you, and prevent any discovery of the people directing the conspiracy; and second, to be able to put you indoors at night and unobserved. Well, I think I have told you all you know yourself now as far as the carriage.

"But there is the Hare and Hounds just in front. We'll pull up here, and I'll get out and see if the coast is clear. I fancy Mr. Kentish would rather you came in unnoticed."

In a few seconds Hewitt was back, and Crockett was conveyed indoors by a side entrance. Hewitt's instructions to the landlord were few, but emphatic. "Don't tell Steggles about it," he said; "make an excuse to get rid of him, and send him out of the house. Take Crockett into some other bedroom, not his own, and let your son look after him. Then come here, and I'll tell you all about it."

Sammy Crockett was undergoing a heavy grooming with white embrocation at the hands of Sergeant Kentish when the landlord returned to Hewitt. "Does Danby know you've got him?" he asked. "How did you do it?"

"Danby doesn't know yet, and with luck he won't know till he sees Crockett running to-morrow. The man who has sold you is Steggles."

"Steggles?"

"Steggles it is. At the very first, when Steggles rushed in to report Sammy Crockett missing, I suspected him. You didn't, I suppose?"

"No. He's always been considered a straight man, and he looked as startled as anybody."

"Yes, I must say he acted it very well. But there was something suspicious in his story. What did he say? Crockett had remarked a chilliness, and asked for a sweater, which Steggles went to fetch. Now, just think. You understand these things. Would any trainer who knew his business (as Steggles does) have gone to bring out a sweater for his man to change for his jersey in the open air, at the very time the man was complaining of chilliness? Of course not. He would have taken his man indoors again and let him change there under shelter. Then supposing Steggles had really been surprised at missing Crockett, wouldn't he have looked about, found the gate open, and *told* you it was open when he first came in? He said nothing of that—we found the gate open for ourselves. So that from the beginning I had a certain opinion of Steggles."

"What you say seems pretty plain now, although it didn't strike me at the time. But, if Steggles was selling us, why couldn't he have drugged the lad? That would have been a deal simpler."

"Because Steggles is a good trainer, and has a certain reputation to keep up. It would have done him no good to have had a runner drugged while under his care; certainly it would have cooked his goose with *you*. It was much the safer thing to connive at kidnapping. That put all the active work into other hands, and left him safe, even if the trick failed. Now, you remember that we traced the prints of Crockett's spiked shoes to within a couple of yards from the fence, and that there they ceased suddenly?"

"Yes. You said it looked as though he had flown up into the air; and so it did."

"But I was sure that it was by that gate that Crockett had left, and by no other. He couldn't have got through the house without being seen, and there was no other way—let alone the evidence of the unbolted gate. Therefore, as the footprints ceased where they did, and were not repeated anywhere in the lane, I knew that he had taken his spiked shoes off—probably changed them for something else, because a runner anxious as to his chances would never risk walking on bare feet, with a chance of cutting them. Ordinary, broad, smooth-soled slippers would leave no impression on the coarse cinders bordering the track, and nothing short of spiked shoes would leave a mark on the hard path in the lane behind. The spike-tracks were leading, not directly toward the door, but in the direction of the fence, when they stopped; somebody had handed, or thrown, the slippers over the fence, and he had changed them on the spot. The enemy had calculated upon the spikes leaving a track in the lane that might lead us in our search, and had arranged accordingly.

"So far so good. I could see no footprints near the gate in the lane. You will remember that I sent Steggles off to watch at the Cop before I went out to the back—merely, of course, to get him out of the way. I went out into the lane, leaving you behind, and walked its whole length, first toward the Old Kilns and then back toward the road. I found nothing to help me except these small pieces of paper—which are here in my pocket-book, by the by. Of course this 'mmy' might have meant 'Jimmy' or 'Tommy' as possibly as 'Sammy,' but they were not to be rejected on that account. Certainly Crockett had been decoyed out of your ground, not taken by force, or there would have been marks of a scuffle in the cinders. And as his request for a sweater was probably an excuse—because it was not at all a cold afternoon—he must have previously designed going out. Inference, a letter received; and here were pieces of a letter. Now, in the light of what I have said, look at these pieces. First, there is the 'mmy'—that I have dealt with. Then see this 'throw them ov'—clearly a part of 'throw them over'; exactly what had probably been done with the slippers. Then the 'poor f,' coming just on the line before, and seen, by joining up with this other piece, might easily be a reference to 'poor feet.' These coincidences, one on the other, went far to establish the identity of the letter, and to confirm my previous impressions. But then there is something else. Two other pieces evidently mean 'left him,' and 'right away,' perhaps; but there is another, containing almost all of the words 'hate his,' with the word 'hate' underlined. Now, who writes 'hate' with the emphasis of underscoring—who but a woman? The writing is large and not very regular; it might easily be that of a half-educated woman. Here was something more—Sammy had been enticed away by a woman.

"Now, I remembered that, when we went into the tap-room on Wednesday, some of his companions were chaffing Crockett about a certain Nancy Webb, and the chaff went home, as was plain to see. The woman, then, who could most easily entice Sammy Crockett away was Nancy Webb. I resolved to find who Nancy Webb was and learn more of her.

"Meantime, I took a look at the road at the end of the lane. It was damper than the lane, being lower, and overhung by trees. There were many wheel-tracks, but only one set that turned in the road and went back the way it came, toward the town; and they were narrow wheels—carriage wheels. Crockett tells me now that they drove him about for a long time before shutting him up; probably the inconvenience of taking him straight to the hiding-place didn't strike them when they first drove off.

"A few inquiries soon set me in the direction of the Plough and Miss Nancy Webb. I had the curiosity to look around the place as I approached, and there, in the garden behind the house, were Steggles and the young lady in earnest confabulation!

"Every conjecture became a certainty. Steggles was the lover of whom Crockett was jealous, and he had employed the girl to bring Sammy out. I watched Steggles home, and gave you a hint to keep him there.

"But the thing that remained was to find Steggles' employer in this business. I was glad to be in when Danby called. He came, of course, to hear if you would blurt out anything, and to learn, if possible, what steps you were taking. He failed. By way of making assurance doubly sure I took a short walk this morning in the character of a deaf gentleman, and got Miss Webb to write me a direction that comprised three of the words on these scraps of paper—'left,' 'right,' and 'lane'; see, they correspond, the peculiar 'f's,' 't's,' and all.

"Now, I felt perfectly sure that Steggles would go for his pay to-day. In the first place, I knew that people mixed up with shady transactions in professional pedestrianism are not apt to trust one another far—they know better. Therefore Steggles wouldn't have had his bribe first. But he would take care to get it before the Saturday heats were run, because once they were over the thing was done, and the principal conspirator might have refused to pay up, and Steggles couldn't have helped himself. Again I hinted he should not go out till I could follow him, and this afternoon, when he went, follow him I did. I saw him go into Danby's house by the side way and come away again. Danby it was, then, who had arranged the business; and nobody was more likely, considering his large pecuniary stake against Crockett's winning this race.

"But now how to find Crockett? I made up my mind he wouldn't be in Danby's own house. That would be a deal too risky, with servants about and so on. I saw that Danby was a builder, and had three shops to let—it was on a paper before his house. What more likely prison than an empty house? I knocked at Danby's door and asked for the keys of those shops. I couldn't have them. The servant told me Danby was out (a manifest lie, for I had just seen him), and that nobody could see the shops till Monday. But I got out of her the address of the shops, and that was all I wanted at the time.

"Now, why was nobody to see those shops till Monday? The interval was suspicious—just enough to enable Crockett to be sent away again and cast loose after the Saturday racing, supposing him to be kept in one of the empty buildings. I went off at once and looked at the shops, forming my conclusions as to which would be the most likely for Danby's purpose. Here I had another confirmation of my ideas. A poor, half-bankrupt baker in one of the shops had, by the bills, the custody of a set of keys; but he, too, told me I couldn't have them; Danby had taken them away—and on Thursday, the very day—with some trivial excuse, and hadn't brought them back. That was all I wanted or could expect in the way of guidance. The whole thing was plain. The rest you know all about."

"Well, you're certainly as smart as they give you credit for, I must say. But suppose Danby had taken down his 'To Let' notice, what would you have done, then?"

"We had our course, even then. We should have gone to Danby, astounded him by telling him all about his little games, terrorized him with threats of the law, and made him throw up his hand and send Crockett back. But, as it is, you see, he doesn't know at this moment— probably won't know till to-morrow afternoon—that the lad is safe and sound here. You will probably use the interval to make him pay for losing the game—by some of the ingenious financial devices you are no doubt familiar with."

"Ay, that I will. He'll give any price against Crockett now, so long as the bet don't come direct from me."

"But about Crockett, now," Hewitt went on. "Won't this confinement be likely to have damaged his speed for a day or two?"

"Ah, perhaps," the landlord replied; "but, bless ye, that won't matter. There's four more in his heat to-morrow. Two I know aren't tryers, and the other two I can hold in at a couple of quid apiece any day. The third round and final won't be till to-morrow week, and he'll be as fit as ever by then. It's as safe as ever it was. How much are you going to have on? I'll lump it on for you safe enough. This is a chance not to be missed; it's picking money up."

"Thank you; I don't think I'll have anything to do with it. This professional pedestrian business doesn't seem a pretty one at all. I don't call myself a moralist, but, if you'll excuse my saying so, the thing is scarcely the game I care to pick tap money at in any way."

"Oh, very well! if you think so, I won't persuade ye, though I don't think so much of your smartness as I did, after that. Still, we won't quarrel; you've done me a mighty good turn, that I must say, and I only feel I aren't level without doing something to pay the debt. Come, now, you've got your trade as I've got mine. Let me have the bill, and I'll pay it like a lord, and feel a deal more pleased than if you made a favor of it—not that I'm above a favor, of course. But I'd prefer paying, and that's a fact."

"My dear sir, you have paid," Hewitt said, with a smile. "You paid in advance. It was a bargain, wasn't it, that I should do your business if you would help me in mine? Very well; a bargain's a bargain, and we've both performed our parts. And you mustn't be offended at what I said just now."

"That I won't! But as to that Raggy Steggles, once those heats are over to-morrow, I'll—well—"

It was on the following Sunday week that Martin Hewitt, in his rooms in London, turned over his paper and read, under the head "Padfield Annual 135 Yards Handicap," this announcement: "Final heat: Crockett, first; Willis, second; Trewby, third; Owen, 0; Howell, 0. A runaway win by nearly three yards."

III. THE CASE OF

MR. FOGGATT

ALMOST the only dogmatism that Martin Hewitt permitted himself in regard to his professional methods was one on the matter of accumulative probabilities. Often when I have remarked upon the apparently trivial nature of the clues by which he allowed himself to be guided—sometimes, to all seeming, in the very face of all likelihood—he has replied that two trivialities, pointing in the same direction, became at once, by their mere agreement, no trivialities at all, but enormously important considerations. "If I were in search of a man," he would say, "of whom I knew nothing but that he squinted, bore a birthmark on his right hand, and limped, and I observed a man who answered to the first peculiarity, so far the clue would be trivial, because thousands of men squint. Now, if that man presently moved and exhibited a birthmark on his right hand, the value of that squint and that mark would increase at once a hundred or a thousand fold. Apart they are little; together much. The weight of evidence is not doubled merely; it would be only doubled if half the men who squinted had right-hand birthmarks; whereas the proportion, if it could be ascertained, would be, perhaps, more like one in ten thousand. The two trivialities, pointing in the same direction, become very strong evidence. And, when the man is seen to walk with a limp, that limp (another triviality), re-enforcing the others, brings the matter to the rank of a practical certainty. The Bertillon system of identification—what is it but a summary of trivialities? Thousands of men are of the same height, thousands of the same length of foot, thousands of the same girth of head—thousands correspond in any separate measurement you may name. It is when the measurements are taken *together* that you have your man identified forever. Just consider how few, if any, of your friends correspond exactly in any two personal peculiarities." Hewitt's dogma received its illustration unexpectedly close at home.

The old house wherein my chambers and Hewitt's office were situated contained, besides my own, two or three more bachelors' dens, in addition to the offices on the ground and first and second floors. At the very top of all, at the back, a fat, middle-aged man, named Foggatt, occupied a set of four rooms. It was only after a long residence, by an accidental remark of the housekeeper's, that I learned the man's name, which was not painted on his door or displayed, with all the others, on the wall of the ground-floor porch.

Mr. Foggatt appeared to have few friends, but lived in something as nearly approaching luxury as an old bachelor living in chambers can live. An ascending case of champagne was a common phenomenon of the staircase, and I have more than once seen a picture, destined for the top floor, of a sort that went far to awaken green covetousness in the heart of a poor journalist.

The man himself was not altogether prepossessing. Fat as he was, he had a way of carrying his head forward on his extended neck and gazing widely about with a pair of the roundest and most prominent eyes I remember to have ever seen, except in a fish. On the whole, his appearance was rather vulgar, rather arrogant, and rather suspicious, without any very pronounced quality of any sort. But certainly he was not pretty. In the end, however, he was found shot dead in his sitting-room.

It was in this way: Hewitt and I had dined together at my club, and late in the evening had returned to my rooms to smoke and discuss whatever came uppermost. I had made a bargain that day with two speculative odd lots at a book sale, each of which contained a hidden prize. We sat talking and turning over these books while time went unperceived, when suddenly we were startled by a loud report. Clearly it was in the building. We listened for a moment, but heard nothing else, and then Hewitt expressed his opinion that the report was that of a gunshot. Gunshots in residential chambers are not common things, wherefore I got up and went to the landing, looking up the stairs and down.

At the top of the next flight I saw Mrs. Clayton, the housekeeper. She appeared to be frightened, and told me that the report came from Mr. Foggatt's room. She thought he might have had an accident with the pistol that usually lay on his mantel-piece. We went upstairs with her, and she knocked at Mr. Foggatt's door.

There was no reply. Through the ventilating fanlight over the door it could be seen that there were lights within, a sign, Mrs. Clayton maintained, that Mr. Foggatt was not out. We knocked again, much more loudly, and called, but still ineffectually. The door was locked, and an application of the housekeeper's key proved that the tenant's key had been left in the lock inside. Mrs.

Clayton's conviction that "something had happened" became distressing, and in the end Hewitt pried open the door with a small poker.

Something *had* happened. In the sitting-room Mr. Foggatt sat with his head bowed over the table, quiet and still. The head was ill to look at, and by it lay a large revolver, of the full-sized army pattern. Mrs. Clayton ran back toward the landing with faint screams.

"Run, Brett!" said Hewitt; "a doctor and a policeman!"

I bounced down the stairs half a flight at a time. "First," I thought, "a doctor. He may not be dead." I could think of no doctor in the immediate neighborhood, but ran up the street away from the Strand, as being the more likely direction for the doctor, although less so for the policeman. It took me a good five minutes to find the medico, after being led astray by a red lamp at a private hotel, and another five to get back, with a policeman.

Foggatt was dead, without a doubt. Probably had shot himself, the doctor thought, from the powder-blackening and other circumstances. Certainly nobody could have left the room by the door, or he must have passed my landing, while the fact of the door being found locked from the inside made the thing impossible. There were two windows to the room, both of which were shut, one being fastened by the catch, while the catch of the other was broken—an old fracture. Below these windows was a sheer drop of fifty feet or more, without a foot or hand-hold near. The windows in the other rooms were shut and fastened. Certainly it seemed suicide—unless it were one of those accidents that will occur to people who fiddle ignorantly with firearms. Soon the rooms were in possession of the police, and we were turned out.

We looked in at the housekeeper's kitchen, where her daughter was reviving and calming Mrs. Clayton with gin and water.

"You mustn't upset yourself, Mrs. Clayton," Hewitt said, "or what will become of us all? The doctor thinks it was an accident."

He took a small bottle of sewing-machine oil from his pocket and handed it to the daughter, thanking her for the loan.

There was little evidence at the inquest. The shot had been heard, the body had been found—that was the practical sum of the matter. No friends or relatives of the dead man came forward. The doctor gave his opinion as to the probability of suicide or an accident, and the police evidence tended in the same direction. Nothing had been found to indicate that any other person had been near the dead man's rooms on the night of the fatality. On the other hand, his papers, bankbook, etc., proved him to be a man of considerable substance, with no apparent motive for suicide. The police had been unable to trace any relatives, or, indeed, any nearer connections than casual acquaintances, fellow-clubmen, and so on. The jury found that Mr. Foggatt had died by accident.

"Well, Brett," Hewitt asked me afterward, "what do you think of the verdict?"

I said that it seemed to be the most reasonable one possible, and to square with the common-sense view of the case.

"Yes," he replied, "perhaps it does. From the point of view of the jury, and on their information, their verdict was quite reasonable. Nevertheless, Mr. Foggatt did not shoot himself. He was shot by a rather tall, active young man, perhaps a sailor, but certainly a gymnast—a young man whom I think I could identify if I saw him."

"But how do you know this?"

"By the simplest possible inferences, which you may easily guess, if you will but think."

"But, then, why didn't you say this at the inquest?"

"My dear fellow, they don't want any inferences and conjectures at an inquest; they only want evidence. If I had traced the murderer, of course then I should·have communicated with the police. As a matter of fact, it is quite possible that the police have observed and know as much as I do—or more. They don't give everything away at an inquest, you know. It wouldn't do."

"But, if you are right, how did the man get away?"

"Come, we are near home now. Let us take a look at the back of the house. He *couldn't* have left by Foggatt's landing door, as we know; and as he *was* there (I am certain of that), and as the chimney is out of the question—for there was a good fire in the grate—he must have gone out by the window. Only one window is possible—that with the broken catch—for all the others were fastened inside. Out of that window, then, he went."

"But how? The window is fifty feet up."

"Of course it is. But why *will* you persist in assuming that the only way of escape by a window is downward? See, now, look up there. The window is at the top floor, and it has a very broad sill. Over the window is nothing but the flat face of the gable-end; but to the right, and a foot or two above the level of the top of the window, an iron gutter ends. Observe, it is not of lead composition, but a strong iron gutter, supported, just at its end, by an iron bracket. If a tall man stood on the end of the window-sill, steadying himself by the left hand and leaning to the right, he could just touch the end of this gutter with his right hand. The full stretch, toe to finger, is seven feet three inches. I have measured it. An active gymnast, or a sailor, could catch the gutter with a slight spring, and by it draw himself upon the roof. You will say he would have to be *very* active, dexterous, and cool. So he would. And that very fact helps us, because it narrows the field of inquiry. We know the sort of man to look for. Because, being certain (as I am) that the man was in the room, I *know* that he left in the way I am telling you. He must have left in some way, and, all the other ways being impossible, this alone remains, difficult as the feat may seem. The fact of his shutting the window behind him further proves his coolness and address at so great a height from the ground."

All this was very plain, but the main point was still dark.

"You say you *know* that another man was in the room," I said; "how do you know that?"

"As I said, by an obvious inference. Come, now, you shall guess how I arrived at that inference. You often speak of your interest in my work, and the attention with which you follow it. This shall be a simple exercise for you. You saw everything in the room as plainly as I myself. Bring the scene back to your memory, and think over the various small objects littering about, and how they would affect the case. Quick observation is the first essential for my work. Did you see a newspaper, for instance?"

"Yes. There was an evening paper on the floor, but I didn't examine it."

"Anything else?"

"On the table there was a whisky decanter, taken from the tantalus-stand on the sideboard, and one glass. That, by the by," I added, "looked as though only one person were present."

"So it did, perhaps, although the inference wouldn't be very strong. Go on!"

"There was a fruit-stand on the sideboard, with a plate beside it containing a few nutshells, a piece of apple, a pair of nut-crackers, and, I think, some orange peel. There was, of course, all the ordinary furniture, but no chair pulled up to the table, except that used by Foggatt himself. That's all I noticed, I think. Stay—there was an ash-tray on the table, and a partly burned cigar near it— only one cigar, though."

"Excellent—excellent, indeed, as far as memory and simple observation go. You saw everything plainly, and you remember everything. Surely *now* you know how I found out that another man had just left?"

"No, I don't; unless there were different kinds of ash in the ash-tray."

"That is a fairly good suggestion, but there were not— there was only a single ash, corresponding in every way to that on the cigar. Don't you remember everything that I did as we went down-stairs?"

"You returned a bottle of oil to the housekeeper's daughter, I think."

"I did. Doesn't that give you a hint? Come, you surely have it now?"

"I haven't."

"Then I sha'n't tell you; you don't deserve it. Think, and don't mention the subject again till you have at least one guess to make. The thing stares you in the face; you see it, you remember it, and yet you *won't* see it. I won't encourage your slovenliness of thought, my boy, by telling you what you can know for yourself if you like. Good-by—I'm off now. There's a case in hand I can't neglect."

"Don't you propose to go further into this, then?"

Hewitt shrugged his shoulders. "I'm not a policeman," he said. "The case is in very good hands. Of course, if anybody comes to me to do it as a matter of business, I'll take it up. It's very interesting, but I can't neglect my regular work for it. Naturally, I shall keep my eyes open and my memory in order. Sometimes these things come into the hands by themselves, as it were; in that case, of course, I am a loyal citizen, and ready to help the law. *Au revoir!*"

I am a busy man myself, and thought little more of Hewitt's conundrum for some time; indeed, when I did think, I saw no way to the answer. A week after the inquest I took a holiday (I had written my nightly leaders regularly every day for the past five years), and saw no more of Hewitt for six weeks. After my return, with still a few days of leave to run, one evening we together turned into Luzatti's, off Coventry Street, for dinner.

"I have been here several times lately," Hewitt said; "they feed you very well. No, not that table"—he seized my arm as I turned to an unoccupied corner—"I fancy it's draughty." He led the way to a longer table where a dark, lithe, and (as well as could be seen) tall young man already sat, and took chairs opposite him.

We had scarcely seated ourselves before Hewitt broke into a torrent of conversation on the subject of bicycling. As our previous conversation had been of a literary sort, and as I had never known Hewitt at any other time to show the slightest interest in bicycling, this rather surprised me. I had, however, such a general outsider's grasp of the subject as is usual in a journalist-of-all-work, and managed to keep the talk going from my side. As we went on I could see the face of the young man opposite brighten with interest. He was a rather fine-looking fellow, with a dark, though very clear skin, but had a hard, angry look of eye, a prominence of cheek-bone, and a squareness of jaw that gave him a rather uninviting aspect. As Hewitt rattled on, however, our neighbor's expression became one of pleasant interest merely.

"Of course," Hewitt said, "we've a number of very capital men just now, but I believe a deal in the forgotten riders of five, ten, and fifteen years back. Osmond, I believe, was better than any man riding now, and I think it would puzzle some of them to beat Furnivall as he was, at his best. But poor old Cortis—really, I believe he was as good as anybody. Nobody ever beat Cortis—except—let me see—I think somebody beat Cortis once—who was it now? I can't remember."

"Liles," said the young man opposite, looking up quickly.

"Ah, yes—Liles it was; Charley Liles. Wasn't it a championship?"

"Mile championship, 1880; Cortis won the other three, though."

"Yes, so he did. I saw Cortis when he first broke the old 2.46 mile record." And straightway Hewitt plunged into a whirl of talk of bicycles, tricycles, records, racing cyclists, Hillier, and Synyer and Noel Whiting, Taylerson and Appleyard—talk wherein the young man opposite bore an animated share, while I was left in the cold.

Our new friend, it seems, had himself been a prominent racing bicyclist a few years back, and was presently, at Hewitt's request, exhibiting a neat gold medal that hung at his watch-guard. That was won, he explained, in the old tall bicycle days, the days of bad tracks, when every racing cyclist carried cinder scars on his face from numerous accidents. He pointed to a blue mark on his forehead, which, he told us, was a track scar, and described a bad fall that had cost him two teeth, and broken others. The gaps among his teeth were plain to see as he smiled.

Presently the waiter brought dessert, and the young man opposite took an apple. Nut-crackers and a fruit-knife lay on our side of the stand, and Hewitt turned the stand to offer him the knife.

"No, thanks," he said; "I only polish a good apple, never peel it. It's a mistake, except with thick-skinned foreign ones."

And he began to munch the apple as only a boy or a healthy athlete can. Presently he turned his head to order coffee. The waiter's back was turned, and he had to be called twice. To my unutterable amazement Hewitt reached swiftly across the table, snatched the half-eaten apple from the young man's plate and pocketed it, gazing immediately, with an abstracted air, at a painted Cupid on the ceiling.

Our neighbor turned again, looked doubtfully at his plate and the table-cloth about it, and then shot a keen glance in the direction of Hewitt. He said nothing, however, but took his coffee and his bill, deliberately drank the former, gazing quietly at Hewitt as he did it, paid the latter, and left.

Immediately Hewitt was on his feet and, taking an umbrella, which stood near, followed. Just as he reached the door he met our late neighbor, who had turned suddenly back.

"Your umbrella, I think?" Hewitt asked, offering it.

"Yes, thanks." But the man's eye had more than its former hardness, and his jaw muscles tightened as I looked. He turned and went. Hewitt came back to me. "Pay the bill," he said, "and go back to your rooms; I will come on later. I must follow this man—it's the Foggatt case." As he went out I heard a cab rattle away, and immediately after it another.

I paid the bill and went home. It was ten o'clock before Hewitt turned up, calling in at his office below on his way up to me.

"Mr. Sidney Mason," he said, "is the gentleman the police will be wanting to-morrow, I expect, for the Foggatt murder. He is as smart a man as I remember ever meeting, and has done me rather neatly twice this evening."

"You mean the man we sat opposite at Luzatti's, of course?"

"Yes, I got his name, of course, from the reverse of that gold medal he was good enough to show me. But I fear he has bilked me over the address. He suspected me, that was plain, and left his umbrella by way of experiment to see if I were watching him sharply enough to notice the circumstance, and to avail myself of it to follow him.

I was hasty and fell into the trap. He cabbed it away from Luzatti's, and I cabbed it after him. He has led me a pretty dance up and down London to-night, and two cabbies have made quite a stroke of business out of us. In the end he entered a house of which, of course, I have taken the address, but I expect he doesn't live there. He is too smart a man to lead me to his den; but the police can certainly find something of him at the house he went in at—and, I expect, left by the back way. By the way, you never guessed that simple little puzzle as to how I found that this *was* a murder, did you? You see it now, of course?"

"Something to do with that apple you stole, I suppose?"

"Something to do with it? I should think so, you worthy innocent. Just ring your bell; we'll borrow Mrs. Clayton's sewing-machine oil again. On the night we broke into Foggatt's room you saw the nutshells and the bitten remains of an apple on the sideboard, and you remembered it; and yet you couldn't see that in that piece of apple possibly lay an important piece of evidence. Of course I never expected you to have arrived at any conclusion, as I had, because I had ten minutes in which to examine that apple, and to do what I did with it. But, at least, you should have seen the possibility of evidence in it.

"First, now, the apple was white. A bitten apple, as you must have observed, turns of a reddish brown color if left to stand long. Different kinds of apples brown with different rapidities, and the browning always begins at the core. This is one of the twenty thousand tiny things that few people take the trouble to notice, but which it is useful for a man in my position to know. A russet will brown quite quickly. The apple on the sideboard was, as near as I could tell, a Newtown pippin or other apple of that kind, which will brown at the core in from twenty minutes to half an hour, and in other parts in a quarter of an hour more. When we saw it, it was white, with barely a tinge of brown about the exposed core. Inference, somebody had been eating it fifteen or twenty minutes before, perhaps a little longer—an inference supported by the fact that it was only partly eaten.

"I examined that apple, and found it bore marks of very irregular teeth. While you were gone, I oiled it over, and, rushing down to my rooms, where I always have a little plaster of Paris handy for such work, took a mold of the part where the teeth had left the clearest marks. I then returned the apple to its place for the police to use if they thought fit. Looking at my mold, it was plain that the person who had bitten that apple had lost two teeth, one at top and one below, not exactly opposite, but nearly so. The other teeth, although they would appear to have been fairly sound, were irregular in size and line. Now, the dead man had, as I saw, a very excellent set of false teeth, regular and sharp, with none missing. Therefore it was plain that somebody *else* had been eating that apple. Do I make myself clear?"

"Quite! Go on!"

"There were other inferences to be made—slighter, but all pointing the same way. For instance, a man of Foggatt's age does not, as a rule, munch an unpeeled apple like a school-boy. Inference, a young man, and healthy. Why I came to the conclusion that he was tall, active, a gymnast, and perhaps a sailor, I have already told you, when we examined the outside of Foggatt's window. It was also pretty clear that robbery was not the motive, since nothing was disturbed, and that a friendly conversation had preceded the murder—witness the drinking and the eating of the apple. Whether or not the police noticed these things I can't say. If they had had their best men on, they certainly would, I think; but the case, to a rough observer, looked so clearly one of accident or suicide that possibly they didn't.

"As I said, after the inquest I was unable to devote any immediate time to the case, but I resolved to keep my eyes open. The man to look for was tall, young, strong and active, with a very irregular set of teeth, a tooth missing from the lower jaw just to the left of the center, and another from the upper jaw a little farther still toward the left. He might possibly be a person I had seen about the premises (I have a good memory for faces), or, of course, he possibly might not.

"Just before you returned from your holiday I noticed a young man at Luzatti's whom I remembered to have seen somewhere about the offices in this building. He was tall, young, and so on, but I had a client with me, and was unable to examine him more narrowly; indeed, as I was not exactly engaged on the case, and as there are several tall young men about, I took little trouble. But to-day, finding the same young man with a vacant seat opposite him, I took the opportunity of making a closer acquaintance."

"You certainly managed to draw him out."

"Oh, yes; the easiest person in the world to draw out is a cyclist. The easiest cyclist to draw out is, of course, the novice, but the next easiest is the veteran. When you see a healthy, well-trained-looking man, who, nevertheless, has a slight stoop in the shoulders, and, maybe, a medal on his watch-guard, it is always a safe card to try him first with a little cycle-racing talk. I soon brought Mr. Mason out of his shell, read his name on his medal, and had a chance of observing his teeth—indeed, he spoke of them himself. Now, as I observed just now, there are several tall, athletic young men about, and also there are several men who have lost teeth. But now I saw that this tall and athletic young man had lost exactly *two* teeth— one from the lower jaw, just to the left of the center, and another from the upper jaw, farther still toward the left! Trivialities, pointing in the same direction, became important considerations. More, his teeth were irregular throughout, and, as nearly as I could remember it, looked remarkably like this little plaster mold of mine."

He produced from his pocket an irregular lump of plaster, about three inches long. On one side of this appeared in relief the likeness of two irregular rows of six or eight teeth, minus one in each row, where a deep gap was seen, in the position spoken of by my friend. He proceeded:

"This was enough at least to set me after this young man. But he gave me the greatest chance of all when he turned and left his apple (eaten unpeeled, remember!— another important triviality) on his plate. I'm afraid I wasn't at all polite, and I ran the risk of arousing his suspicions, but I couldn't resist the temptation to steal it. I did, as you saw, and here it is."

He brought the apple from his coat-pocket. One bitten side, placed against the upper half of the mold, fitted precisely, a projection of apple filling exactly the deep gap. The other side similarly fitted the lower half.

"There's no getting behind that, you see," Hewitt remarked. "Merely observing the man's teeth was a guide, to some extent, but this is as plain as his signature or his thumb impression. You'll never find two men *bite* exactly alike, no matter whether they leave distinct teeth-marks or not. Here, by the by, is Mrs. Clayton's oil. We'll take another mold from this apple, and compare *them*."

He oiled the apple, heaped a little plaster in a newspaper, took my water-jug, and rapidly pulled off a hard mold. The parts corresponding to the merely broken places in the apple were, of course, dissimilar; but as to the teeth-marks, the impressions were identical.

"That will do, I think," Hewitt said. "Tomorrow morning, Brett, I shall put up these things in a small parcel, and take them round to Bow Street."

"But are they sufficient evidence?"

"Quite sufficient for the police purpose. There is the man, and all the rest—his movements on the day and so forth—are simple matters of inquiry; at any rate, that is police business."

I had scarcely sat down to my breakfast on the following morning when Hewitt came into the room and put a long letter before me.

"From our friend of last night," he said; "read it."

This letter began abruptly, and undated, and was as follows:

> *"TO MARTIN HEWITT, ESQ.*
> *"SIR: I must compliment you on the adroitness you exhibited this evening in extracting from me my name. The address I was able to balk*

you of for the time being, although by the time you read this you will probably have found it through the Law List, as I am an admitted solicitor. That, however, will be of little use to you, for I am removing myself, I think, beyond the reach even of your abilities of search. I knew you well by sight, and was, perhaps, foolish to allow myself to be drawn as I did. Still, I had no idea that it would be dangerous, especially after seeing you, as a witness with very little to say, at the inquest upon the scoundrel I shot. Your somewhat discourteous seizure of my apple at first amazed me—indeed, I was a little doubtful as to whether you had really taken it—but it was my first warning that you might be playing a deep game against me, incomprehensible as the action was to my mind. I subsequently reflected that I had been eating an apple, instead of taking the drink he first offered me, in the dead wretch's rooms on the night he came to his merited end. From this I assume that your design was in some way to compare what remained of the two apples—although I do not presume to fathom the depths of your detective system. Still, I have heard of many of your cases, and profoundly admire the keenness you exhibit. I am thought to be a keen man myself, but, although I was able, to some extent, to hold my own to-night, I admit that your acumen in this case alone is something beyond me.

    "I do not know by whom you are commissioned to hunt me, nor to what extent

*you may be acquainted with my connection with
the creature I killed. I have sufficient respect for
you, however, to wish that you should not regard
me as a vicious criminal, and a couple of hours
to spare in which to offer you an explanation
that will convince you that such is not altogether
the case. A hasty and violent temper I admit
possessing; but even now I can not forget the
one crime it has led me into—for it is, I suppose,
strictly speaking, a crime. For it was the man
Foggatt who made a felon of my father before the
eyes of the world, and killed him with shame. It
was he who murdered my mother, and none the
less murdered her because she died of a broken
heart. That he was also a thief and a hypocrite
might have concerned me little but for that.*

*"Of my father I remember very little. He
must, I fear, have been a weak and incapable
man in many respects. He had no business
abilities—in fact, was quite unable to understand
the complicated business matters in which he
largely dealt. Foggatt was a consummate master
of all those arts of financial jugglery that make
so many fortunes, and ruin so many others,
in matters of company promoting, stocks, and
shares. He was unable to exercise them, however,
because of a great financial disaster in which he
had been mixed up a few years before, and which
made his name one to be avoided in future. In
these circumstances he made a sort of secret
and informal partnership with my father, who,
ostensibly alone in the business, acted throughout*

on the directions of Foggatt, understanding
as little what he did, poor, simple man, as a
schoolboy would have done. The transactions
carried on went from small to large, and,
unhappily from honorable to dishonorable. My
father relied on the superior abilities of Foggatt
with an absolute trust, carrying out each day
the directions given him privately the previous
evening, buying, selling, printing prospectuses,
signing whatever had to be signed, all with sole
responsibility and as sole partner, while Foggatt,
behind the scenes absorbed the larger share of the
profits. In brief, my unhappy and foolish father
was a mere tool in the hands of the cunning
scoundrel who pulled all the wires of the business,
himself unseen and irresponsible. At last three
companies, for the promotion of which my father
was responsible, came to grief in a heap. Fraud
was written large over all their history, and, while
Foggatt retired with his plunder, my father was
left to meet ruin, disgrace, and imprisonment.
From beginning to end he, and he only, was
responsible. There was no shred of evidence to
connect Foggatt with the matter, and no means
of escape from the net drawn about my father. He
lived through three years of imprisonment, and
then, entirely abandoned by the man who had
made use of his simplicity, he died—of nothing
but shame and a broken heart.

"Of this I knew nothing at the time. Again and
again, as a small boy, I remember asking of my
mother why I had no father at home, as other boys

had—unconscious of the stab I thus inflicted on her gentle heart. Of her my earliest, as well as my latest, memory is that of a pale, weeping woman, who grudged to let me out of her sight.

"Little by little I learned the whole cause of my mother's grief, for she had no other confidant, and I fear my character developed early, for my first coherent remembrance of the matter is that of a childish design to take a table-knife and kill the bad man who had made my father die in prison and caused my mother to cry.

"One thing, however, I never knew—the name of that bad man. Again and again, as I grew older, I demanded to know, but my mother always withheld it from me, with a gentle reminder that vengeance was for a greater hand than mine.

"I was seventeen years of age when my mother died. I believe that nothing but her strong attachment to myself and her desire to see me safely started in life kept her alive so long. Then I found that through all those years of narrowed means she had contrived to scrape and save a little money—sufficient, as it afterward proved, to see me through the examinations for entrance to my profession, with the generous assistance of my father's old legal advisers, who gave me my articles, and who have all along treated me with extreme kindness.

"For most of the succeeding years my life does not concern the matter in hand. I was a lawyer's clerk in my benefactors' service, and afterward

*a qualified man among their assistants. All
through the firm were careful, in pursuance of
my poor mother's wishes, that I should not learn
the name or whereabouts of the man who had
wrecked her life and my father's. I first met the
man himself at the Clifton Club, where I had gone
with an acquaintance who was a member. It was
not till afterward that I understood his curious
awkwardness on that occasion. A week later I
called (as I had frequently done) at the building
in which your office is situated, on business with
a solicitor who has an office on the floor above
your own. On the stairs I almost ran against Mr.
Foggatt. He started and turned pale, exhibiting
signs of alarm that I could not understand, and
asked me if I wished to see him.*

*"'No,' I replied, 'I didn't know you lived here. I
am after somebody else just now. Aren't you well?'*

*"He looked at me rather doubtfully, and said
he was not very well.*

*"I met him twice or thrice after that, and on
each occasion his manner grew more friendly,
in a servile, flattering, and mean sort of way—a
thing unpleasant enough in anybody, but doubly
so in the intercourse of a man with another young
enough to be his own son. Still, of course, I treated
the man civilly enough. On one occasion he asked
me into his rooms to look at a rather fine picture
he had lately bought, and observed casually, lifting
a large revolver from the mantel-piece:*

*"'You see, I am prepared for any unwelcome
visitors to my little den! He! He!' Conceiving him,*

*of course, to refer to burglars, I could not help
wondering at the forced and hollow character
of his laugh. As we went down the stairs he said:
'I think we know one another pretty well now,
Mr. Mason, eh? And if I could do anything to
advance your professional prospects, I should be
glad of the chance, of course. I understand the
struggles of a young professional man—he! he!' It
was the forced laugh again, and the man spoke
nervously. 'I think,' he added, 'that if you will
drop in to-morrow evening, perhaps I may have a
little proposal to make. Will you?'*

"I assented, wondering what this proposal
could be. Perhaps this eccentric old gentleman
was a good fellow, after all, anxious to do me a
good turn, and his awkwardness was nothing but
a natural delicacy in breaking the ice. I was not so
flush of good friends as to be willing to lose one. He
might be desirous of putting business in my way.

"I went, and was received with cordiality that
even then seemed a little over-effusive. We sat
and talked of one thing and another for a long
while, and I began to wonder when Mr. Foggatt
was coming to the point that most interested me.
Several times he invited me to drink and smoke,
but long usage to athletic training has given me
a distaste for both practices, and I declined. At
last he began to talk about myself. He was afraid
that my professional prospects in this country
were not great, but he had heard that in some of
the colonies—South Africa, for example—young
lawyers had brilliant opportunities.

"'If you'd like to go there,' he said, 'I've no doubt, with a little capital, a clever man like you could get a grand practice together very soon. Or you might buy a share in some good established practice. I should be glad to let you have £500, or even a little more, if that wouldn't satisfy you, and—'

"I stood aghast. Why should this man, almost a stranger, offer me £500, or even more, 'if that wouldn't satisfy' me? What claim had I on him? It was very generous of him, of course, but out of the question. I was, at least, a gentleman, and had a gentleman's self-respect. Meanwhile, he had gone maundering on, in a halting sort of way, and presently let slip a sentence that struck me like a blow between the eyes.

"'I shouldn't like you to bear ill-will because of what has happened in the past,' he said. 'Your late—your late lamented mother—I'm afraid—she had unworthy suspicions—I'm sure—it was best for all parties—your father always appreciated—'

"I set back my chair and stood erect before him. This groveling wretch, forcing the words through his dry lips, was the thief who had made another of my father and had brought to miserable ends the lives of both my parents! Everything was clear. The creature went in fear of me, never imagining that I did not know him, and sought to buy me off—to buy me from the remembrance of my dead mother's broken heart for £500—£500 that he had made my father steal

*for him! I said not a word. But the memory of all
my mother's bitter years, and a savage sense of
this crowning insult to myself, took a hold upon
me, and I was a tiger. Even then I verily believe
that one word of repentance, one tone of honest
remorse, would have saved him. But he drooped
his eyes, snuffled excuses, and stammered of
'unworthy suspicions' and 'no ill-will.' I let him
stammer. Presently he looked up and saw my
face; and fell back in his chair, sick with terror.
I snatched the pistol from the mantel-piece, and,
thrusting it in his face, shot him where he sat.*

"*My subsequent coolness and quietness
surprise me now. I took my hat and stepped
toward the door. But there were voices on the
stairs. The door was locked on the inside, and
I left it so. I went back and quietly opened a
window. Below was a clear drop into darkness,
and above was plain wall; but away to one
side, where the slope of the gable sprang from
the roof, an iron gutter ended, supported by a
strong bracket. It was the only way. I got upon
the sill and carefully shut the window behind me,
for people were already knocking at the lobby
door. From the end of the sill, holding on by the
reveal of the window with one hand, leaning
and stretching my utmost, I caught the gutter,
swung myself clear, and scrambled on the roof.
I climbed over many roofs before I found, in an
adjoining street, a ladder lashed perpendicularly
against the front of a house in course of repair.
This, to me, was an easy opportunity of descent,*

*notwithstanding the boards fastened over the face
of the ladder, and I availed myself of it.*

*"I have taken some time and trouble in order
that you (so far as I am aware the only human
being beside myself who knows me to be the
author of Foggatt's death) shall have at least the
means of appraising my crime at its just value
of culpability. How much you already know of
what I have told you I can not guess. I am wrong,
hardened, and flagitious, I make no doubt, but
I speak of the facts as they are. You see the thing,
of course, from your own point of view—I from
mine. And I remember my mother!*

*"Trusting that you will forgive the odd freak
of a man—a criminal, let us say—who makes a
confidant of the man set to hunt him down, I beg
leave to be, sir, your obedient servant,*

"SIDNEY MASON."

I read the singular document through and handed it
back to Hewitt.

"How does it strike you?" Hewitt asked.

"Mason would seem to be a man of very marked
character," I said. "Certainly no fool. And, if his tale is
true, Foggatt is no great loss to the world."

"Just so—if the tale is true. Personally I am disposed
to believe it is."

"Where was the letter posted?"

"It wasn't posted. It was handed in with the others
from the front-door letter-box this morning in an
unstamped envelope. He must have dropped it in
himself during the night. Paper," Hewitt proceeded,

holding it up to the light, "Turkey mill, ruled foolscap. Envelope, blue, official shape, Pirie's watermark. Both quite ordinary and no special marks."

"Where do you suppose he's gone?"

"Impossible to guess. Some might think he meant suicide by the expression 'beyond the reach even of your abilities of search,' but I scarcely think he is the sort of man to do that. No, there is no telling. Something may be got by inquiring at his late address, of course; but, when such a man tells you he doesn't think you will find him, you may count upon its being a difficult job. His opinion is not to be despised."

"What shall you do?"

"Put the letter in the box with the casts for the police. *Fiat justitia*, you know, without any question of sentiment. As to the apple, I really think, if the police will let me, I'll make you a present of it. Keep it somewhere as a souvenir of your absolute deficiency in reflective observation in this case, and look at it whenever you feel yourself growing dangerously conceited. It should cure you."

This is the history of the withered and almost petrified half apple that stands in my cabinet among a number of flint implements and one or two rather fine old Roman vessels. Of Mr. Sidney Mason we never heard another word. The police did their best, but he had left not a track behind him. His rooms were left almost undisturbed, and he had gone without anything in the way of elaborate preparation for his journey, and without leaving a trace of his intentions.

IV. THE CASE OF THE

DIXON TORPEDO

HEWITT was very apt, in conversation, to dwell upon the many curious chances and coincidences that he had observed, not only in connection with his own cases, but also in matters dealt with by the official police, with whom he was on terms of pretty regular, and, indeed, friendly, acquaintanceship. He has told me many an anecdote of singular happenings to Scotland Yard officials with whom he has exchanged experiences. Of Inspector Nettings, for instance, who spent many weary months in a search for a man wanted by the American Government, and in the end found, by the merest accident (a misdirected call), that the man had been lodging next door to himself the whole of the time; just as ignorant, of course, as was the inspector himself as to the enemy at the other side of the party-wall. Also of another inspector, whose name I can not recall, who, having been given rather meager and insufficient details of a man whom he anticipated having great difficulty in finding, went straight down the stairs of the office where he had received instructions, and actually *fell over* the man near the door, where he had stooped down to tie his shoe-lace! There were cases, too, in which, when a great and notorious crime had been committed, and various persons had been arrested on suspicion, some were found among them who had long been badly wanted for some other crime altogether. Many criminals had met their deserts by venturing out of their own particular line of crime into another; often a man who got into trouble over something comparatively small found himself in for a startlingly larger trouble, the result of some previous misdeed that otherwise would have gone unpunished. The ruble note-forger Mirsky might never have been handed over to the Russian authorities had he confined his genius to forgery alone. It was generally supposed at the time of his extradition that he had communicated with the Russian Embassy, with a view to giving himself up—a foolish proceeding on his part, it would seem, since his whereabouts, indeed even his identity as the forger, had not been suspected. He *had* communicated with the Russian Embassy, it is true, but for quite a different purpose, as Martin Hewitt well understood at the time. What that purpose was is now for the first time published.

The time was half-past one in the afternoon, and Hewitt sat in his inner office examining and comparing the handwriting of two letters by the aid of a large lens. He put down the lens and glanced at the clock on the mantel-piece with a premonition of lunch; and as he did so his clerk quietly entered the room with one of those printed slips which were kept for the announcement of unknown visitors. It was filled up in a hasty and almost illegible hand, thus:

Name of visitor: *F. Graham Dixon*.
Address: *Chancery Lane*.
Business: *Private and urgent*.

"Show Mr. Dixon in," said Martin Hewitt.

Mr. Dixon was a gaunt, worn-looking man of fifty or so, well, although rather carelessly, dressed, and carrying in his strong, though drawn, face and dullish eyes the look that characterizes the life-long strenuous brain-worker. He leaned forward anxiously in the chair which Hewitt offered him, and told his story with a great deal of very natural agitation.

"You may possibly have heard, Mr. Hewitt—I know there are rumors—of the new locomotive torpedo which the government is about adopting; it is, in fact, the Dixon torpedo, my own invention, and in every respect—not merely in my own opinion, but in that of the government experts—by far the most efficient and certain yet produced. It will travel at least four hundred yards farther than any torpedo now made, with perfect accuracy of aim (a very great desideratum, let me tell you), and will carry an unprecedentedly heavy charge. There are other advantages—speed, simple discharge, and so forth—that I needn't bother you about. The machine is the result of many years of work and disappointment, and its design has only been arrived at by a careful balancing of principles and means, which are expressed on the only four existing sets of drawings. The whole thing, I need hardly tell you, is a profound secret, and you may judge of my present state of mind when I tell you that one set of drawings has been stolen."

"From your house?"

"From my office, in Chancery Lane, this morning. The four sets of drawings were distributed thus: Two were at the Admiralty Office, one being a finished set on thick paper, and the other a set of tracings therefrom; and the other two were at my own office, one being a penciled set, uncolored—a sort of finished draft, you understand—and the other a set of tracings similar to those at the Admiralty. It is this last set that has gone. The two sets were kept together in one drawer in my room. Both were there at ten this morning; of that I am sure, for I had to go to that very drawer for something else when I first arrived. But at twelve the tracings had vanished."

"You suspect somebody, probably?"

"I can not. It is a most extraordinary thing. Nobody has left the office (except myself, and then only to come to you) since ten this morning, and there has been no visitor. And yet the drawings are gone!"

"But have you searched the place?"

"Of course I have! It was twelve o'clock when I first discovered my loss, and I have been turning the place upside down ever since—I and my assistants. Every drawer has been emptied, every desk and table turned over, the very carpet and linoleum have been taken up, but there is not a sign of the drawings. My men even insisted on turning all their pockets inside out, although I never for a moment suspected either of them, and it would take a pretty big pocket to hold the drawings, doubled up as small as they might be."

"You say your men—there are two, I understand—had neither left the office?"

"Neither; and they are both staying in now. Worsfold suggested that it would be more satisfactory if they did not leave till something was done toward clearing the mystery up, and, although, as I have said, I don't suspect either in the least, I acquiesced."

"Just so. Now—I am assuming that you wish me to undertake the recovery of these drawings?"

The engineer nodded hastily.

"Very good; I will go round to your office. But first perhaps you can tell me something about your assistants—something it might be awkward to tell me in their presence, you know. Mr. Worsfold, for instance?"

"He is my draughtsman—a very excellent and intelligent man, a very smart man, indeed, and, I feel sure, quite beyond suspicion. He has prepared many important drawings for me (he has been with me nearly ten years now), and I have always found him trustworthy. But, of course, the temptation in this case would be enormous. Still, I can not suspect Worsfold. Indeed, how can I suspect anybody in the circumstances?"

"The other, now?"

"His name's Ritter. He is merely a tracer, not a fully skilled draughtsman. He is quite a decent young fellow, and I have had him two years. I don't consider him particularly smart, or he would have learned a little more of his business by this time. But I don't see the least reason to suspect him. As I said before, I can't reasonably suspect anybody."

"Very well; we will get to Chancery Lane now, if you please, and you can tell me more as we go."

"I have a cab waiting. What else can I tell you?"

"I understand the position to be succinctly this: The drawings were in the office when you arrived. Nobody came out, and nobody went in; and *yet* they vanished. Is that so?"

"That is so. When I say that absolutely nobody came in, of course I except the postman. He brought a couple of letters during the morning. I mean that absolutely nobody came past the barrier in the outer office—the usual thing, you know, like a counter, with a frame of ground glass over it."

"I quite understand that. But I think you said that the drawings were in a drawer in your *own* room—not the outer office, where the draughtsmen are, I presume?"

"That is the case. It is an inner room, or, rather, a room parallel with the other, and communicating with it; just as your own room is, which we have just left."

"But, then, you say you never left your office, and yet the drawings vanished—apparently by some unseen agency— while you were there in the room?"

"Let me explain more clearly." The cab was bowling

smoothly along the Strand, and the engineer took out a pocket-book and pencil. "I fear," he proceeded, "that I am a little confused in my explanation—I am naturally rather agitated. As you will see presently, my offices consist of three rooms, two at one side of a corridor, and the other opposite—thus." He made a rapid pencil sketch.

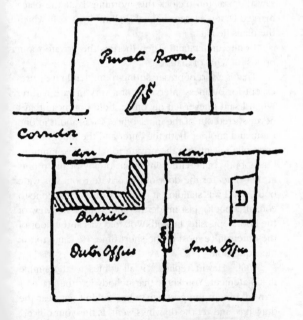

"In the outer office my men usually work. In the inner office I work myself. These rooms communicate, as you see, by a door. Our ordinary way in and out of the place is by the door of the outer office leading into the corridor, and we first pass through the usual lifting flap in the barrier. The door leading from the *inner* office to the corridor is always kept locked on the inside, and I don't suppose I unlock it once in three months. It has not been unlocked all the morning. The drawer in which the missing drawings were kept, and in which I saw them at ten o'clock this morning, is at the place marked D; it is a large chest of shallow drawers in which the plans lie flat."

"I quite understand. Then there is the private room opposite. What of that?"

"That is a sort of private sitting-room that I rarely use, except for business interviews of a very private nature. When I said I never left my office, I did not mean that I never stirred out of the inner office. I was about in one room and another, both the outer and the inner offices, and once I went into the private room for five minutes, but nobody came either in or out of any of the rooms at that time, for the door of the private room was wide open, and I was standing at the book-case (I had gone to consult a book), just inside the door, with a full view of the doors opposite. Indeed, Worsfold was at the door of the outer office most of the short time. He came to ask me a question."

"Well," Hewitt replied, "it all comes to the simple first statement. You know that nobody left the place or arrived, except the postman, who couldn't get near the drawings, and yet the drawings went. Is this your office?"

The cab had stopped before a large stone building. Mr. Dixon alighted and led the way to the first-floor. Hewitt took a casual glance round each of the three rooms. There was a sort of door in the frame of ground glass over the barrier to admit of speech with visitors. This door Hewitt pushed wide open, and left so.

He and the engineer went into the inner office. "Would you like to ask Worsfold and Ritter any questions?" Mr. Dixon inquired.

"Presently. Those are their coats, I take it, hanging just to the right of the outer office door, over the umbrella stand?"

"Yes, those are all their things—coats, hats, stick, and umbrella."

"And those coats were searched, you say?"

"Yes."

"And this is the drawer—thoroughly searched, of course?"

"Oh, certainly; every drawer was taken out and turned over."

"Well, of course I must assume you made no mistake in your hunt. Now tell me, did anybody know where these plans were, beyond yourself and your two men?"

"As far as I can tell, not a soul."

"You don't keep an office boy?"

"No. There would be nothing for him to do except to post a letter now and again, which Ritter does quite well for."

"As you are quite sure that the drawings were there at ten o'clock, perhaps the thing scarcely matters. But I may as well know if your men have keys of the office?"

"Neither. I have patent locks to each door and I keep all the keys myself. If Worsfold or Ritter arrive before me in the morning they have to wait to be let in; and I am always present myself when the rooms are cleaned. I have not neglected precautions, you see."

"No. I suppose the object of the theft—assuming it is a theft—is pretty plain: the thief would offer the drawings for sale to some foreign government?"

"Of course. They would probably command a great sum. I have been looking, as I need hardly tell you, to that invention to secure me a very large fortune, and I shall be ruined, indeed, if the design is taken abroad. I am under the strictest engagements to secrecy with the Admiralty, and not only should I lose all my labor, but I should lose all the confidence reposed in me at headquarters; should, in fact, be subject to penalties for breach of contract, and my career stopped forever. I can not tell you what a serious business this is for me. If you can not help me, the consequences will be terrible. Bad for the service of the country, too, of course."

"Of course. Now tell me this: It would, I take it, be necessary for the thief to *exhibit* these drawings to anybody anxious to buy the secret—I mean, he couldn't describe the invention by word of mouth."

"Oh, no, that would be impossible. The drawings are of the most complicated description, and full of figures upon which the whole thing depends. Indeed, one would have to be a skilled expert to properly appreciate the design at all. Various principles of hydrostatics, chemistry, electricity, and pneumatics are most delicately manipulated and adjusted, and the smallest error or omission in any part would upset the whole. No, the drawings are necessary to the thing, and they are gone."

At this moment the door of the outer office was heard to open and somebody entered. The door between the two offices was ajar, and Hewitt could see right through to the glass door left open over the barrier and into the space beyond. A well-dressed, dark, bushy-bearded man stood there carrying a hand-bag, which he placed on the ledge before him. Hewitt raised his hand to enjoin silence. The man spoke in a rather high-pitched voice and with a slight accent. "Is Mr. Dixon now within?" he asked.

"He is engaged," answered one of the draughtsmen; "very particularly engaged. I am afraid you won't be able to see him this afternoon. Can I give him any message?"

"This is two—the second time I have come to-day. Not two hours ago Mr. Dixon himself tells me to call again. I have a very important—very excellent steam-packing to show him that is very cheap and the best of the market." The man tapped his bag. "I have just taken orders from the largest railway companies. Can not I see him, for one second only? I will not detain him."

"Really, I'm sure you can't this afternoon; he isn't seeing anybody. But if you'll leave your name—"

"My name is Hunter; but what the good of that? He ask me to call a little later, and I come, and now he is engaged. It is a very great pity." And the man snatched up his bag and walking-stick, and stalked off, indignantly.

Hewitt stood still, gazing through the small aperture in the doorway.

"You'd scarcely expect a man with such a name as Hunter to talk with that accent, would you?" he observed, musingly. "It isn't a French accent, nor a German; but it seems foreign. You don't happen to know him, I suppose?"

"No, I don't. He called here about half-past twelve, just while we were in the middle of our search and I was frantic over the loss of the drawings. I was in the outer office myself, and told him to call later. I have lots of such agents here, anxious to sell all sorts of engineering appliances. But what will you do now? Shall you see my men?"

"I think," said Hewitt, rising—"I think I'll get you to question them yourself."

"Myself?"

"Yes, I have a reason. Will you trust me with the 'key' of the private room opposite? I will go over there for a little, while you talk to your men in this room. Bring them in here and shut the door; I can look after the office from across the corridor, you know. Ask them each to detail his exact movements about the office this morning, and get them to recall each visitor who has been here from the beginning of the week. I'll let you know the reason of this later. Come across to me in a few minutes."

Hewitt took the key and passed through the outer office into the corridor.

Ten minutes later Mr. Dixon, having questioned his draughtsmen, followed him. He found Hewitt standing before the table in the private room, on which lay several drawings on tracing-paper.

"See here, Mr. Dixon," said Hewitt, "I think these are the drawings you are anxious about?"

The engineer sprang toward them with a cry of delight. "Why, yes, yes," he exclaimed, turning them over, "every one of them! But where—how—they must have been in the place after all, then? What a fool I have been!"

Hewitt shook his head. "I'm afraid you're not quite so lucky as you think, Mr. Dixon," he said. "These drawings have most certainly been out of the house for a little while. Never mind how—we'll talk of that after. There is no time to lose. Tell me—how long would it take a good draughtsman to copy them?"

"They couldn't possibly be traced over properly in less than two or two and a half long days of very hard work," Dixon replied with eagerness.

"Ah! then it is as I feared. These tracings have been photographed, Mr. Dixon, and our task is one of every possible difficulty. If they had been copied in the ordinary way, one might hope to get hold of the copy. But photography upsets everything. Copies can be multiplied with such amazing facility that, once the thief gets a decent start, it is almost hopeless to checkmate him. The only chance is to get at the negatives before copies are taken. I must act at once; and I fear, between ourselves, it may be necessary for me to step very distinctly over the line of the law in the matter. You see, to get at those negatives may involve something very like house-breaking. There must be no delay, no waiting for legal procedure, or the mischief is done. Indeed, I very much question whether you have any legal remedy, strictly speaking."

"Mr. Hewitt, I implore you, do what you can. I need not say that all I have is at your disposal. I will guarantee to hold you harmless for anything that may happen. But do, I entreat you, do everything possible. Think of what the consequences may be!"

"Well, yes, so I do," Hewitt remarked, with a smile. "The consequences to me, if I were charged with house-breaking, might be something that no amount of guarantee could mitigate. However, I will do what I can, if only from patriotic motives. Now, I must see your tracer, Ritter. He is the traitor in the camp."

"Ritter? But how?"

"Never mind that now. You are upset and agitated, and had better not know more than is necessary for a little while, in case you say or do something unguarded. With Ritter I must take a deep course; what I don't know I must appear to know, and that will seem more likely to him if I disclaim acquaintance with what I do know. But first put these tracings safely away out of sight."

Dixon slipped them behind his book-case.

"Now," Hewitt pursued, "call Mr. Worsfold and give him something to do that will keep him in the inner office across the way, and tell him to send Ritter here."

Mr. Dixon called his chief draughtsman and requested him to put in order the drawings in the drawers of the inner room that had been disarranged by the search, and to send Ritter, as Hewitt had suggested.

Ritter walked into the private room with an air of respectful attention. He was a puffy-faced, unhealthy-looking young man, with very small eyes and a loose, mobile mouth.

"Sit down, Mr. Ritter," Hewitt said, in a stern voice. "Your recent transactions with your friend Mr. Hunter are well known both to Mr. Dixon and myself."

Ritter, who had at first leaned easily back in his chair, started forward at this, and paled.

"You are surprised, I observe; but you should be more careful in your movements out of doors if you do not wish your acquaintances to be known. Mr. Hunter, I believe, has the drawings which Mr. Dixon has lost, and, if so, I am certain that you have given them to him. That, you know, is theft, for which the law provides a severe penalty."

Ritter broke down completely and turned appealingly to Mr. Dixon.

"Oh, sir," he pleaded, "it isn't so bad, I assure you. I was tempted, I confess, and hid the drawings; but they are still in the office, and I can give them to you—really, I can."

"Indeed?" Hewitt went on. "Then, in that case, perhaps you'd better get them at once. Just go and fetch them in; we won't trouble to observe your hiding-place. I'll only keep this door open, to be sure you don't lose your way, you know—down the stairs, for instance."

The wretched Ritter, with hanging head, slunk into the office opposite. Presently he reappeared, looking, if possible, ghastlier than before. He looked irresolutely down the corridor, as if meditating a run for it, but Hewitt stepped toward him and motioned him back to the private room.

"You mustn't try any more of that sort of humbug," Hewitt said with increased severity. "The drawings are gone, and you have stolen them; you know that well enough. Now attend to me. If you received your deserts, Mr. Dixon would send for a policeman this moment, and have you hauled off to the jail that is your proper place. But, unfortunately, your accomplice, who calls himself Hunter—but who has other names besides that—as I happen to know—has the drawings, and it is absolutely necessary that these should be recovered. I am afraid that it will be necessary, therefore, to come to some arrangement with this scoundrel—to square him, in fact. Now, just take that pen and paper, and write to your confederate as I dictate. You know the alternative if you cause any difficulty."

Ritter reached tremblingly for the pen.

"Address him in your usual way," Hewitt proceeded. "Say this: 'There has been an alteration in the plans.'"

Have you got that? 'There has been an alteration in the plans. I shall be alone here at six o'clock. Please come, without fail.' Have you got it? Very well; sign it, and address the envelope. He must come here, and then we may arrange matters. In the meantime, you will remain in the inner office opposite."

The note was written, and Martin Hewitt, without glancing at the address, thrust it into his pocket. When Ritter was safely in the inner office, however, he drew it out and read the address. "I see," he observed, "he uses the same name, Hunter; 27 Little Carton Street, Westminster, is the address, and there I shall go at once with the note. If the man comes here, I think you had better lock him in with Ritter, and send for a policeman— it may at least frighten him. My object is, of course, to get the man away, and then, if possible, to invade his house, in some way or another, and steal or smash his negatives if they are there and to be found. Stay here, in any case, till I return. And don't forget to lock up those tracings."

It was about six o'clock when Hewitt returned, alone, but with a smiling face that told of good fortune at first sight.

"First, Mr. Dixon," he said, as he dropped into an easy chair in the private room, "let me ease your mind by the information that I have been most extraordinarily lucky; in fact, I think you have no further cause for anxiety. Here are the negatives. They were not all quite dry when I—well, what?—stole them, I suppose I must say; so that they have stuck together a bit, and probably the films are damaged. But you don't mind that, I suppose?"

He laid a small parcel, wrapped in a newspaper, on the table. The engineer hastily tore away the paper and took up five or six glass photographic negatives, of a half-plate size, which were damp, and stuck together by the gelatine films in couples. He held them, one after another, up to the light of the window, and glanced through them. Then, with a great sigh of relief, he placed them on the hearth and pounded them to dust and fragments with the poker.

For a few seconds neither spoke. Then Dixon, flinging himself into a chair, said:

"Mr. Hewitt, I can't express my obligation to you. What would have happened if you had failed, I prefer not to think of. But what shall we do with Ritter now? The other man hasn't been here yet, by the by."

"No; the fact is I didn't deliver the letter. The worthy gentleman saved me a world of trouble by taking himself out of the way." Hewitt laughed. "I'm afraid he has rather got himself into a mess by trying two kinds of theft at once, and you may not be sorry to hear that his attempt on your torpedo plans is likely to bring him a dose of penal servitude for something else. I'll tell you what has happened.

"Little Carton Street, Westminster, I found to be a seedy sort of place—one of those old streets that have seen much better days. A good many people seem to live in each house—they are fairly large houses, by the way—and there is quite a company of bell-handles on each doorpost, all down the side like organ-stops. A barber had possession of the ground floor front of No. 27 for trade purposes, so to him I went. 'Can you tell me,' I said, 'where in this house I can find Mr. Hunter?' He looked doubtful, so I went on: 'His friend will do, you know—I can't think of his name; foreign gentleman, dark, with a bushy beard.'

"The barber understood at once. 'Oh, that's Mirsky, I expect,' he said. 'Now, I come to think of it, he has had letters addressed to Hunter once or twice; I've took 'em in. Top floor back.'

"This was good so far. I had got at 'Mr. Hunter's' other alias. So, by way of possessing him with the idea that I knew all about him, I determined to ask for him as Mirsky before handing over the letter addressed to him as Hunter. A little bluff of that sort is invaluable at the right time. At the top floor back I stopped at the door and tried to open it at once, but it was locked. I could hear somebody scuttling about within, as though carrying things about, and I knocked again. In a little while the door opened about a foot, and there stood Mr. Hunter— or Mirsky, as you like—the man who, in the character of a traveler in steam-packing, came here twice to-day. He was in his shirt-sleeves, and cuddled something under his arm, hastily covered with a spotted pocket-handkerchief.

"'I have called to see M. Mirsky,' I said, 'with a confidential letter—'

"'Oh, yas, yas,' he answered hastily; 'I know—I know. Excuse me one minute.' And he rushed off down-stairs with his parcel.

"Here was a noble chance. For a moment I thought of following him, in case there might be something interesting in the parcel. But I had to decide in a moment, and I decided on trying the room. I slipped inside the door, and, finding the key on the inside, locked it. It was a confused sort of room, with a little iron bedstead in one corner and a sort of rough boarded inclosure in another. This I rightly conjectured to be the photographic dark-room, and made for it at once.

"There was plenty of light within when the door was left open, and I made at once for the drying-rack that was fastened over the sink. There were a number of negatives in it, and I began hastily examining them one after another. In the middle of this our friend Mirsky returned and tried the door. He rattled violently at the handle and pushed. Then he called.

"At this moment I had come upon the first of the negatives you have just smashed. The fixing and washing had evidently only lately been completed, and the negative was drying on the rack. I seized it, of course, and the others which stood by it.

"'Who are you, there, inside?' Mirsky shouted indignantly from the landing. 'Why for you go in my room like that? Open this door at once, or I call the police!'

"I took no notice. I had got the full number of negatives, one for each drawing, but I was not by any means sure that he had not taken an extra set; so I went on hunting down the rack. There were no more, so I set to work to turn out all the undeveloped plates. It was quite possible, you see, that the other set, if it existed, had not yet been developed.

"Mirsky changed his tune. After a little more banging and shouting I could hear him kneel down and try the key-hole. I had left the key there, so that he could see nothing. But he began talking softly and rapidly through the hole in a foreign language. I did not know it in the least, but I believe it was Russian. What had led him to believe I understood Russian I could not at the time imagine, though I have a notion now. I went on ruining his stock of plates. I found several boxes, apparently of new plates, but, as there was no means of telling whether they were really unused or were merely undeveloped, but with the chemical impress of your drawings on them, I dragged every one ruthlessly from its hiding-place and laid it out in the full glare of the sunlight—destroying it thereby, of course, whether it was unused or not.

"Mirsky left off talking, and I heard him quietly sneaking off. Perhaps his conscience was not sufficiently clear to warrant an appeal to the police, but it seemed to me rather probable at the time that that was what he was going for. So I hurried on with my work. I found three dark slides—the parts that carried the plates in the back of the camera, you know—one of them fixed in the camera itself. These I opened, and exposed the plates to ruination as before. I suppose nobody ever did so much devastation in a photographic studio in ten minutes as I managed.

"I had spoiled every plate I could find, and had the developed negatives safely in my pocket, when I happened to glance at a porcelain washing-well under the sink. There was one negative in that, and I took it up. It was *not* a negative of a drawing of yours, but of a Russian twenty-ruble note!

"This *was* a discovery. The only possible reason any man could have for photographing a bank-note was the manufacture of an etched plate for the production of forged copies. I was almost as pleased as I had been at the discovery of *your* negatives. He might bring the police now as soon as he liked; I could turn the tables on him completely. I began to hunt about for anything else relating to this negative.

"I found an inking-roller, some old pieces of blanket (used in printing from plates), and in a corner on the floor, heaped over with newspapers and rubbish, a small copying-press. There was also a dish of acid, but not an etched plate or a printed note to be seen. I was looking at the press, with the negative in one hand and the inking-roller in the other, when I became conscious of a shadow across the window. I looked up quickly, and there was Mirsky hanging over from some ledge or projection to the side of the window, and staring straight at me, with a look of unmistakable terror and apprehension.

"The face vanished immediately. I had to move a table to get at the window, and by the time I had opened it there was no sign or sound of the rightful tenant of the room. I had no doubt now of his reason for carrying a parcel down-stairs. He probably mistook me for another visitor he was expecting, and, knowing he must take this visitor into his room, threw the papers and rubbish over the press, and put up his plates and papers in a bundle and secreted them somewhere down-stairs, lest his occupation should be observed.

"Plainly, my duty now was to communicate with the police. So, by the help of my friend the barber down-stairs, a messenger was found and a note sent over to Scotland Yard. I awaited, of course, for the arrival of the police, and occupied the interval in another look round—finding nothing important, however. When the official detective arrived, he recognized at once the importance of the case. A large number of forged Russian notes have been put into circulation on the Continent lately, it seems, and it was suspected that they came from London. The Russian Government have been sending urgent messages to the police here on the subject.

"Of course I said nothing about your business; but, while I was talking with the Scotland Yard man, a letter was left by a messenger, addressed to Mirsky. The letter will be examined, of course, by the proper authorities, but I was not a little interested to perceive that the envelope bore the Russian imperial arms above the words 'Russian Embassy.' Now, why should Mirsky communicate with the Russian Embassy? Certainly not to let the officials know that he was carrying on a very extensive and lucrative business in the manufacture of spurious Russian notes. I think it is rather more than possible that he wrote—probably before he actually got your drawings—to say that he could sell information of the highest importance, and that this letter was a reply. Further, I think it quite possible that, when I asked for him by his Russian name and spoke of 'a confidential letter,' he at once concluded that *I* had come from the embassy in answer to his letter. That would account for his addressing me in Russian through the key-hole; and, of course, an official from the Russian Embassy would be the very last person in the world whom he would like to observe any indications of his little etching experiments. But, anyhow, be that as it may," Hewitt concluded, "your drawings are safe now, and if once Mirsky is caught, and I think it likely, for a man in his shirt-sleeves, with scarcely any start, and, perhaps, no money about him, hasn't a great chance to get away—if he is caught, I say, he will probably get something handsome at St. Petersburg in the way of imprisonment, or Siberia, or what not; so that you will be amply avenged."

"Yes, but I don't at all understand this business of the drawings even now. How in the world were they taken out of the place, and how in the world did you find it out?"

"Nothing could be simpler; and yet the plan was rather ingenious. I'll tell you exactly how the thing revealed itself to me. From your original description of the case many people would consider that an impossibility had been performed. Nobody had gone out and nobody had come in, and yet the drawings had been taken away. But an impossibility is an impossibility, after all, and as drawings don't run away of themselves, plainly somebody had taken them, unaccountable as it might seem. Now, as they were in your inner office, the only people who could have got at them besides yourself were your assistants, so that it was pretty clear that one of them, at least, had something to do with the business. You told me that Worsfold was an excellent and intelligent draughtsman. Well, if such a man as that meditated treachery, he would probably be able to carry away the design in his head—at any rate, a little at a time—and would be under no necessity to run the risk of stealing a set of the drawings. But Ritter, you remarked, was an inferior sort of man. 'Not particularly smart,' I think, were your words—only a mechanical sort of tracer. *He* would be unlikely to be able to carry in his head the complicated details of such designs as yours, and, being in a subordinate position, and continually overlooked, he would find it impossible to make copies of the plans in the office. So that, to begin with, I thought I saw the most probable path to start on.

"When I looked round the rooms, I pushed open the glass door of the barrier and left the door to the inner office ajar, in order to be able to see any thing that *might* happen in any part of the place, without actually expecting any definite development. While we were talking, as it happened, our friend Mirsky (or Hunter—as you please) came into the outer office, and my attention was instantly called to him by the first thing he did. Did you notice anything peculiar yourself?"

"No, really, I can't say I did. He seemed to behave much as any traveler or agent might."

"Well, what I noticed was the fact that as soon as he entered the place he put his walking-stick into the umbrella-stand over there by the door, close by where he stood, a most unusual thing for a casual caller to do, before even knowing whether you were in. This made me watch him closely. I perceived with increased interest that the stick was exactly of the same kind and pattern as one already standing there, also a curious thing. I kept my eyes carefully on those sticks, and was all the more interested and edified to see, when he left, that he took the *other* stick—not the one he came with—from the stand, and carried it away, leaving his own behind. I might have followed him, but I decided that more could be learned by staying, as, in fact, proved to be the case. This, by the by, is the stick he carried away with him. I took the liberty of fetching it back from Westminster, because I conceive it to be Ritter's property."

Hewitt produced the stick. It was an ordinary, thick Malacca cane, with a buck-horn handle and a silver band. Hewitt bent it across his knee and laid it on the table.

"Yes," Dixon answered, "that is Ritter's stick. I think I have often seen it in the stand. But what in the world—"

"One moment; I'll just fetch the stick Mirsky left behind." And Hewitt stepped across the corridor.

He returned with another stick, apparently an exact facsimile of the other, and placed it by the side of the other.

"When your assistants went into the inner room, I carried this stick off for a minute or two. I knew it was not Worsfold's, because there was an umbrella there with his initial on the handle. Look at this."

Martin Hewitt gave the handle a twist and rapidly unscrewed it from the top. Then it was seen that the stick was a mere tube of very thin metal, painted to appear like a Malacca cane.

"It was plain at once that this was no Malacca cane—it wouldn't bend. Inside it I found your tracings, rolled up tightly. You can get a marvelous quantity of thin tracing-paper into a small compass by tight rolling."

"And this—this was the way they were brought back!" the engineer exclaimed. "I see that clearly. But how did they get away? That's as mysterious as ever."

"Not a bit of it! See here. Mirsky gets hold of Ritter, and they agree to get your drawings and photograph them. Ritter is to let his confederate have the drawings, and Mirsky is to bring them back as soon as possible, so that they sha'n't be missed for a moment. Ritter habitually carries this Malacca cane, and the cunning of Mirsky at once suggests that this tube should be made in outward facsimile. This morning Mirsky keeps the actual stick, and Ritter comes to the office with the tube. He seizes the first opportunity—probably when you were in this private room, and Worsfold was talking to you from the corridor—to get at the tracings, roll them up tightly, and put them in the tube, putting the tube back into the umbrella-stand. At half-past twelve, or whenever it was, Mirsky turns up for the first time with the actual stick and exchanges them, just as he afterward did when he brought the drawings back."

"Yes, but Mirsky came half an hour after they were—
Oh, yes, I see. What a fool I was! I was forgetting. Of
course, when I first missed the tracings, they were in this
walking-stick, safe enough, and I was tearing my hair out
within arm's reach of them!"

"Precisely. And Mirsky took them away before your
very eyes. I expect Ritter was in a rare funk when he
found that the drawings were missed. He calculated, no
doubt, on your not wanting them for the hour or two
they would be out of the office."

"How lucky that it struck me to jot a pencil-note
on one of them! I might easily have made my note
somewhere else, and then I should never have known
that they had been away."

"Yes, they didn't give you any too much time to miss
them. Well, I think the rest pretty clear. I brought the
tracings in here, screwed up the sham stick and put it
back. You identified the tracings and found none missing,
and then my course was pretty clear, though it looked
difficult. I knew you would be very naturally indignant
with Ritter, so, as I wanted to manage him myself, I told
you nothing of what he had actually done, for fear that, in
your agitated state, you might burst out with something
that would spoil my game. To Ritter I pretended to know
nothing of the return of the drawings or *how* they had
been stolen—the only things I did know with certainty.
But I *did* pretend to know all about Mirsky—or Hunter—
when, as a matter of fact, I knew nothing at all, except
that he probably went under more than one name. That
put Ritter into my hands completely. When he found the
game was up, he began with a lying confession. Believing
that the tracings were still in the stick and that we knew

nothing of their return, he said that they had not been away, and that he would fetch them—as I had expected he would. I let him go for them alone, and, when he returned, utterly broken up by the discovery that they were not there, I had him altogether at my mercy. You see, if he had known that the drawings were all the time behind your book-case, he might have brazened it out, sworn that the drawings had been there all the time, and we could have done nothing with him. We couldn't have sufficiently frightened him by a threat of prosecution for theft, because there the things were in your possession, to his knowledge.

"As it was he answered the helm capitally: gave us Mirsky's address on the envelope, and wrote the letter that was to have got him out of the way while I committed burglary, if that disgraceful expedient had not been rendered unnecessary. On the whole, the case has gone very well."

"It has gone marvelously well, thanks to yourself. But what shall I do with Ritter?"

"Here's his stick—knock him down-stairs with it, if you like. I should keep the tube, if I were you, as a memento. I don't suppose the respectable Mirsky will ever call to ask for it. But I should certainly kick Ritter out of doors—or out of window, if you like—without delay."

Mirsky was caught, and, after two remands at the police-court, was extradited on the charge of forging Russian notes. It came out that he had written to the embassy, as Hewitt had surmised, stating that he had certain valuable information to offer, and the letter which Hewitt had seen delivered was an acknowledgment, and a request for more definite particulars. This was what gave rise to the impression that Mirsky had himself informed the Russian authorities of his forgeries. His real intent was very different, but was never guessed.

"I wonder," Hewitt has once or twice observed, "whether, after all, it would not have paid the Russian authorities better on the whole if I had never investigated Mirsky's little note factory. The Dixon torpedo was worth a good many twenty-ruble notes."

V. THE QUINTON
JEWEL AFFAIR

IT WAS COMPARATIVELY RARELY that Hewitt came into contact with members of the regular criminal class—those, I mean, who are thieves, of one sort or another, by exclusive profession. Still, nobody could have been better prepared than Hewitt for encountering this class when it became necessary. By some means, which I never quite understood, he managed to keep abreast of the very latest fashions in the ever-changing slang dialect of the fraternity, and he was a perfect master of the more modern and debased form of Romany. So much so that frequently a gypsy who began (as they always do) by pretending that he understood nothing, and never heard of a gypsy language, ended by confessing that Hewitt could *rokker* better than most Romany *chals* themselves.

By this acquaintance with their habits and talk Hewitt was sometimes able to render efficient service in cases of especial importance. In the Quinton jewel affair Hewitt came into contact with a very accomplished thief.

The case will probably be very well remembered. Sir Valentine Quinton, before he married, had been as poor as only a man of rank with an old country establishment to keep up can be. His marriage, however, with the daughter of a wealthy financier had changed all that, and now the Quinton establishment was carried on on as lavish a scale as might be; and, indeed, the extravagant habits of Lady Quinton herself rendered it an extremely lucky thing that she had brought a fortune with her.

Among other things her jewels made quite a collection, and chief among them was the great ruby, one of the very few that were sent to this country to be sold (at an average price of somewhere about twenty thousand pounds apiece, I believe) by the Burmese king before the annexation of his country. Let but a ruby be of a great size and color, and no equally fine diamond can approach its value. Well, this great ruby (which was set in a pendant, by the by), together with a necklace, brooches, bracelets, ear-rings—indeed, the greater part of Lady Quinton's collection—were stolen. The robbery was effected at the usual time and in the usual way in cases of carefully planned jewelry robberies. The time was early evening— dinner-time, in fact—and an entrance had been made by the window to Lady Quinton's dressing-room, the door screwed up on the inside, and wires artfully stretched about the grounds below to overset anybody who might observe and pursue the thieves.

On an investigation by London detectives, however, a feature of singularity was brought to light. There had plainly been only one thief at work at Radcot Hall, and no other had been inside the grounds. Alone he had planted the wires, opened the window, screwed the door, and picked the lock of the safe. Clearly this was a thief of the most accomplished description.

Some few days passed, and, although the police had made various arrests, they appeared to be all mistakes, and the suspected persons were released one after another. I was talking of the robbery with Hewitt at lunch, and asked him if he had received any commission to hunt for the missing jewels.

"No," Hewitt replied, "I haven't been commissioned. They are offering an immense reward however—a very pleasant sum, indeed. I have had a short note from Radcot Hall informing me of the amount, and that's all. Probably they fancy that I may take the case up as a speculation, but that is a great mistake. I'm not a beginner, and I must be commissioned in a regular manner, hit or miss, if I am to deal with the case. I've quite enough commissions going now, and no time to waste hunting for a problematical reward."

But we were nearer a clue to the Quinton jewels than we then supposed.

We talked of other things, and presently rose and left the restaurant, strolling quietly toward home. Some little distance from the Strand, and near our own door, we passed an excited Irishman—without doubt an Irishman by appearance and talk—who was pouring a torrent of angry complaints in the ears of a policeman. The policeman obviously thought little of the man's grievances, and with an amused smile appeared to be advising him to go home quietly and think no more about it. We passed on and mounted our stairs. Something interesting in our conversation made me stop for a little while at Hewitt's office door on my way up, and, while I stood there, the Irishman we had seen in the street mounted the stairs. He was a poorly dressed but sturdy-looking fellow, apparently a laborer, in a badly-worn best suit of clothes. His agitation still held him, and without a pause he immediately burst out:

"Which of ye jintlemen will be Misther Hewitt, sor?"

"This is Mr. Hewitt," I said. "Do you want him?"

"It's protecshin I want, sor—protecshin! I spake to the polis, an' they laff at me, begob. Foive days have I lived in London, an' 'tis nothin' but battle, murdher, an' suddhen death for me here all day an' ivery day! An' the polis say I'm dhrunk!"

He gesticulated wildly, and to me it seemed just possible that the police might be right.

"They say I'm drunk, sor," he continued, "but, begob, I b'lieve they think I'm mad. An' me being thracked an' folleyed an' dogged an' waylaid an' poisoned an' blandandhered an' kidnapped an' murdhered, an' for why I do not know!"

"And who's doing all this?'

"Sthrangers, sor—sthrangers. 'Tis a sthranger here I am mesilf, an' fwy they do it bates me, onless I do be so like the Prince av Wales or other crowned head they thry to slaughter me. They're layin' for me in the sthreet now, I misdoubt not, and fwat they may thry next I can tell no more than the Lord Mayor. An' the polis won't listen to me!"

This, I thought, must be one of the very common cases of mental hallucination which one hears of every day—the belief of the sufferer that he is surrounded by enemies and followed by spies. It is probably the most usual delusion of the harmless lunatic.

"But what have these people done?" Hewitt asked, looking rather interested, although amused. "What actual assaults have they committed, and when? And who told you to come here?"

"Who towld me, is ut? Who but the payler outside—in the street below! I explained to 'um, an' sez he: 'Ah, you go an' take a slape,' sez he; 'you go an' take a good slape, an' they'll be all gone whin ye wake up.' 'But they'll murdher me,' sez I. 'Oh, no!' sez he, smilin' behind av his ugly face. 'Oh, no, they won't; you take ut aisy, me frind, an' go home!' 'Take it aisy, is ut, an' go home!' sez I; 'why, that's just where they've been last, a-ruinationin' an' a-turnin' av the place upside down, an' me strook on the head onsensible a mile away. Take ut aisy, is ut, ye say, whin all the demons in this unholy place is jumpin' on me every minut in places promiscuous till I can't tell where to turn, descendin' an' vanishin' marvelious an' onaccountable? Take ut aisy, is ut?' sez I. 'Well, me frind,' sez he, 'I can't help ye; that's the marvelious an' onaccountable departmint up the stairs forninst ye. Misther Hewitt ut is,' sez he, 'that attinds to the onaccountable departmint, him as wint by a minut ago. You go an' bother him.' That's how I was towld, sor."

Hewitt smiled.

"Very good," he said; "and now what are these extraordinary troubles of yours? Don't declaim," he added, as the Irishman raised his hand and opened his mouth, preparatory to another torrent of complaint; "just say in ten words, if you can, what they've done to you."

"I will, sor. Wan day had I been in London, sor—wan day only, an' a low scutt thried to poison me dhrink; next day some udther thief av sin shoved me off av a railway platform undher a train, malicious and purposeful; glory be, he didn't kill me! but the very dochter that felt me bones thried to pick me pockut, I du b'lieve. Sunday night I was grabbed outrageous in a darrk turnin', rowled on the groun', half strangled, an' me pockuts nigh ripped out av me trousies. An' this very blessed mornin' av light I was strook onsensible an' left a livin' corpse, an' my lodgin's penethrated an' all the thruck mishandled an' bruk up behind me back. Is that a panjandhery for the polis to laff at, sor?"

Had Hewitt not been there I think I should have done my best to quiet the poor fellow with a few soothing words and to persuade him to go home to his friends. His excited and rather confused manner, his fantastic story of a sort of general conspiracy to kill him, and the absurd reference to the doctor who tried to pick his pocket seemed to me plainly to confirm my first impression that he was insane. But Hewitt appeared strangely interested.

"Did they steal anything?" he asked.

"Divil a shtick but me door-key, an' that they tuk home an' lift in the door."

Hewitt opened his office door.

"Come in," he said, "and tell me all about this. You come, too, Brett."

The Irishman and I followed him into the inner office, where, shutting the door, Hewitt suddenly turned on the Irishman and exclaimed sharply: "*Then you've still got it?*"

He looked keenly in the man's eyes, but the only expression there was one of surprise.

"Got ut?" said the Irishman. "Got fwhat, sor? Is ut you're thinkin' I've got the horrors, as well as the polis?"

Hewitt's gaze relaxed. "Sit down, sit down!" he said. "You've still got your watch and money, I suppose, since you weren't robbed?"

"Oh, that? Glory be, I have ut still! though for how long—or me own head, for that matter—in this state of besiegement, I can not say."

"Now," said Hewitt, "I want a full, true, and particular account of yourself and your doings for the last week. First, your name?"

"Leamy's my name, sor—Michael Leamy."

"Lately from Ireland?"

"Over from Dublin this last blessed Wednesday, and a crooil bad poundherin' tit was in the boat, too—shpakin' av that same."

"Looking for work?"

"That is my purshuit at prisint, sor."

"Did anything noticeable happen before these troubles of yours began—anything here in London or on the journey?"

"Sure," the Irishman smiled, "part av the way I thraveled first-class by favor av the gyard, an' I got a small job before I lift the train."

"How was that? Why did you travel first-class part of the way?"

"There was a station fwhere we shtopped afther a long run, an' I got down to take the cramp out av me joints, an' take a taste av dhrink. I over-shtayed somehow, an', whin I got to the train, begob, it was on the move. There was a first-class carr'ge door opin right forninst me, an' into that the gyard crams me holus-bolus. There was a juce of a foine jintleman sittin' there, an' he stares at me umbrageous, but I was not dishcommoded, bein' onbashful by natur'. We thravelled along a heap av miles more, till we came near London. Afther we had shtopped at a station where they tuk tickets we wint ahead again, an' prisintly, as we rips through some udther station, up jumps the jintleman opposite, swearin' hard undher his tongue, an' looks out at the windy. 'I thought this train shtopped here,' sez he."

"Chalk Farm," observed Hewitt, with a nod.

"The name I do not know, sor, but that's fwhat he

said. Then he looks at me onaisy for a little, an' at last he sez: 'Wud ye loike a small job, me good man, well paid?'

"'Faith,' sez I, ''tis that will suit me well.'

"'Then, see here,' sez he, 'I should have got out at that station, havin' particular business; havin' missed, I must sen' a telegrammer from Euston. Now, here's a bag,' sez he, 'a bag full of imporrtant papers for my solicitor—imporrtant to me, ye ondershtand, not worth the shine av a brass farden to a sowl else—an' I want 'em tuk on to him. Take you this bag,' he sez, 'an' go you straight out wid it at Euston an' get a cab. I shall stay in the station a bit to see to the telegrammer. Dhrive out av the station, across the road outside, an' wait there five minuts by the clock. Ye ondershtand? Wait five minuts, an, maybe I'll come an' join ye. If I don't 'twill be bekase I'm detained onexpected, an' then ye'll dhrive to my solicitor straight. Here's his address, if ye can read writin',' an' he put ut on a piece av paper. He gave me half-a-crown for the cab, an' I tuk his bag."

"One moment—have you the paper with the address now?"

"I have not, sor. I missed ut afther the blayguards overset me yesterday; but the solicitor's name was Hollams, an' a liberal jintleman wid his money he was, too, by that same token."

"What was his address?"

"'Twas in Chelsea, and 'twas Gold or Golden something, which I know by the good token av fwhat he gave me; but the number I misremember."

Hewitt turned to his directory. "Gold Street is the place, probably," he said, "and it seems to be a street chiefly of private houses. You would be able to point out the house if you were taken there, I suppose?"

"I should that, sor; indade, I was thinkin' av goin' there an' tellin' Misther Hollams all my throubles, him havin' been so kind."

"Now tell me exactly what instructions the man in the train gave you, and what happened?"

"He sez: 'You ask for Misther Hollams, an' see nobody else. Tell him ye've brought the sparks from Misther W.'"

I fancied I could see a sudden twinkle in Hewitt's eye, but he made no other sign, and the Irishman proceeded.

"'Sparks?' sez I. 'Yes, sparks,' sez he. 'Misther Hollams will know; 'tis our jokin' word for 'em; sometimes papers is sparks when they set a lawsuit ablaze,' and he laffed. 'But be sure ye say the *sparks from Misther W.*,' he sez again, 'bekase then he'll know ye're jinuine an' he'll pay ye han'some. Say Misther W. sez you're to have your reg'lars, if ye like. D'ye mind that?'

"'Ay,' sez I, 'that I'm to have me reg'lars.'

"Well, sor, I tuk the bag and wint out of the station, tuk the cab, an' did all as he towld me. I waited the foive minuts, but he niver came, so off I druv to Misther Hollams, and he threated me han'some, sor."

"Yes, but tell me exactly all he did."

"'Misther Hollams, sor?' sez I. 'Who are ye?' sez he. 'Mick Leamy, sor,' sez I, 'from Misther W. wid the sparks.' 'Oh,' sez he, 'thin come in.' I wint in. 'They're in here, are they?' sez he, takin' the bag. 'They are, sor,' sez I, 'an' Misther W. sez I'm to have me reg'lars.' 'You shall,' sez he. 'What shall we say, now—afinnip?' 'Fwhat's that, sor?' sez I. 'Oh,' sez he, 'I s'pose ye're a new hand; five quid—ondershtand that?'"

"Begob, I did ondershtand it, an' moighty plazed I was to have come to a place where they pay five-pun' notes for

carryin' bags. So whin he asked me was I new to London
an' shud I kape in the same line av business, I towld him
I shud for certin, or any thin' else payin' like it. 'Right,'
sez he; 'let me know whin ye've got any thin'—ye'll find
me all right.' An' he winked frindly. 'Faith, that I know
shall, sor,' sez I, wid the money safe in me pockut; an'
I winked him back, conjanial. 'I've a smart family about
me,' sez he, 'an' I treat 'em all fair an' liberal.' An', saints
I thought it likely his family 'ud have all they wanted
seein' he was so free-handed wid a stranger. Thin he
asked me where I was a livin' in London, and, when I
towld him nowhere, he towld me av a room in Mussor
Street, here by Drury Lane, that was to let, in a house his
fam'ly knew very well, an' I wint straight there an' tuk ut
an' there I do be stayin' still, sor."

I hadn't understood at first why Hewitt took so much
interest in the Irishman's narrative, but the latter part of
it opened my eyes a little. It seemed likely that Leamy
had, in his innocence, been made a conveyer of stolen
property. I knew enough of thieves' slang to know that
"sparks" meant diamonds or other jewels; that "regulars"
was the term used for a payment made to a brother thief
who gave assistance in some small way, such as carrying
the booty; and that the "family" was the time-honored
expression for a gang of thieves.

"This was all on Wednesday, I understand," said
Hewitt. "Now tell me what happened on Thursday—the
poisoning, or drugging, you know?"

"Well, sor, I was walking out, an' toward the evenin' I
lost mesilf. Up comes a man, seemin'ly a sthranger, and
shmacks me on the showldher. 'Why, Mick!' sez he; 'it's
Mick Leamy, I du b'lieve!'

"'I am that,' sez I, 'but you I do not know.'

"'Not know me?' sez he. 'Why, I wint to school wid ye.' An' wid that he hauls me off to a bar, blarneyin' and minowdherin', an' orders dhrinks.

"'Can ye rache me a poipe-loight?' sez he, an' I turned to get ut, but, lookin' back suddent, there was that onblushin' thief av the warl' tippin' a paperful of phowder stuff into me glass."

"What did you do?" Hewitt asked.

"I knocked the dhirty face av him, sor, an' can ye blame me? A mane scutt, thryin' for to poison a well-manin' sthranger. I knocked the face av him, an' got away home."

"Now the next misfortune?"

"Faith, that was av a sort likely to turn out the last of all misfortunes. I wint that day to the Crystal Palace, bein' dishposed for a little sphort, seein' as I was new to London. Comin' home at night, there was a juce av a crowd on the station platform, consekins of a late thrain. Sthandin' by the edge av the platform at the fore end, just as thrain came in, some onvisible murdherer gives me a stupenjus drive in the back, and over I wint on the line, mid-betwixt the rails. The engine came up an' wint half over me widout givin' me a scratch, bekase av my centraleous situation, an' then the porther-men pulled me out, nigh sick wid fright, sor, as ye may guess. A jintleman in the crowd sings out: 'I'm a medical man!' an' they tuk me in the waitin'-room, an' he investigated me, havin' turned everybody else out av the room. There wuz no bones bruk, glory be! and the docthor-man he was tellin' me so, after feelin' me over, whin I felt his hand in me waistcoat pockut.

"'An' fwhat's this, sor?' sez I. 'Do you be lookin' for your fee that thief's way?'

"He laffed, and said: 'I want no fee from ye, me man, an' I did but feel your ribs,' though on me conscience he had done that undher me waistcoat already. An' so I came home."

"What did they do to you on Saturday?"

"Saturday, sor, they gave me a whole holiday, and I began to think less of things; but on Saturday night, in a dark place, two blayguards tuk me throat from behind, nigh choked me, flung me down, an' wint through all me pockuts in about a quarter av a minut."

"And they took nothing, you say?"

"Nothing, sor. But this mornin' I got my worst dose. I was trapesing along distreshful an' moighty sore, in a street just away off the Strand here, when I observed the docthor-man that was at the Crystal Palace station a-smilin' an' beckonin' at me from a door.

"'How are ye now?' sez he. 'Well,' sez I, 'I'm mighty sore an' sad bruised,' sez I. 'Is that so?' sez he. 'Sthep in here.' So I sthepped in, an' before I could wink there dhropped a crack on the back av me head that sent me off as unknowledgable as a corrpse. I knew no more for a while, sor, whether half an hour or an hour, an' thin I got up in a room av the place, marked 'To Let.' 'Twas a house full av offices, by the same token, like this. There was a sore bad lump on me head—see ut, sor?—an' the whole warl' was shpinnin' roun' rampageous. The things out av me pockuts were lyin' on the flure by me—all barrin' the key av me room. So that the demons had been through me posseshins again, bad luck to 'em."

"You are quite sure, are you, that everything was there except the key?" Hewitt asked.

"Certin, sor? Well, I got along to me room, sick an' sorry enough, an' doubtsome whether I might get in wid no key. But there was the key in the open door, an', by this an' that, all the shtuff in the room—chair, table, bed, an' all—was shtandin' on their heads twisty-ways, an' the bedclothes an' every thin' else; such a disgraceful stramash av conglomerated thruck as ye niver dhreamt av. The chist av drawers was lyin' on uts face, wid all the dhrawers out an' emptied on the flure. 'Twas as though an arrmy had been lootin', sor!"

"But still nothing was gone?"

"Nothin', so far as I investigated, sor. But I didn't shtay. I came out to spake to the polis, an' two av them laffed at me—wan afther another!"

"It has certainly been no laughing matter for you. Now, tell me—have you anything in your possession—documents, or valuables, or anything—that any other person, to your knowledge, is anxious to get hold of?"

"I have not, sor—divil a document! As to valuables, thim an' me is the cowldest av sthrangers."

"Just call to mind, now, the face of the man who tried to put powder in your drink, and that of the doctor who attended to you in the railway station. Were they at all alike, or was either like anybody you have seen before?"

Leamy puckered his forehead and thought.

"Faith," he said presently, "they were a bit alike, though one had a beard an' the udther whiskers only."

"Neither happened to look like Mr. Hollams, for instance?"

Leamy started. "Begob, but they did! They'd ha' been mortal like him if they'd been shaved." Then, after a pause, he suddenly added: "Holy saints! is ut the fam'ly he talked av?"

Hewitt laughed. "Perhaps it is," he said. "Now, as to the man who sent you with the bag. Was it an old bag?"

"Bran' cracklin' new—a brown leather bag."

"Locked?"

"That I niver thried, sor. It was not my consarn."

"True. Now, as to this Mr. W. himself." Hewitt had been rummaging for some few minutes in a portfolio, and finally produced a photograph, and held it before the Irishman's eye. "Is that like him?" he asked.

"Shure it's the man himself! Is he a friend av yours, sor?"

"No, he's not exactly a friend of mine," Hewitt answered, with a grim chuckle. "I fancy he's one of that very respectable *family* you heard about at Mr. Hollams'. Come along with me now to Chelsea, and see if you can point out that house in Gold Street. I'll send for a cab."

He made for the outer office, and I went with him.

"What is all this, Hewitt?" I asked. "A gang of thieves with stolen property?"

Hewitt looked in my face and replied: "*It's the Quinton ruby!*"

"What! The ruby? Shall you take the case up, then?"

"I shall. It is no longer a speculation."

"Then do you expect to find it at Hollams' house in Chelsea?" I asked.

"No, I don't, because it isn't there—else why are they trying to get it from this unlucky Irishman? There has been bad faith in Hollams' gang, I expect, and Hollams has missed the ruby and suspects Leamy of having taken it from the bag."

"Then who is this Mr. W. whose portrait you have in your possession?"

"See here!" Hewitt turned over a small pile of recent newspapers and selected one, pointing at a particular paragraph. "I kept that in my mind, because to me it seemed to be the most likely arrest of the lot," he said.

It was an evening paper of the previous Thursday, and the paragraph was a very short one, thus:

"The man Wilks, who was arrested at Euston Station yesterday, in connection with the robbery of Lady Quinton's jewels, has been released, nothing being found to incriminate him."

"How does that strike you?" asked Hewitt. "Wilks is a man well known to the police—one of the most accomplished burglars in this country, in fact. I have had no dealings with him as yet, but I found means, some time ago, to add his portrait to my little collection, in case I might want it, and to-day it has been quite useful."

The thing was plain now. Wilks must have been bringing his booty to town, and calculated on getting out at Chalk Farm and thus eluding the watch which he doubtless felt pretty sure would be kept (by telegraphic instruction) at Euston for suspicious characters arriving from the direction of Radcot. His transaction with Leamy was his only possible expedient to save himself from being hopelessly taken with the swag in his possession. The paragraph told me why Leamy had waited in vain for "Mr. W." in the cab.

"What shall you do now?" I asked.

"I shall go to the Gold Street house and find out what I can as soon as this cab turns up."

There seemed a possibility of some excitement in the adventure, so I asked: "Will you want any help?"

Hewitt smiled. "I *think* I can get through it alone," he said.

"Then may I come to look on?" I said. "Of course I don't want to be in your way, and the result of the business, whatever it is, will be to your credit alone. But I am curious."

"Come, then, by all means. The cab will be a four-wheeler, and there will be plenty of room."

Gold Street was a short street of private houses of very fair size and of a half-vanished pretension to gentility. We drove slowly through, and Leamy had no difficulty in pointing out the house wherein he had been paid five pounds for carrying a bag. At the end the cab turned the corner and stopped, while Hewitt wrote a short note to an official of Scotland Yard.

"Take this note," he instructed Leamy, "to Scotland Yard in the cab, and then go home. I will pay the cabman now."

"I will, sor. An' will I be protected?"

"Oh, yes! Stay at home for the rest of the day, and I expect you'll be left alone in future. Perhaps I shall have something to tell you in a day or two; if I do, I'll send. Good-by."

The cab rolled off, and Hewitt and I strolled back along Gold Street. "I think," Hewitt said, "we will drop in on Mr. Hollams for a few minutes while we can. In a few hours I expect the police will have him, and his house, too, if they attend promptly to my note."

"Have you ever seen him?"

"Not to my knowledge, though I may know him by some other name. Wilks I know by sight, though he doesn't know me."

"What shall we say?"

"That will depend on circumstances. I may not get my cue till the door opens, or even till later. At worst, I can easily apply for a reference as to Leamy, who, you remember, is looking for work."

But we were destined not to make Mr. Hollams' acquaintance, after all. As we approached the house a great uproar was heard from the lower part giving on to the area, and suddenly a man, hatless, and with a sleeve of his coat nearly torn away burst through the door and up the area steps, pursued by two others. I had barely time to observe that one of the pursuers carried a revolver, and that both hesitated and retired on seeing that several people were about the street, when Hewitt, gripping my arm and exclaiming: "That's our man!" started at a run after the fugitive.

We turned the next corner and saw the man thirty yards before us, walking, and pulling up his sleeve at the shoulder, so as to conceal the rent. Plainly he felt safe from further molestation.

"That's Sim Wilks," Hewitt explained, as we followed, "the 'juce of a foine jintleman' who got Leamy to carry his bag, and the man who knows where the Quinton ruby is, unless I am more than usually mistaken. Don't stare after him, in case he looks round. Presently, when we get into the busier streets, I shall have a little chat with him."

But for some time the man kept to the back streets. In time, however, he emerged into the Buckingham Palace Road, and we saw him stop and look at a hat-shop. But after a general look over the window and a glance in at the door he went on.

"Good sign!" observed Hewitt; "got no money with him—makes it easier for us."

In a little while Wilks approached a small crowd gathered about a woman fiddler. Hewitt touched my arm, and a few quick steps took us past our man and to the opposite side of the crowd. When Wilks emerged, he met us coming in the opposite direction.

"What, Sim!" burst out Hewitt with apparent delight. "I haven't piped your mug[1] for a stretch;[2] I thought you'd fell.[3] Where's your cady?[4]"

Wilks looked astonished and suspicious. "I don't know you," he said. "You've made a mistake."

Hewitt laughed. "I'm glad you don't know me," he said. "If you don't, I'm pretty sure the reelers[5] won't. I think I've faked my mug pretty well, and my clobber too. Look here: I'll stand you a new cady. Strange blokes don't do that, eh?"

Wilks was still suspicious. "I don't know what you mean," he said. Then, after a pause, he added: "Who are you, then?"

Hewitt winked and screwed his face genially aside. "Hooky!" he said. "I've had a lucky touch[6] and I'm Mr. Smith till I've melted the pieces.[7] You come and damp it."

"I'm off," Wilks replied. "Unless you're pal enough to lend me a quid," he added, laughing.

"I am that," responded Hewitt, plunging his hand in his pocket. "I'm flush, my boy, flush, and I've been wetting it

1. Seen your face
2. A year
3. Been imprisoned
4. Hat
5. Police
6. Robbery
7. Spent the money

pretty well to-day. I feel pretty jolly now, and I shouldn't wonder if I went home cannon.[8] Only a quid? Have two, if you want 'em—or three; there's plenty more, and you'll do the same for me some day. Here y'are."

Hewitt had, of a sudden, assumed the whole appearance, manners, and bearing of a slightly elevated rowdy. Now he pulled his hand from his pocket and extended it, full of silver, with five or six sovereigns interspersed, toward Wilks.

"I'll have three quid," Wilks said, with decision, taking the money; "but I'm blowed if I remember you. Who's your pal?"

Hewitt jerked his hand in my direction, winked, and said, in a low voice: "He's all right. Having a rest. Can't stand Manchester," and winked again.

Wilks laughed and nodded, and I understood from that that Hewitt had very flatteringly given me credit for being "wanted" by the Manchester police.

We lurched into a public house, and drank a very little very bad whisky and water. Wilks still regarded us curiously, and I could see him again and again glancing doubtfully in Hewitt's face. But the loan of three pounds had largely reassured him. Presently Hewitt said:

"How about our old pal down in Gold Street? Do anything with him now? Seen him lately?"

Wilks looked up at the ceiling and shook his head.

"That's a good job. It 'ud be awkward if you were about there to-day, I can tell you."

"Why?"

"Never mind, so long as you're not there. I know something, if I *have* been away. I'm glad I haven't had any truck with Gold Street lately, that's all."

---

8. Drunk

"D'you mean the reelers are on it?"

Hewitt looked cautiously over his shoulder, leaned toward Wilks, and said: "Look here: this is the straight tip. I know this—I got it from the very nark[9] that's given the show away: By six o'clock No. 8 Gold Street will be turned inside out, like an old glove, and everyone in the place will be—" He finished the sentence by crossing his wrists like a handcuffed man. "What's more," he went on, "they know all about what's gone on there lately, and everybody that's been in or out for the last two moons[10] will be wanted particular—and will be found, I'm told." Hewitt concluded with a confidential frown, a nod, and a wink, and took another mouthful of whisky. Then he added, as an after-thought: "So I'm glad you haven't been there lately."

Wilks looked in Hewitt's face and asked: "Is that straight?"

"*Is* it?" replied Hewitt with emphasis. "You go and have a look, if you ain't afraid of being smugged yourself. Only *I* shan't go near No. 8 just yet—I know that."

Wilks fidgeted, finished his drink, and expressed his intention of going. "Very well, if you *won't* have another—" replied Hewitt. But he had gone.

"Good!" said Hewitt, moving toward the door; "he has suddenly developed a hurry. I shall keep him in sight, but you had better take a cab and go straight to Euston. Take tickets to the nearest station to Radcot—Kedderby, I think it is—and look up the train arrangements. Don't show yourself too much, and keep an eye on the entrance. Unless I am mistaken, Wilks will be there pretty

9. Police spy
10. Months

soon, and I shall be on his heels. If I *am* wrong, then you won't see the end of the fun, that's all."

Hewitt hurried after Wilks, and I took the cab and did as he wished. There was an hour and a few minutes, I found, to wait for the next train, and that time I occupied as best I might, keeping a sharp lookout across the quadrangle. Barely five minutes before the train was to leave, and just as I was beginning to think about the time of the next, a cab dashed up and Hewitt alighted. He hurried in, found me, and drew me aside into a recess, just as another cab arrived.

"Here he is," Hewitt said. "I followed him as far as Euston Road and then got my cabby to spurt up and pass him. He had had his mustache shaved off, and I feared you mightn't recognize him, and so let him see you."

From our retreat we could see Wilks hurry into the booking-office. We watched him through to the platform and followed. He wasted no time, but made the best of his way to a third-class carriage at the extreme fore end of the train.

"We have three minutes," Hewitt said, "and everything depends on his not seeing us get into this train. Take this cap. Fortunately, we're both in tweed suits."

He had bought a couple of tweed cricket caps, and these we assumed, sending our "bowler" hats to the cloak-room. Hewitt also put on a pair of blue spectacles, and then walked boldly up the platform and entered a first-class carriage. I followed close on his heels, in such a manner that a person looking from the fore end of the train would be able to see but very little of me.

"So far so good," said Hewitt, when we were seated and the train began to move off. "I must keep a lookout at each station, in case our friend goes off unexpectedly."

"I waited some time," I said; "where did you both go to?"

"First he went and bought that hat he is wearing. Then he walked some distance, dodging the main thoroughfares and keeping to the back streets in a way that made following difficult, till he came to a little tailor's shop. There he entered and came out in a quarter of an hour with his coat mended. This was in a street in Westminster. Presently he worked his way up to Tothill Street, and there he plunged into a barber's shop. I took a cautious peep at the window, saw two or three other customers also waiting, and took the opportunity to rush over to a 'notion' shop and buy these blue spectacles, and to a hatter's for these caps—of which I regret to observe that yours is too big. He was rather a long while in the barber's, and finally came out, as you saw him, with no mustache. This was a good indication. It made it plainer than ever that he had believed my warning as to the police descent on the house in Gold Street and its frequenters; which was right and proper, for what I told him was quite true. The rest you know. He cabbed to the station, and so did I."

"And now perhaps," I said, "after giving me the character of a thief wanted by the Manchester police, forcibly depriving me of my hat in exchange for this all-too-large cap, and rushing me off out of London without any definite idea of when I'm coming back, perhaps you'll tell me what we're after?"

Hewitt laughed. "You wanted to join in, you know," he said, "and you must take your luck as it comes. As a matter of fact there is scarcely anything in my profession so uninteresting and so difficult as this watching and following business. Often it lasts for weeks. When we alight, we shall have to follow Wilks again, under the most difficult possible conditions, in the country. There it is often quite impossible to follow a man unobserved. It is only because it is the only way that I am undertaking it now. As to what we're after, you know that as well as I— the Quinton ruby. Wilks has hidden it, and without his help it would be impossible to find it. We are following him so that he will find it for us."

"He must have hidden it, I suppose, to avoid sharing with Hollams?"

"Of course, and availed himself of the fact of Leamy having carried the bag to direct Hollams's suspicion to him. Hollams found out by his repeated searches of Leamy and his lodgings, that this was wrong, and this morning evidently tried to persuade the ruby out of Wilks' possession with a revolver. We saw the upshot of that."

Kedderby Station was about forty miles out. At each intermediate stopping station Hewitt watched earnestly, but Wilks remained in the train. "What I fear," Hewitt observed, "is that at Kedderby he may take a fly. To stalk a man on foot in the country is difficult enough; but you *can't* follow one vehicle in another without being spotted. But if he's so smart as I think, he won't do it. A man traveling in a fly is noticed and remembered in these places."

He did *not* take a fly. At Kedderby we saw him jump out quickly and hasten from the station. The train stood for a few minutes, and he was out of the station before we alighted. Through the railings behind the platform we could see him walking briskly away to the right. From the ticket collector we ascertained that Radcot lay in that direction, three miles off.

To my dying day I shall never forget that three miles. They seemed three hundred. In the still country almost every footfall seemed audible for any distance, and in the long stretches of road one could see half a mile behind or before. Hewitt was cool and patient, but I got into a fever of worry, excitement, want of breath, and back-ache. At first, for a little, the road zig-zagged, and then the chase was comparatively easy. We waited behind one bend till Wilks had passed the next, and then hurried in his trail, treading in the dustiest parts of the road or on the side grass, when there was any, to deaden the sound of our steps.

At the last of these short bends we looked ahead and saw a long, white stretch of road with the dark form of Wilks a couple of hundred yards in front. It would never do to let him get to the end of this great stretch before following, as he might turn off at some branch road out of sight and be lost. So we jumped the hedge and scuttled along as we best might on the other side, with backs bent, and our feet often many inches deep in wet clay. We had to make continual stoppages to listen and peep out, and on one occasion, happening, incautiously, to stand erect, looking after him, I was much startled to see Wilks, with his face toward me, gazing down the road. I ducked like lightning, and, fortunately, he seemed not to have observed me, but went on as before. He had probably heard some slight noise, but looked straight along the road for its explanation, instead of over the hedge. At hilly parts of the road there was extreme difficulty; indeed, on approaching a rise it was usually necessary to lie down under the hedge till Wilks had passed the top, since from the higher ground he could have seen us easily. This improved neither my clothes, my comfort, nor my temper. Luckily we never encountered the difficulty of a long and high wall, but once we were nearly betrayed by a man who shouted to order us off his field.

At last we saw, just ahead, the square tower of an old church, set about with thick trees. Opposite this Wilks paused, looked irresolutely up and down the road, and then went on. We crossed the road, availed ourselves of the opposite hedge, and followed. The village was to be seen some three or four hundred yards farther along the road, and toward it Wilks sauntered slowly. Before he actually reached the houses he stopped and turned back.

"The churchyard!" exclaimed Hewitt, under his breath. "Lie close and let him pass."

Wilks reached the churchyard gate, and again looked irresolutely about him. At that moment a party of children, who had been playing among the graves, came chattering and laughing toward and out of the gate, and Wilks walked hastily away again, this time in the opposite direction.

"That's the place, clearly," Hewitt said. "We must slip across quietly, as soon as he's far enough down the road. Now!"

We hurried stealthily across, through the gate, and into the churchyard, where Hewitt threw his blue spectacles away. It was now nearly eight in the evening, and the sun was setting. Once again Wilks approached the gate, and did not enter, because a laborer passed at the time. Then he came back and slipped through.

The grass about the graves was long, and under the trees it was already twilight. Hewitt and I, two or three yards apart, to avoid falling over one another in case of sudden movement, watched from behind gravestones. The form of Wilks stood out large and black against the fading light in the west as he stealthily approached through the long grass. A light cart came clattering along the road, and Wilks dropped at once and crouched on his knees till it had passed. Then, staring warily about him, he made straight for the stone behind which Hewitt waited.

I saw Hewitt's dark form swing noiselessly round to the other side of the stone. Wilks passed on and dropped on his knee beside a large, weather-worn slab that rested on a brick under-structure a foot or so high. The long grass largely hid the bricks, and among it Wilks plunged his hand, feeling along the brick surface. Presently he drew out a loose brick, and laid it on the slab. He felt again in the place, and brought forth a small dark object. I saw Hewitt rise erect in the gathering dusk, and with extended arm step noiselessly toward the stooping man. Wilks made a motion to place the dark object in his pocket, but checked himself, and opened what appeared to be a lid, as though to make sure of the safety of the contents. The last light, straggling under the trees, fell on a brilliantly sparkling object within, and like a flash Hewitt's hand shot over Wilks' shoulder and snatched the jewel.

The man actually screamed—one of those curious sharp little screams that one may hear from a woman very suddenly alarmed. But he sprang at Hewitt like a cat, only to meet a straight drive of the fist that stretched him on his back across the slab. I sprang from behind my stone, and helped Hewitt to secure his wrists with a pocket-handkerchief. Then we marched him, struggling and swearing, to the village.

When, in the lights of the village, he recognized us, he had a perfect fit of rage, but afterward he calmed down, and admitted that it was a "very clean cop." There was some difficulty in finding the village constable, and Sir Valentine Quinton was dining out and did not arrive for at least an hour. In the interval Wilks grew communicative.

"How much d'ye think I'll get?" he asked.

"Can't guess," Hewitt replied. "And as we shall probably have to give evidence, you'll be giving yourself away if you talk too much."

"Oh, I don't care; that'll make no difference. It's a fair cop, and I'm in for it. You got at me nicely, lending me three quid. I never knew a reeler do that before. That blinded me. But was it kid about Gold Street?"

"No, it wasn't. Mr. Hollams is safely shut up by this time, I expect, and you are avenged for your little trouble with him this afternoon."

"What did you know about that? Well, you've got it up nicely for me, I must say. S'pose you've been following me all the time?"

"Well, yes; I haven't been far off. I guessed you'd want to clear out of town if Hollams was taken, and I knew this"—Hewitt tapped his breast pocket—"was what you'd take care to get hold of first. You hid it, of course, because you knew that Hollams would probably have you searched for it if he got suspicious?"

"Yes, he did, too. Two blokes went over my pockets one night, and somebody got into my room. But I expected that, Hollams is such a greedy pig. Once he's got you under his thumb he don't give you half your makings, and, if you kick, he'll have you smugged. So that I wasn't going to give him *that* if I could help it. I s'pose it ain't any good asking how you got put on to our mob?"

"No," said Hewitt, "it isn't."

We didn't get back till the next day, staying for the night, despite an inconvenient want of requisites, at the Hall. There were, in fact, no late trains. We told Sir Valentine the story of the Irishman, much to his amusement.

"Leamy's tale sounded unlikely, of course," Hewitt said, "but it was noticeable that every one of his misfortunes pointed in the same direction—that certain persons were tremendously anxious to get at something they supposed he had. When he spoke of his adventure with the bag, I at once remembered Wilks' arrest and subsequent release. It was a curious coincidence, to say the least, that this should happen at the very station to which the proceeds of this robbery must come, if they came to London at all, and on the day following the robbery itself. Kedderby is one of the few stations on this line where no trains would stop after the time of the robbery, so that the thief would have to wait till the next day to get back. Leamy's recognition of Wilks' portrait made me feel pretty certain. Plainly, he had carried stolen property; the poor, innocent fellow's conversation with Hollams showed that, as, in fact, did the sum, five pounds, paid to him by way of 'regulars,' or customary toll, from the plunder of services of carriage. Hollams obviously took Leamy for a criminal friend of

Wilks', because of his use of the thieves' expressions 'sparks' and 'regulars,' and suggested, in terms which Leamy misunderstood, that he should sell any plunder he might obtain to himself, Hollams. Altogether it would have been very curious if the plunder were *not* that from Radcot Hall, especially as no other robbery had been reported at the time.

"Now, among the jewels taken, only one was of a very pre-eminent value—the famous ruby. It was scarcely likely that Hollams would go to so much trouble and risk, attempting to drug, injuring, waylaying, and burgling the rooms of the unfortunate Leamy, for a jewel of small value—for any jewel, in fact, but the ruby. So that I felt a pretty strong presumption, at all events, that it was the ruby Hollams was after. Leamy had not had it, I was convinced, from his tale and his manner, and from what I judged of the man himself. The only other person was Wilks, and certainly he had a temptation to keep this to himself, and avoid, if possible, sharing with his London director, or principal; while the carriage of the bag by the Irishman gave him a capital opportunity to put suspicion on him, with the results seen. The most daring of Hollams' attacks on Leamy was doubtless the attempted maiming or killing at the railway station, so as to be able, in the character of a medical man, to search his pockets. He was probably desperate at the time, having, I have no doubt, been following Leamy about all day at the Crystal Palace without finding an opportunity to get at his pockets.

"The struggle and flight of Wilks from Hollams' confirmed my previous impressions. Hollams, finally satisfied that very morning that Leamy certainly had not the jewel, either on his person or at his lodging, and knowing, from having so closely watched him, that he had been nowhere where it could be disposed of, concluded that Wilks was cheating him, and attempted to extort the ruby from him by the aid of another ruffian and a pistol. The rest of my way was plain. Wilks, I knew, would seize the opportunity of Hollams' being safely locked up to get at and dispose of the ruby. I supplied him with funds and left him to lead us to his hiding-place. He did it, and I think that's all."

"He must have walked straight away from my house to the churchyard," Sir Valentine remarked, "to hide that pendant. That was fairly cool."

"Only a cool hand could carry out such a robbery single-handed," Hewitt answered. "I expect his tools were in the bag that Leamy carried, as well as the jewels. They must have been a small and neat set."

They were. We ascertained on our return to town the next day that the bag, with all its contents intact, including the tools, had been taken by the police at their surprise visit to No. 8 Gold Street, as well as much other stolen property.

Hollams and Wilks each got very wholesome doses of penal servitude, to the intense delight of Mick Leamy. Leamy himself, by the by, is still to be seen, clad in a noble uniform, guarding the door of a well-known London restaurant. He has not had any more five-pound notes for carrying bags, but knows London too well now to expect it.

VI. THE STANWAY
CAMEO MYSTERY

IT IS NOW a fair number of years back since the loss of the famous Stanway Cameo made its sensation, and the only person who had the least interest in keeping the real facts of the case secret has now been dead for some time, leaving neither relatives nor other representatives. Therefore no harm will be done in making the inner history of the case public; on the contrary, it will afford an opportunity of vindicating the professional reputation of Hewitt, who is supposed to have completely failed to make anything of the mystery surrounding the case. At the present time connoisseurs in ancient objects of art are often heard regretfully to wonder whether the wonderful cameo, so suddenly discovered and so quickly stolen, will ever again be visible to the public eye. Now this question need be asked no longer.

The cameo, as may be remembered from the many descriptions published at the time, was said to be absolutely the finest extant. It was a sardonyx of three strata—one of those rare sardonyx cameos in which it has been possible for the artist to avail himself of three different colors of superimposed stone—the lowest for the ground and the two others for the middle and high relief of the design. In size it was, for a cameo, immense, measuring seven and a half inches by nearly six. In subject it was similar to the renowned Gonzaga Cameo—now the property of the Czar of Russia—a male and a female head with imperial insignia; but in this case supposed to represent Tiberius Claudius and Messalina. Experts considered it probably to be the work of Athenion, a famous gem-cutter of the first Christian century, whose most notable other work now extant is a smaller cameo, with a mythological subject, preserved in the Vatican.

The Stanway Cameo had been discovered in an obscure Italian village by one of those traveling agents who scour all Europe for valuable antiquities and objects of art. This man had hurried immediately to London with his prize, and sold it to Mr. Claridge of St. James Street, eminent as a dealer in such objects. Mr. Claridge, recognizing the importance and value of the article, lost no opportunity of making its existence known, and very soon the Claudius Cameo, as it was at first usually called, was as famous as any in the world. Many experts in ancient art examined it, and several large bids were made for its purchase.

In the end it was bought by the Marquis of Stanway for five thousand pounds for the purpose of presentation to the British Museum. The marquis kept the cameo at his town house for a few days, showing it to his friends, and then returned it to Mr. Claridge to be finally and carefully cleaned before passing into the national collection. Two nights after Mr. Claridge's premises were broken into and the cameo stolen.

Such, in outline, was the generally known history of the Stanway Cameo. The circumstances of the burglary in detail were these: Mr. Claridge had himself been the last to leave the premises at about eight in the evening, at dusk, and had locked the small side door as usual. His assistant, Mr. Cutler, had left an hour and a half earlier. When Mr. Claridge left, everything was in order, and the policeman on fixed-point duty just opposite, who bade Mr. Claridge good-evening as he left, saw nothing suspicious during the rest of his term of duty, nor did his successors at the point throughout the night.

In the morning, however, Mr. Cutler, the assistant, who arrived first, soon after nine o'clock, at once perceived that something unlooked-for had happened. The door, of which he had a key, was still fastened, and had not been touched; but in the room behind the shop Mr. Claridge's private desk had been broken open, and the contents turned out in confusion. The door leading on to the staircase had also been forced. Proceeding up the stairs, Mr. Cutler found another door open, leading from the top landing to a small room; this door had been opened by the simple expedient of unscrewing and taking off the lock, which had been on the inside. In the ceiling of this room was a trap-door, and this was six or eight inches open, the edge resting on the half-wrenched-off bolt, which had been torn away when the trap was levered open from the outside.

Plainly, then, this was the path of the thief or thieves. Entrance had been made through the trap-door, two more doors had been opened, and then the desk had been ransacked. Mr. Cutler afterward explained that at this time he had no precise idea what had been stolen, and did not know where the cameo had been left on the previous evening. Mr. Claridge had himself undertaken the cleaning, and had been engaged on it, the assistant said, when he left.

There was no doubt, however, after Mr. Claridge's arrival at ten o'clock—the cameo was gone. Mr. Claridge, utterly confounded at his loss, explained incoherently, and with curses on his own carelessness, that he had locked the precious article in his desk on relinquishing work on it the previous evening, feeling rather tired, and not taking the trouble to carry it as far as the safe in another part of the house.

The police were sent for at once, of course, and every investigation made, Mr. Claridge offering a reward of five hundred pounds for the recovery of the cameo. The affair was scribbled off at large in the earliest editions of the evening papers, and by noon all the world was aware of the extraordinary theft of the Stanway Cameo, and many people were discussing the probabilities of the case, with very indistinct ideas of what a sardonyx cameo precisely was.

It was in the afternoon of this day that Lord Stanway called on Martin Hewitt. The marquis was a tall, upstanding man of spare figure and active habits, well known as a member of learned societies and a great patron of art. He hurried into Hewitt's private room as soon as his name had been announced, and, as soon as Hewitt had given him a chair, plunged into business.

"Probably you already guess my business with you, Mr. Hewitt—you have seen the early evening papers? Just so; then I needn't tell you again what you already know. My cameo is gone, and I badly want it back. Of course the police are hard at work at Claridge's, but I'm not quite satisfied. I have been there myself for two or three hours, and can't see that they know any more about it than I do myself. Then, of course, the police, naturally and properly enough from their point of view, look first to find the criminal, regarding the recovery of the property almost as a secondary consideration. Now, from *my* point of view, the chief consideration is the property. Of course I want the thief caught, if possible, and properly punished; but still more I want the cameo."

"Certainly it is a considerable loss. Five thousand pounds—"

"Ah, but don't misunderstand me! It isn't the monetary value of the thing that I regret. As a matter of fact, I am indemnified for that already. Claridge has behaved most honorably—more than honorably. Indeed, the first intimation I had of the loss was a check from him for five thousand pounds, with a letter assuring me that the restoration to me of the amount I had paid was the least he could do to repair the result of what he called his unpardonable carelessness. Legally, I'm not sure that I could demand anything of him, unless I could prove very flagrant neglect indeed to guard against theft."

"Then I take it, Lord Stanway," Hewitt observed, "that you much prefer the cameo to the money?"

"Certainly. Else I should never have been willing to pay the money for the cameo. It was an enormous price—perhaps much above the market value, even for such a valuable thing—but I was particularly anxious that it should not go out of the country. Our public collections here are not so fortunate as they should be in the possession of the very finest examples of that class of work. In short, I had determined on the cameo, and, fortunately, happen to be able to carry out determinations of that sort without regarding an extra thousand pounds or so as an obstacle. So that, you see, what I want is not the value, but the thing itself. Indeed, I don't think I can possibly keep the money Claridge has sent me; the affair is more his misfortune than his fault. But I shall say nothing about returning it for a little while; it may possibly have the effect of sharpening everybody in the search."

"Just so. Do I understand that you would like me to look into the case independently, on your behalf?"

"Exactly. I want you, if you can, to approach the matter entirely from my point of view—your sole object being to find the cameo. Of course, if you happen on the thief as well, so much the better. Perhaps, after all, looking for the one is the same thing as looking for the other?"

"Not always; but usually it is, or course; even if they are not together, they certainly *have* been at one time, and to have one is a very long step toward having the other. Now, to begin with, is anybody suspected?"

"Well, the police are reserved, but I believe the fact is they've nothing to say. Claridge won't admit that he suspects any one, though he believes that whoever it was must have watched him yesterday evening through the back window of his room, and must have seen him put the cameo away in his desk; because the thief would seem to have gone straight to the place. But I half fancy that, in his inner mind, he is inclined to suspect one of two people. You see, a robbery of this sort is different from others. That cameo would never be stolen, I imagine, with the view of its being sold—it is much too famous a thing; a man might as well walk about offering to sell the Tower of London. There are only a very few people who buy such things, and every one of them knows all about it. No dealer would touch it; he could never even show it, much less sell it, without being called to account. So that it really seems more likely that it has been taken by somebody who wishes to keep it for mere love of the thing—a collector, in fact—who would then have to keep it secretly at home, and never let a soul besides himself see it, living in the consciousness that at his death it must be found and this theft known; unless, indeed, an ordinary vulgar burglar has taken it without knowing its value."

"That isn't likely," Hewitt replied. "An ordinary burglar, ignorant of its value, wouldn't have gone straight to the cameo and have taken it in preference to many other things of more apparent worth, which must be lying near in such a place as Claridge's."

"True—I suppose he wouldn't. Although the police seem to think that the breaking in is clearly the work of a regular criminal—from the jimmy-marks, you know, and so on."

"Well, but what of the two people you think Mr. Claridge suspects?"

"Of course I can't say that he does suspect them—I only fancied from his tone that it might be possible; he himself insists that he can't, in justice, suspect anybody. One of these men is Hahn, the traveling agent who sold him the cameo. This man's character does not appear to be absolutely irreproachable; no dealer trusts him very far. Of course Claridge doesn't say what he paid him for the cameo; these dealers are very reticent about their profits, which I believe are as often something like five hundred per cent as not. But it seems Hahn bargained to have something extra, depending on the amount

Claridge could sell the carving for. According to the appointment he should have turned up this morning, but he hasn't been seen, and nobody seems to know exactly where he is."

"Yes; and the other person?"

"Well, I scarcely like mentioning him, because he is certainly a gentleman, and I believe, in the ordinary way, quite incapable of anything in the least degree dishonorable; although, of course, they say a collector has no conscience in the matter of his own particular hobby, and certainly Mr. Wollett is as keen a collector as any man alive. He lives in chambers in the next turning past Claridge's premises—can, in fact, look into Claridge's back windows if he likes. He examined the cameo several times before I bought it, and made several high offers—appeared, in fact, very anxious indeed to get it. After I had bought it he made, I understand, some rather strong remarks about people like myself 'spoiling the market' by paying extravagant prices, and altogether cut up 'crusty,' as they say, at losing the specimen." Lord Stanway paused a few seconds, and then went on: "I'm not sure that I ought to mention Mr. Woollett's name for a moment in connection with such a matter; I am personally perfectly certain that he is as incapable of anything like theft as myself. But I am telling you all I know."

"Precisely. I can't know too much in a case like this. It can do no harm if I know all about fifty innocent people, and may save me from the risk of knowing nothing about the thief. Now, let me see: Mr. Wollett's rooms, you say, are near Mr. Claridge's place of business? Is there any means of communication between the roofs?"

"Yes, I am told that it is perfectly possible to get from one place to the other by walking along the leads."

"Very good! Then, unless you can think of any other information that may help me, I think, Lord Stanway, I will go at once and look at the place."

"Do, by all means. I think I'll come back with you. Somehow, I don't like to feel idle in the matter, though I suppose I can't do much. As to more information, I don't think there is any."

"In regard to Mr. Claridge's assistant, now: Do you know anything of him?"

"Only that he has always seemed a very civil and decent sort of man. Honest, I should say, or Claridge wouldn't have kept him so many years—there are a good many valuable things about at Claridge's. Besides, the man has keys of the place himself, and, even if he were a thief, he wouldn't need to go breaking in through the roof."

"So that," said Hewitt, "we have, directly connected with this cameo, besides yourself, these people: Mr. Claridge, the dealer; Mr. Cutler, the assistant in Mr. Claridge's business; Hahn, who sold the article to Claridge, and Mr. Woollett, who made bids for it. These are all?"

"All that I know of. Other gentlemen made bids, I believe, but I don't know them."

"Take these people in their order. Mr. Claridge is out of the question, as a dealer with a reputation to keep up would be, even if he hadn't immediately sent you this five thousand pounds—more than the market value, I understand, of the cameo. The assistant is a reputable man, against whom nothing is known, who would never

need to break in, and who must understand his business
well enough to know that he could never attempt to
sell the missing stone without instant detection. Hahn
is a man of shady antecedents, probably clever enough
to know as well as anybody how to dispose of such
plunder—if it be possible to dispose of it at all; also,
Hahn hasn't been to Claridge's to-day, although he had
an appointment to take money. Lastly, Mr. Woollett is a
gentleman of the most honorable record, but a perfectly
rabid collector, who had made every effort to secure the
cameo before you bought it; who, moreover, could have
seen Mr. Claridge working in his back room, and who
has perfectly easy access to Mr. Claridge's roof. If we
find it can't be none of these, then we must look where
circumstances indicate."

There was unwonted excitement at Mr. Claridge's
place when Hewitt and his client arrived. It was a dull
old building, and in the windows there was never more
show than an odd blue china vase or two, or, mayhap, a
few old silver shoe-buckles and a curious small sword.
Nine men out of ten would have passed it without a
glance; but the tenth at least would probably know it
for a place famous through the world for the number
and value of the old and curious objects of art that had
passed through it.

On this day two or three loiterers, having heard of
the robbery, extracted what gratification they might from
staring at nothing between the railings guarding the
windows. Within, Mr. Claridge, a brisk, stout, little old
man, was talking earnestly to a burly police-inspector in
uniform, and Mr. Cutler, who had seized the opportunity
to attempt amateur detective work on his own account,

was groveling perseveringly about the floor, among old porcelain and loose pieces of armor, in the futile hope of finding any clue that the thieves might have considerately dropped.

Mr. Claridge came forward eagerly.

"The leather case has been found, I am pleased to be able to tell you, Lord Stanway, since you left."

"Empty, of course?"

"Unfortunately, yes. It had evidently been thrown away by the thief behind a chimney-stack a roof or two away, where the police have found it. But it is a clue, of course."

"Ah, then this gentleman will give me his opinion of it," Lord Stanway said, turning to Hewitt. "This, Mr. Claridge, is Mr. Martin Hewitt, who has been kind enough to come with me here at a moment's notice. With the police on the one hand and Mr. Hewitt on the other we shall certainly recover that cameo, if it is to be recovered, I think."

Mr. Claridge bowed, and beamed on Hewitt through his spectacles. "I'm very glad Mr. Hewitt has come," he said. "Indeed, I had already decided to give the police till this time to-morrow, and then, if they had found nothing, to call in Mr. Hewitt myself."

Hewitt bowed in his turn, and then asked: "Will you let me see the various breakages? I hope they have not been disturbed."

"Nothing whatever has been disturbed. Do exactly as seems best. I need scarcely say that everything here is perfectly at your disposal. You know all the circumstances, of course?"

"In general, yes. I suppose I am right in the belief that you have no resident housekeeper?"

"No," Claridge replied, "I haven't. I had one housekeeper who sometimes pawned my property in the evening, and then another who used to break my most valuable china, till I could never sleep or take a moment's ease at home for fear my stock was being ruined here. So I gave up resident housekeepers. I felt some confidence in doing it because of the policeman who is always on duty opposite."

"Can I see the broken desk?"

Mr. Claridge led the way into the room behind the shop. The desk was really a sort of work-table, with a lifting top and a lock. The top had been forced roughly open by some instrument which had been pushed in below it and used as a lever, so that the catch of the lock was torn away. Hewitt examined the damaged parts and the marks of the lever, and then looked out at the back window.

"There are several windows about here," he remarked, "from which it might be possible to see into this room. Do you know any of the people who live behind them?"

"Two or three I know," Mr. Claridge answered, "but there are two windows—the pair almost immediately before us—belonging to a room or office which is to let. Any stranger might get in there and watch."

"Do the roofs above any of those windows communicate in any way with yours?"

"None of those directly opposite. Those at the left do; you may walk all the way along the leads."

"And whose windows are they?"

Mr. Claridge hesitated. "Well," he said, "they're Mr. Woollett's, an excellent customer of mine. But he's a gentleman, and—well, I really think it's absurd to suspect him."

"In a case like this," Hewitt answered, "one must disregard nothing but the impossible. Somebody—whether Mr. Woollett himself or another person—could possibly have seen into this room from those windows, and equally possibly could have reached this room from that one. Therefore we must not forget Mr. Woollett. Have any of your neighbors been burgled during the night? I mean that strangers anxious to get at your trap-door would probably have to begin by getting into some other house close by, so as to reach your roof."

"No," Mr. Claridge replied; "there has been nothing of that sort. It was the first thing the police ascertained."

Hewitt examined the broken door and then made his way up the stairs with the others. The unscrewed lock of the door of the top back-room required little examination. In the room below the trap-door was a dusty table on which stood a chair, and at the other side of the table sat Detective-Inspector Plummer, whom Hewitt knew very well, and who bade him "good-day" and then went on with his docket.

"This chair and table were found as they are now, I take it?" Hewitt asked.

"Yes," said Mr. Claridge; "the thieves, I should think, dropped in through the trap-door, after breaking it open, and had to place this chair where it is to be able to climb back."

Hewitt scrambled up through the trap-way and examined it from the top. The door was hung on long external barn-door hinges, and had been forced open in a similar manner to that practiced on the desk. A jimmy had been pushed between the frame and the door near the bolt, and the door had been pried open, the bolt being torn away from the screws in the operation.

Presently Inspector Plummer, having finished his docket, climbed up to the roof after Hewitt, and the two together went to the spot, close under a chimney-stack on the next roof but one, where the case had been found. Plummer produced the case, which he had in his coat-tail pocket, for Hewitt's inspection.

"I don't see anything particular about it; do you?" he said. "It shows us the way they went, though, being found just here."

"Well, yes," Hewitt said; "if we kept on in this direction, we should be going toward Mr. Woollett's house, and *his* trap-door, shouldn't we!"

The inspector pursed his lips, smiled, and shrugged his shoulders. "Of course we haven't waited till now to find that out," he said.

"No, of course. And, as you say, I didn't think there is much to be learned from this leather case. It is almost new, and there isn't a mark on it." And Hewitt handed it back to the inspector.

"Well," said Plummer, as he returned the case to his pocket, "what's your opinion?"

"It's rather an awkward case."

"Yes, it is. Between ourselves—I don't mind telling you—I'm having a sharp lookout kept over there"—Plummer jerked his head in the direction of Mr. Woollett's chambers—"because the robbery's an unusual one. There's only two possible motives—the sale of the cameo or the keeping of it. The sale's out of the question, as you know; the thing's only salable to those who would collar the thief at once, and who wouldn't have the thing in their places now for anything. So that it must be taken to keep, and that's a thing nobody but the maddest of collectors would do, just such persons as—" and the inspector nodded again toward Mr. Woollett's quarters. "Take that with the other circumstances," he added, "and I think you'll agree it's worth while looking a little farther that way. Of course some of the work—taking off the lock and so on—looks rather like a regular burglar, but it's just possible that any one badly wanting the cameo would like to hire a man who was up to the work."

"Yes, it's possible."

"Do you know anything of Hahn, the agent?" Plummer asked, a moment later.

"No, I don't. Have you found him yet?"

"I haven't yet, but I'm after him. I've found he was at Charing Cross a day or two ago, booking a ticket for the Continent. That and his failing to turn up to-day seem to make it worth while not to miss *him* if we can help it. He isn't the sort of man that lets a chance of drawing a bit of money go for nothing."

They returned to the room. "Well," said Lord Stanway, "what's the result of the consultation? We've been waiting here very patiently, while you two clever men have been discussing the matter on the roof."

On the wall just beneath the trap-door a very dusty old tall hat hung on a peg. This Hewitt took down and examined very closely, smearing his fingers with the dust from the inside lining. "Is this one of your valuable and crusted old antiques?" he asked, with a smile, of Mr. Claridge.

"That's only an old hat that I used to keep here for use in bad weather," Mr. Claridge said, with some surprise at the question. "I haven't touched it for a year or more."

"Oh, then it couldn't have been left here by your last night's visitor," Hewitt replied, carelessly replacing it on the hook. "You left here at eight last night, I think?"

"Eight exactly—or within a minute or two."

"Just so. I think I'll look at the room on the opposite side of the landing, if you'll let me."

"Certainly, if you'd like to," Claridge replied; "but they haven't been there—it is exactly as it was left. Only a lumber-room, you see," he concluded, flinging the door open.

A number of partly broken-up packing-cases littered about this room, with much other rubbish. Hewitt took the lid of one of the newest-looking packing-cases, and glanced at the address label. Then he turned to a rusty old iron box that stood against a wall. "I should like to see behind this," he said, tugging at it with his hands. "It is heavy and dirty. Is there a small crowbar about the house, or some similar lever?"

Mr. Claridge shook his head. "Haven't such a thing in the place," he said.

"Never mind," Hewitt replied, "another time will do to shift that old box, and perhaps, after all, there's little reason for moving it. I will just walk round to the police-station, I think, and speak to the constables who were on duty opposite during the night. I think, Lord Stanway, I have seen all that is necessary here."

"I suppose," asked Mr. Claridge, "it is too soon yet to ask if you have formed any theory in the matter?"

"Well—yes, it is," Hewitt answered. "But perhaps I may be able to surprise you in an hour or two; but that I don't promise. By the by," he added suddenly, "I suppose you're sure the trap-door was bolted last night?"

"Certainly," Mr. Claridge answered, smiling. "Else how could the bolt have been broken? As a matter of fact, I believe the trap hasn't been opened for months. Mr. Cutler, do you remember when the trap-door was last opened?"

Mr. Cutler shook his head. "Certainly not for six months," he said.

"Ah, very well; it's not very important," Hewitt replied.

As they reached the front shop a fiery-faced old gentleman bounced in at the street door, stumbling over an umbrella that stood in a dark corner, and kicking it three yards away.

"What the deuce do you mean," he roared at Mr. Claridge, "by sending these police people smelling about my rooms and asking questions of my servants? What do you mean, sir, by treating me as a thief? Can't a gentleman come into this place to look at an article without being suspected of stealing it, when it disappears through your wretched carelessness? I'll ask my solicitor, sir, if there isn't a remedy for this sort of thing. And if I catch another of your spy fellows on my staircase, or crawling about my roof, I'll—I'll shoot him!"

"Really, Mr. Woollett—" began Mr. Claridge, somewhat abashed, but the angry old man would hear nothing.

"Don't talk to me, sir; you shall talk to my solicitor. And am I to understand, my lord"—turning to Lord Stanway—"that these things are being done with your approval?"

"Whatever is being done," Lord Stanway answered, "is being done by the police on their own responsibility, and entirely without prompting, I believe, by Mr. Claridge—certainly without a suggestion of any sort from myself. I think that the personal opinion of Mr. Claridge—certainly my own—is that anything like a suspicion of your position in this wretched matter is ridiculous. And if you will only consider the matter calmly—"

"Consider it calmly? Imagine yourself considering such a thing calmly, Lord Stanway. I *won't* consider it calmly. I'll—I'll—I won't have it. And if I find another man on my roof, I'll pitch him off!" And Mr. Woollett bounced into the street again.

"Mr. Woollett is annoyed," Hewitt observed, with a smile. "I'm afraid Plummer has a clumsy assistant somewhere."

Mr. Claridge said nothing, but looked rather glum, for Mr. Woollett was a most excellent customer.

Lord Stanway and Hewitt walked slowly down the street, Hewitt staring at the pavement in profound thought. Once or twice Lord Stanway glanced at his face, but refrained from disturbing him. Presently, however, he observed: "You seem, at least, Mr. Hewitt, to have noticed something that has set you thinking. Does it look like a clue?"

Hewitt came out of his cogitation at once. "A clue?" he said; "the case bristles with clues. The extraordinary thing to me is that Plummer, usually a smart man, doesn't seem to have seen one of them. He must be out of sorts, I'm afraid. But the case is decidedly a most remarkable one."

"Remarkable in what particular way?"

"In regard to motive. Now it would seem, as Plummer was saying to me just now on the roof, that there were only two possible motives for such a robbery. Either the man who took all this trouble and risk to break into Claridge's place must have desired to sell the cameo at a good price, or he must have desired to keep it for himself, being a lover of such things. But neither of these has been the actual motive."

"Perhaps he thinks he can extort a good sum from me by way of ransom?"

"No, it isn't that. Nor is it jealousy, nor spite, nor anything of that kind. I know the motive, I *think*—but I wish we could get hold of Hahn. I will shut myself up alone and turn it over in my mind for half an hour presently."

"Meanwhile, what I want to know is, apart from all your professional subtleties—which I confess I can't understand—can you get back the cameo?"

"That," said Hewitt, stopping at the corner of the street, "I am rather afraid I can not—nor anybody else. But I am pretty sure I know the thief."

"Then surely that will lead you to the cameo?"

"It *may*, of course; but, then, it is just possible that by this evening you may not want to have it back, after all."

Lord Stanway stared in amazement.

"Not want to have it back!" he exclaimed. "Why, of course I shall want to have it back. I don't understand you in the least; you talk in conundrums. Who is the thief you speak of?"

"I think, Lord Stanway," Hewitt said, "that perhaps I had better not say until I have quite finished my inquiries, in case of mistakes. The case is quite an extraordinary one, and of quite a different character from what one would at first naturally imagine, and I must be very careful to guard against the possibility of error. I have very little fear of a mistake, however, and I hope I may wait on you in a few hours at Piccadilly with news. I have only to see the policemen."

"Certainly, come whenever you please. But why see the policemen? They have already most positively stated that they saw nothing whatever suspicious in the house or near it."

"I shall not ask them anything at all about the house," Hewitt responded. "I shall just have a little chat with them—about the weather." And with a smiling bow he turned away, while Lord Stanway stood and gazed after him, with an expression that implied a suspicion that his special detective was making a fool of him.

In rather more than an hour Hewitt was back in Mr. Claridge's shop. "Mr. Claridge," he said, "I think I must ask you one or two questions in private. May I see you in your own room?"

They went there at once, and Hewitt, pulling a chair before the window, sat down with his back to the light. The dealer shut the door, and sat opposite him, with the light full in his face.

"Mr. Claridge," Hewitt proceeded slowly, "*when did you first find that Lord Stanway's cameo was a forgery?*"

Claridge literally bounced in his chair. His face paled, but he managed to stammer sharply: "What—what—what d'you mean? Forgery? Do you mean to say I sell forgeries? Forgery? It wasn't a forgery!"

"Then," continued Hewitt in the same deliberate tone, watching the other's face the while, "if it wasn't a forgery, *why did you destroy it and burst your trap-door and desk to imitate a burglary?*"

The sweat stood thick on the dealer's face, and he

gasped. But he struggled hard to keep his faculties together, and ejaculated hoarsely: "Destroy it? What— what—I didn't—didn't destroy it!"

"Threw it into the river, then—don't prevaricate about details."

"No—no—it's a lie! Who says that? Go away! You're insulting me!" Claridge almost screamed.

"Come, come, Mr. Claridge," Hewitt said more placably, for he had gained his point; "don't distress yourself, and don't attempt to deceive me—you can't, I assure you. I know everything you did before you left here last night—everything."

Claridge's face worked painfully. Once or twice he appeared to be on the point of returning an indignant reply, but hesitated, and finally broke down altogether.

"Don't expose me, Mr. Hewitt!" he pleaded; "I beg you won't expose me! I haven't harmed a soul but myself. I've paid Lord Stanway every penny back, and I never knew the thing was a forgery till I began to clean it. I'm an old man, Mr. Hewitt, and my professional reputation has been spotless until now. I beg you won't expose me."

Hewitt's voice softened. "Don't make an unnecessary trouble of it," he said. "I see a decanter on your sideboard—let me give you a little brandy and water. Come, there's nothing criminal, I believe, in a man's breaking open his own desk, or his own trap-door, for that matter. Of course I'm acting for Lord Stanway in this affair, and I must, in duty, report to him without reserve. But Lord Stanway is a gentleman, and I'll undertake he'll do nothing inconsiderate of your feelings, if you're disposed to be frank. Let us talk the affair over; tell me about it."

"It was that swindler Hahn who deceived me in the beginning," Claridge said. "I have never made a mistake with a cameo before, and I never thought so close an imitation was possible. I examined it most carefully, and was perfectly satisfied, and many experts examined it afterward, and were all equally deceived. I felt as sure as I possibly could feel that I had bought one of the finest, if not actually the finest, cameos known to exist. It was not until after it had come back from Lord Stanway's, and I was cleaning it the evening before last, that in course of my work it became apparent that the thing was nothing but a consummately clever forgery. It was made of three layers of molded glass, nothing more nor less. But the glass was treated in a way I had never before known of, and the surface had been cunningly worked on till it defied any ordinary examination. Some of the glass imitation cameos made in the latter part of the last century, I may tell you, are regarded as marvelous pieces of work, and, indeed, command very fair prices, but this was something quite beyond any of those.

"I was amazed and horrified. I put the thing away and went home. All that night I lay awake in a state of distraction, quite unable to decide what to do. To let the cameo go out of my possession was impossible. Sooner or later the forgery would be discovered, and my reputation—the highest in these matters in this country, I may safely claim, and the growth of nearly fifty years of honest application and good judgment—this reputation would be gone forever. But without considering this, there was the fact that I had taken five thousand pounds of Lord Stanway's money for a mere piece of glass, and that money I must, in mere common honesty as well

as for my own sake, return. But how? The name of the
Stanway Cameo had become a household word, and to
confess that the whole thing was a sham would ruin my
reputation and destroy all confidence—past, present,
and future—in me and in my transactions. Either way
spelled ruin. Even if I confided in Lord Stanway privately,
returned his money, and destroyed the cameo, what
then? The sudden disappearance of an article so famous
would excite remark at once. It had been presented to
the British Museum, and if it never appeared in that
collection, and no news were to be got of it, people
would guess at the truth at once. To make it known that I
myself had been deceived would have availed nothing. It
is my business *not* to be deceived; and to have it known
that my most expensive specimens might be forgeries
would equally mean ruin, whether I sold them cunningly
as a rogue or ignorantly as a fool. Indeed, my pride, my
reputation as a connoisseur, is a thing near to my heart,
and it would be an unspeakable humiliation to me to have
it known that I had been imposed on by such a forgery.
What could I do? Every expedient seemed useless but
one—the one I adopted. It was not straightforward, I
admit; but, oh! Mr. Hewitt, consider the temptation—
and remember that it couldn't do a soul any harm. No
matter who might be suspected, I knew there could not
possibly be evidence to make them suffer. All the next
day—yesterday—I was anxiously worrying out the thing
in my mind and carefully devising the—the trick, I'm
afraid you'll call it, that you by some extraordinary means
have seen through. It seemed the only thing—what else
was there? More I needn't tell you; you know it. I have
only now to beg that you will use your best influence

with Lord Stanway to save me from public derision and exposure. I will do anything—-pay anything—anything but exposure, at my age, and with my position."

"Well, you see," Hewitt replied thoughtfully, "I've no doubt Lord Stanway will show you every consideration, and certainly I will do what I can to save you in the circumstances; though you must remember that you *have* done some harm—you have caused suspicions to rest on at least one honest man. But as to reputation, I've a professional reputation of my own. If I help to conceal your professional failure, I shall appear to have failed in *my* part of the business."

"But the cases are different, Mr. Hewitt. Consider. You are not expected—it would be impossible—to succeed invariably; and there are only two or three who know you have looked into the case. Then your other conspicuous successes—"

"Well, well, we shall see. One thing I don't know, though—whether you climbed out of a window to break open the trap-door, or whether you got up through the trap-door itself and pulled the bolt with a string through the jamb, so as to bolt it after you."

"There was no available window. I used the string, as you say. My poor little cunning must seem very transparent to you, I fear. I spent hours of thought over the question of the trap-door—how to break it open so as to leave a genuine appearance, and especially how to bolt it inside after I had reached the roof. I thought I had succeeded beyond the possibility of suspicion; how you penetrated the device surpasses my comprehension. How, to begin with, could you possibly know that the cameo was a forgery? Did you ever see it?"

"Never. And, if I had seen it, I fear I should never have been able to express an opinion on it; I'm not a connoisseur. As a matter of fact, I *didn't* know that the thing was a forgery in the first place; what I knew in the first place was that it was *you* who had broken into the house. It was from that that I arrived at the conclusion, after a certain amount of thought, that the cameo must have been forged. Gain was out of the question. You, beyond all men, could never sell the Stanway Cameo again, and, besides, you had paid back Lord Stanway's money. I knew enough of your reputation to know that you would never incur the scandal of a great theft at your place for the sake of getting the cameo for yourself, when you might have kept it in the beginning, with no trouble and mystery. Consequently I had to look for another motive, and at first another motive seemed an impossibility. Why should you wish to take all this trouble to lose five thousand pounds? You had nothing to gain; perhaps you had something to save—your professional reputation, for instance. Looking at it so, it was plain that you were *suppressing* the cameo—burking it; since, once taken as you had taken it, it could never come to light again. That suggested the solution of the mystery at once—you had discovered, after the sale, that the cameo was not genuine."

"Yes, yes—I see; but you say you began with the knowledge that I broke into the place myself. How did you know that? I can not imagine a trace—"

"My dear sir, you left traces everywhere. In the first place, it struck me as curious, before I came here, that you had sent off that check for five thousand pounds to Lord Stanway an hour or so after the robbery was discovered; it looked so much as though you were sure of the cameo never coming back, and were in a hurry to avert suspicion. Of course I understood that, so far as I then knew the case, you were the most unlikely person in the world, and that your eagerness to repay Lord Stanway might be the most creditable thing possible. But the point was worth remembering, and I remembered it.

"When I came here, I saw suspicious indications in many directions, but the conclusive piece of evidence was that old hat hanging below the trap-door."

"But I never touched it; I assure you, Mr. Hewitt, I never touched the hat; haven't touched it for months—"

"Of course. If you *had* touched it, I might never have got the clue. But we'll deal with the hat presently; that wasn't what struck me at first. The trap-door first took my attention. Consider, now: Here was a trap-door, most insecurely hung on *external* hinges; the burglar had a screwdriver, for he took off the door-lock below with it. Why, then, didn't he take this trap off by the hinges, instead of making a noise and taking longer time and trouble to burst the bolt from its fastenings? And why, if he were a stranger, was he able to plant his jimmy from the outside just exactly opposite the interior bolt? There was only one mark on the frame, and that precisely in the proper place.

"After that I saw the leather case. It had not been thrown away, or some corner would have shown signs of the fall. It had been put down carefully where it was found. These things, however, were of small importance compared with the hat. The hat, as you know, was exceedingly thick with dust—the accumulation of months. But, on the top side, presented toward the trap-door, were a score or so of *raindrop marks*. That was all. They were new marks, for there was no dust over them; they had merely had time to dry and cake the dust they had fallen on. *Now, there had been no rain since a sharp shower just after seven o'clock last night*. At that time you, by your own statement, were in the place. You left at eight, and the rain was all over at ten minutes or a quarter past seven. The trap-door, you also told me, had not been opened for months. The thing was plain. You, or somebody who was here when you were, had opened that trap-door during, or just before, that shower. I said little then, but went, as soon as I had left, to the police-station. There I made perfectly certain that there had been no rain during the night by questioning the policemen who were on duty outside all the time. There had been none. I knew everything.

"The only other evidence there was pointed with all the rest. There were no rain-marks on the leather case; it had been put on the roof as an after-thought when there was no rain. A very poor after-thought, let me tell you, for no thief would throw away a useful case that concealed his booty and protected it from breakage, and throw it away just so as to leave a clue as to what direction he had gone in. I also saw, in the lumber-room, a number of packing-cases—one with a label dated two days back—which had been opened with an iron lever; and yet, when I made an excuse to ask for it, you said there was no such thing in the place. Inference, you didn't want me to compare it with the marks on the desks and doors. That is all, I think."

Mr. Claridge looked dolorously down at the floor. "I'm afraid," he said, "that I took an unsuitable rôle when I undertook to rely on my wits to deceive men like you. I thought there wasn't a single vulnerable spot in my defense, but you walk calmly through it at the first attempt. Why did I never think of those raindrops?"

"Come," said Hewitt, with a smile, "that sounds unrepentant. I am going, now, to Lord Stanway's. If I were you, I think I should apologize to Mr. Woollett in some way."

Lord Stanway, who, in the hour or two of reflection left him after parting with Hewitt, had come to the belief that he had employed a man whose mind was not always in order, received Hewitt's story with natural astonishment. For some time he was in doubt as to whether he would be doing right in acquiescing in anything but a straightforward public statement of the facts connected with the disappearance of the cameo, but in the end was persuaded to let the affair drop, on receiving an assurance from Mr. Woollett that he unreservedly accepted the apology offered him by Mr. Claridge.

As for the latter, he was at least sufficiently punished in loss of money and personal humiliation for his escapade. But the bitterest and last blow he sustained when the unblushing Hahn walked smilingly into his office two days later to demand the extra payment agreed on in consideration of the sale. He had been called suddenly away, he exclaimed, on the day he should have come, and hoped his missing the appointment had occasioned no inconvenience. As to the robbery of the cameo, of course he was very sorry, but "pishness was pishness," and he would be glad of a check for the sum agreed on. And the unhappy Claridge was obliged to pay it, knowing that the man had swindled him, but unable to open his mouth to say so.

The reward remained on offer for a long time; indeed, it was never publicly withdrawn, I believe, even at the time of Claridge's death. And several intelligent newspapers enlarged upon the fact that an ordinary burglar had completely baffled and defeated the boasted acumen of Mr. Martin Hewitt, the well-known private detective.

VII. THE AFFAIR OF
THE TORTOISE

VERY OFTEN Hewitt was tempted, by the fascination of some particularly odd case, to neglect his other affairs to follow up a matter that from a business point of view was of little or no value to him. As a rule, he had a sufficient regard for his own interests to resist such temptations, but in one curious case, at least, I believe he allowed it largely to influence him. It was certainly an extremely odd case—one of those affairs that, coming to light at intervals, but more often remaining unheard of by the general public, convince one that, after all, there is very little extravagance about Mr. R.L. Stevenson's bizarre imaginings of doings in London in his "New Arabian Nights." "There is nothing in this world that is at all possible," I have often heard Martin Hewitt say, "that has not happened or is not happening in London." Certainly he had opportunities of knowing.

The case I have referred to occurred some time before my own acquaintance with him began—in 1878, in fact. He had called one Monday morning at an office in regard to something connected with one of those uninteresting, though often difficult, cases which formed, perhaps, the bulk of his practice, when he was informed of a most mysterious murder that had taken place in another part of the same building on the previous Saturday afternoon.

Owing to the circumstances of the case, only the vaguest account had appeared in the morning papers, and even this, as it chanced, Hewitt had not read.

The building was one of a new row in a partly rebuilt street near the National Gallery. The whole row had been built by a speculator for the purpose of letting out in flats, suites of chambers, and in one or two cases, on the ground floors, offices. The rooms had let very well, and to desirable tenants, as a rule. The least satisfactory tenant, the proprietor reluctantly admitted, was a Mr. Rameau, a negro gentleman, single, who had three rooms on the top floor but one of the particular building that Hewitt was visiting. His rent was paid regularly, but his behavior had produced complaints from other tenants. He got uproariously drunk, and screamed and howled in unknown tongues. He fell asleep on the staircase, and ladies were afraid to pass. He bawled rough chaff down the stairs and along the corridors at butcher-boys and messengers, and played on errand-boys brutal practical jokes that ended in police-court summonses. He once had a way of sliding down the balusters, shouting: "Ho! ho! ho! yah!" as he went, but as he was a big, heavy man, and the balusters had been built for different treatment, he had very soon and very firmly been requested to stop it. He had plenty of money, and spent it freely; but it was generally felt that there was too much of the light-hearted savage about him to fit him to live among quiet people.

How much longer the landlord would have stood this sort of thing, Hewitt's informant said, was a matter of conjecture, for on the Saturday afternoon in question the tenancy had come to a startling full-stop. Rameau had been murdered in his room, and the body had, in the most unaccountable fashion, been secretly removed from the premises.

The strongest possible suspicion pointed to a man who had been employed in shoveling and carrying coals, cleaning windows, and chopping wood for several of the buildings, and who had left that very Saturday. The crime had, in fact, been committed with this man's chopper, and the man himself had been heard, again and again, to threaten Rameau, who, in his brutal fashion, had made a butt of him. This man was a Frenchman, Victor Goujon by name, who had lost his employment as a watchmaker by reason of an injury to his right hand, which destroyed its steadiness, and so he had fallen upon evil days and odd jobs.

He was a little man of no great strength, but extraordinarily excitable, and the coarse gibes and horse-play of the big negro drove him almost to madness. Rameau would often, after some more than ordinarily outrageous attack, contemptuously fling Goujon a shilling, which the little Frenchman, although wanting a shilling badly enough, would hurl back in his face, almost weeping with impotent rage. "Pig! *Canaille*!" he would scream. "Dirty pig of Africa! Take your sheelin' to vere you 'ave stole it! *Voleur*! Pig!"

There was a tortoise living in the basement, of which Goujon had made rather a pet, and the negro would sometimes use this animal as a missile, flinging it at the little Frenchman's head. On one such occasion the tortoise struck the wall so forcibly as to break its shell, and then Goujon seized a shovel and rushed at his tormentor with such blind fury that the latter made a bolt of it. These were but a few of the passages between

Rameau and the fuel-porter, but they illustrate the state of feeling between them.

Goujon, after correspondence with a relative in France who offered him work, gave notice to leave, which expired on the day of the crime. At about three that afternoon a housemaid, proceeding toward Rameau's rooms, met Goujon as he was going away. Goujon bade her good-by, and, pointing in the direction of Rameau's rooms, said exultantly: "Dere shall be no more of the black pig for me; vit 'im I 'ave done for. Zut! I mock me of 'im! 'E vill never *tracasser* me no more." And he went away.

The girl went to the outer door of Rameau's rooms, knocked, and got no reply. Concluding that the tenant was out, she was about to use her keys, when she found that the door was unlocked. She passed through the lobby and into the sitting-room, and there fell in a dead faint at the sight that met her eyes. Rameau lay with his back across the sofa and his head—drooping within an inch of the ground. On the head was a fearful gash, and below it was a pool of blood.

The girl must have lain unconscious for about ten minutes. When she came to her senses, she dragged herself, terrified, from the room and up to the housekeeper's apartments, where, being an excitable and nervous creature, she only screamed "Murder!" and immediately fell in a fit of hysterics that lasted three-quarters of an hour. When at last she came to herself, she told her story, and, the hall-porter having been summoned, Rameau's rooms were again approached.

The blood still lay on the floor, and the chopper, with which the crime had evidently been committed, rested against the fender; but the body had vanished! A search was at once made, but no trace of it could be seen anywhere. It seemed impossible that it could have been carried out of the building, for the hall-porter must at once have noticed anybody leaving with so bulky a burden. Still, in the building it was not to be found.

When Hewitt was informed of these things on Monday, the police were, of course, still in possession of Rameau's rooms. Inspector Nettings, Hewitt was told, was in charge of the case, and as the inspector was an acquaintance of his, and was then in the rooms upstairs, Hewitt went up to see him.

Nettings was pleased to see Hewitt, and invited him to look around the rooms. "Perhaps you can spot something we have overlooked," he said. "Though it's not a case there can be much doubt about."

"You think it's Goujon, don't you?"

"Think? Well, rather! Look here! As soon as we got here on Saturday, we found this piece of paper and pin on the floor. We showed it to the housemaid, and then she remembered—she was too much upset to think of it before—that when she was in the room the paper was laying on the dead man's chest—pinned there, evidently. It must have dropped off when they removed the body. It's a case of half-mad revenge on Goujon's part, plainly. See it; you read French, don't you?"

The paper was a plain, large half-sheet of note-paper, on which a sentence in French was scrawled in red ink in a large, clumsy hand, thus:

puni par un vengeur de la tortue.

"*Puni par un vengeur de la tortue*," Hewitt repeated musingly. "'Punished by an avenger of the tortoise,' That seems odd."

"Well, rather odd. But you understand the reference, of course. Have they told you about Rameau's treatment of Goujon's pet tortoise?"

"I think it was mentioned among his other pranks. But this is an extreme revenge for a thing of that sort, and a queer way of announcing it."

"Oh, he's mad—mad with Rameau's continual ragging and baiting," Nettings answered. "Anyway, this is a plain indication—plain as though he'd left his own signature. Besides, it's in his own language—French. And there's his chopper, too."

"Speaking of signatures," Hewitt remarked, "perhaps you have already compared this with other specimens of Goujon's writing?"

"I did think of it, but they don't seem to have a specimen to hand, and, anyway, it doesn't seem very important. There's 'avenger of the tortoise' plain enough, in the man's own language, and that tells everything. Besides, handwritings are easily disguised."

"Have you got Goujon?"

"Well, no; we haven't. There seems to be some little difficulty about that. But I expect to have him by this time to-morrow. Here comes Mr. Styles, the landlord."

Mr. Styles was a thin, querulous, and withered-looking little man, who twitched his eyebrows as he spoke, and spoke in short, jerky phrases.

"No news, eh, inspector, eh? eh? Found out nothing else, eh? Terrible thing for my property—terrible! Who's your friend?"

Nettings introduced Hewitt.

"Shocking thing this, eh, Mr. Hewitt? Terrible! Comes of having anything to do with these blood-thirsty

foreigners, eh? New buildings and all—character ruined.
No one come to live here now, eh? Tenants—noisy
niggers—murdered by my own servants—terrible! *You*
formed any opinion, eh?"

"I dare say I might if I went into the case."

"Yes, yes—same opinion as inspector's, eh? I mean
an opinion of your own?" The old man scrutinized
Hewitt's face sharply.

"If you'd like me to look into the matter—"
Hewitt began.

"Eh? Oh, look into it! Well, I can't commission you,
you know—matter for the police. Mischief's done. Police
doing very well, I think—must be Goujon. But look
about the place, certainly, if you like. If you see anything
likely to serve *my* interests, tell me, and—and—perhaps
I'll employ you, eh, eh? Good-afternoon."

The landlord vanished, and the inspector laughed.
"Likes to see what he's buying, does Mr. Styles," he said.

Hewitt's first impulse was to walk out of the place
at once. But his interest in the case had been roused,
and he determined, at any rate, to examine the rooms,
and this he did very minutely. By the side of the lobby
was a bath-room, and in this was fitted a tip-up wash-
basin, which Hewitt inspected with particular attention.
Then he called the housekeeper, and made inquiries
about Rameau's clothes and linen. The housekeeper
could give no idea of how many overcoats or how much
linen he had had. He had all a negro's love of display,
and was continually buying new clothes, which, indeed,
were lying, hanging, littering, and choking up the
bedroom in all directions. The housekeeper, however,
on Hewitt's inquiring after such a garment in particular,

did remember one heavy black ulster, which Rameau had very rarely worn—only in the coldest weather.

"After the body was discovered," Hewitt asked the housekeeper, "was any stranger observed about the place—whether carrying anything or not?"

"No, sir," the housekeeper replied. "There's been particular inquiries about that. Of course, after we knew what was wrong and the body was gone, nobody was seen, or he'd have been stopped. But the hall-porter says he's certain no stranger came or went for half an hour or more before that—the time about when the housemaid saw the body and fainted."

At this moment a clerk from the landlord's office arrived and handed Nettings a paper. "Here you are," said Nettings to Hewitt; "they've found a specimen of Goujon's handwriting at last, if you'd like to see it. I don't want it; I'm not a graphologist, and the case is clear enough for me anyway."

Hewitt took the paper. "This" he said, "is a different sort of handwriting from that on the paper. The red-ink note about the avenger of the tortoise is in a crude, large, clumsy, untaught style of writing. This is small, neat, and well formed—except that it is a trifle shaky, probably because of the hand injury."

"That's nothing," contended Nettings. "handwriting clues are worse than useless, as a rule. It's so easy to disguise and imitate writing; and besides, if Goujon is such a good penman as you seem to say, why, he could all the easier alter his style. Say now yourself, can any fiddling question of handwriting get over this thing about 'avenging the tortoise'—practically a written confession—to say nothing of the chopper, and what he said to the housemaid as he left?"

"Well," said Hewitt, "perhaps not; but we'll see. Meantime"—turning to the landlord's clerk—"possibly you will be good enough to tell me one or two things. First, what was Goujon's character?"

"Excellent, as far as we know. We never had a complaint about him except for little matters of carelessness—leaving coal-scuttles on the staircases for people to fall over, losing shovels, and so on. He was certainly a bit careless, but, as far as we could see, quite a decent little fellow. One would never have thought him capable of committing murder for the sake of a tortoise, though he was rather fond of the animal."

"The tortoise is dead now, I understand?"

"Yes."

"Have you a lift in this building?"

"Only for coals and heavy parcels. Goujon used to work it, sometimes going up and down in it himself with coals, and so on; it goes into the basement."

"And are the coals kept under this building?"

"No. The store for the whole row is under the next two houses—the basements communicate."

"Do you know Rameau's other name?"

"César Rameau he signed in our agreement."

"Did he ever mention his relations?"

"No. That is to say, he did say something one day when he was very drunk; but, of course, it was all rot. Some one told him not to make such a row—he was a beastly tenant—and he said he was the best man in the place, and his brother was Prime Minister, and all sorts of things. Mere drunken rant! I never heard of his saying anything sensible about relations. We know nothing of his connections; he came here on a banker's reference."

"Thanks. I think that's all I want to ask. You notice," Hewitt proceeded, turning to Nettings, "the only ink in this place is scented and violet, and the only paper is tinted and scented, too, with a monogram—characteristic of a negro with money. The paper that was pinned on Rameau's breast is in red ink on common and rather grubby paper, therefore it was written somewhere else and brought here. Inference, premeditation."

"Yes, yes. But are you an inch nearer with all these speculations? Can you get nearer than I am now without them?"

"Well, perhaps not," Hewitt replied. "I don't profess at this moment to know the criminal; you do. I'll concede you that point for the present. But you don't offer an opinion as to who removed Rameau's body—which I think I know."

"Who was it, then?"

"Come, try and guess that yourself. It wasn't Goujon; I don't mind letting you know that. But it was a person quite within your knowledge of the case. You've mentioned the person's name more than once."

Nettings stared blankly. "I don't understand you in the least," he said. "But, of course, you mean that this mysterious person you speak of as having moved the body committed the murder?"

"No, I don't. Nobody could have been more innocent of that."

"Well," Nettings concluded with resignation, "I'm afraid one of us is rather thick-headed. What will you do?"

"Interview the person who took away the body," Hewitt replied, with a smile.

"But, man alive, why? Why bother about the person if it isn't the criminal?"

"Never mind—never mind; probably the person will be a most valuable witness."

"Do you mean you think this person—whoever it is—saw the crime?"

"I think it very probable indeed."

"Well, I won't ask you any more. I shall get hold of Goujon; that's simple and direct enough for me. I prefer to deal with the heart of the case—the murder itself—when there's such clear evidence as I have."

"I shall look a little into that, too, perhaps," Hewitt said, "and, if you like, I'll tell you the first thing I shall do."

"What's that?"

"I shall have a good look at a map of the West Indies, and I advise you to do the same. Good-morning."

Nettings stared down the corridor after Hewitt, and continued staring for nearly two minutes after he had disappeared. Then he said to the clerk, who had remained: "What was he talking about?"

"Don't know," replied the clerk. "Couldn't make head nor tail of it."

"I don't believe there *is* a head to it," declared Nettings; "nor a tail either. He's kidding us."

Nettings was better than his word, for within two hours of his conversation with Hewitt, Goujon was captured and safe in a cab bound for Bow Street. He had been stopped at Newhaven in the morning on his way to Dieppe, and was brought back to London. But now Nettings met a check.

Late that afternoon he called on Hewitt to explain matters. "We've got Goujon," he said, gloomily, "but there's a difficulty. He's got two friends who can swear an *alibi*. Rameau was seen alive at half-past one on Saturday, and the girl found him dead about three. Now, Goujon's two friends, it seems, were with him from one o'clock till four in the afternoon, with the exception of five minutes when the girl saw him, and then he left them to take a key or something to the housekeeper before finally leaving. They were waiting on the landing below when Goujon spoke to the housemaid, heard him speaking, and had seen him go all the way up to the housekeeper's room and back, as they looked up the wide well of the staircase. They are men employed near the place, and seem to have good characters. But perhaps we shall find something unfavorable about them. They were drinking with Goujon, it seems, by way of 'seeing him off.'"

"Well," Hewitt said, "I scarcely think you need trouble to damage these men's characters. They are probably telling the truth. Come, now, be plain. You've come here to get a hint as to whether my theory of the case helps you, haven't you?"

"Well, if you can give me a friendly hint, although, of course, I may be right, after all. Still, I wish you'd explain a bit as to what you meant by looking at a map and all that mystery. Nice thing for me to be taking a lesson in my own business after all these years! But perhaps I deserve it."

"See, now," quoth Hewitt, "you remember what map I told you to look at?"

"The West Indies."

"Right! Well, here you are." Hewitt reached an atlas from his book-shelf. "Now, look here: the biggest island of the lot on this map, barring Cuba, is Hayti. You know as well as I do that the western part of that island is peopled by the black republic of Hayti, and that the country is in a degenerate state of almost unexampled savagery, with a ridiculous show of civilization. There are revolutions all the time; the South American republics are peaceful and prosperous compared to Hayti. The state of the country is simply awful—read Sir Spenser St. John's book on it. President after president of the vilest sort forces his way to power and commits the most horrible and bloodthirsty excesses, murdering his opponents by the hundred and seizing their property for himself and his satellites, who are usually as bad, if not worse, than the president himself. Whole families—men, women, and children— are murdered at the instance of these ruffians, and, as a consequence, the most deadly feuds spring up, and the presidents and their followers are always themselves in danger of reprisals from others. Perhaps the very worst of these presidents in recent times has been the notorious Domingue, who was overthrown by an insurrection, as they all are sooner or later, and compelled to fly the country. Domingue and his nephews, one of whom was Chief Minister, while in power committed the cruellest bloodshed, and many members of the opposite party sought refuge in a small island lying just to the north of Hayti, but were sought out there and almost exterminated. Now, I will show you that island on the map. What is its name?"

"Tortuga."

"It is. 'Tortuga,' however, is only the old Spanish name; the Haytians speak French—Creole French. Here is a French atlas: now see the name of that island."

"La Tortue!"

"La Tortue it is—the tortoise. Tortuga means the same thing in Spanish. But that island is always spoken of in Hayti as La Tortue. Now, do you see the drift of that paper pinned to Rameau's breast?"

"Punished by an avenger of—or from—the tortoise or La Tortue—clear enough. It would seem that the dead man had something to do with the massacre there, and somebody from the island is avenging it. The thing's most extraordinary."

"And now listen. The name of Domingue's nephew, who was Chief Minister, was *Septimus Rameau*."

"And this was César Rameau—his brother, probably. I see. Well, this *is* a case."

"I think the relationship probable. Now you understand why I was inclined to doubt that Goujon was the man you wanted."

"Of course, of course! And now I suppose I must try to get a nigger—the chap who wrote that paper. I wish he hadn't been such an ignorant nigger. If he'd only have put the capitals to the words 'La Tortue,' I might have thought a little more about them, instead of taking it for granted that they meant that wretched tortoise in the basement of the house. Well, I've made a fool of a start, but I'll be after that nigger now."

"And I, as I said before," said Hewitt, "shall be after the person that carried off Rameau's body. I have had something else to do this afternoon, or I should have begun already."

"You said you thought he saw the crime. How did you judge that?"

Hewitt smiled. "I think I'll keep that little secret to myself for the present," he said. "You shall know soon."

"Very well," Nettings replied, with resignation. "I suppose I mustn't grumble if you don't tell me everything. I feel too great a fool altogether over this case to see any farther than you show me." And Inspector Nettings left on his search; while Martin Hewitt, as soon as he was alone, laughed joyously and slapped his thigh.

There was a cab-rank and shelter at the end of the street where Mr. Styles' building stood, and early that evening a man approached it and hailed the cabmen and the waterman. Any one would have known the new-comer at once for a cabman taking a holiday. The brim of the hat, the bird's-eye neckerchief, the immense coat-buttons, and, more than all, the rolling walk and the wrinkled trousers, marked him out distinctly.

"Watcheer!" he exclaimed, affably, with the self-possessed nod only possible to cabbies and 'busmen. "I'm a-lookin' for a bilker. I'm told one o' the blokes off this rank carried 'im last Saturday, and I want to know where he went. I ain't 'ad a chance o' gettin' 'is address yet. Took a cab just as it got dark, I'm told. Tallish chap, muffled up a lot, in a long black overcoat. Any of ye seen 'im?"

The cabbies looked at one another and shook their heads; it chanced that none of them had been on that particular rank at that time. But the waterman said: "'Old on—I bet 'e's the bloke wot old Bill Stammers took. Yorkey was fust on the rank, but the bloke wouldn't 'ave a 'ansom—wanted a four-wheeler, so old Bill took 'im. Biggish chap in a long black coat, collar up an' muffled thick; soft wide-awake 'at, pulled over 'is eyes; and he was in a 'urry, too. Jumped in sharp as a weasel."

"Didn't see 'is face, did ye?"

"No—not an inch of it; too much muffled. Couldn't tell if he 'ad a face."

"Was his arm in a sling?"

"Ay, it looked so. Had it stuffed through the breast of his coat, like as though there might be a sling inside."

"That's 'im. Any of ye tell me where I might run across old Bill Stammers? He'll tell me where my precious bilker went to."

As to this there was plenty of information, and in five minutes Martin Hewitt, who had become an unoccupied cabman for the occasion, was on his way to find old Bill Stammers. That respectable old man gave him full particulars as to the place in the East End where he had driven his muffled fare on Saturday, and Hewitt then begun an eighteen, or twenty hours' search beyond Whitechapel.

At about three on Tuesday afternoon, as Nettings was in the act of leaving Bow Street Police Station, Hewitt drove up in a four-wheeler. Some prisoner appeared to be crouching low in the vehicle, but, leaving him to take care of himself, Hewitt hurried into the station and shook Nettings by the hand. "Well," he said, "have you got the murderer of Rameau yet?"

"No," Nettings growled. "Unless—well, Goujon's under remand still, and, after all, I've been thinking that he may know something—"

"Pooh, nonsense!" Hewitt answered. "You'd better let him go. Now, I *have* got somebody." Hewitt laughed and slapped the inspector's shoulder. "I've got the man who carried Rameau's body away!"

"The deuce you have! Where? Bring him in. We must have him—"

"All right, don't be in a hurry; he won't bolt." And Hewitt stepped out to the cab and produced his prisoner, who, pulling his hat farther over his eyes, hurried furtively into the station. One hand was stowed in the breast of his long coat, and below the wide brim of his hat a small piece of white bandage could be seen; and, as he lifted his face, it was seen to be that of a negro.

"Inspector Nettings," Hewitt said ceremoniously, "allow me to introduce Mr. César Rameau!"

Nettings gasped.

"What!" he at length ejaculated. "What! You—you're Rameau?"

The negro looked round nervously, and shrank farther from the door.

"Yes," he said; "but please not so loud—please not loud. Zey may be near, and I'm 'fraid."

"You will certify, will you not," asked Hewitt, with malicious glee, "not only that you were not murdered last Saturday by Victor Goujon, but that, in fact, you were not murdered at all? Also, that you carried your own body away in the usual fashion, on your own legs."

"Yes, yes," responded Rameau, looking haggardly about; "but is not zis—zis room publique? I should not be seen."

"Nonsense!" replied Hewitt rather testily; "you exaggerate your danger and your own importance, and your enemies' abilities as well. You're safe enough."

"I suppose, then," Nettings remarked slowly, like a man on whose mind something vast was beginning to dawn, "I suppose—why, hang it, you must have just got up while that fool of a girl was screaming and fainting upstairs, and walked out. They say there's nothing so hard as a nigger's skull, and yours has certainly made a fool of me. But, then, *somebody* must have chopped you over the head; who was it?"

"My enemies—my great enemies—enemies politique. I am a great man"—this with a faint revival of vanity amid his fear—"a great man in my countree. Zey have great secret club-sieties to kill me—me and my fren's; and one enemy coming in my rooms does zis—one, two"—he indicated wrist and head—"wiz a choppa."

Rameau made the case plain to Nettings, so far as the actual circumstances of the assault on himself were concerned. A negro whom he had noticed near the place more than once during the previous day or two had attacked him suddenly in his rooms, dealing him two savage blows with a chopper. The first he had caught on his wrist, which was seriously damaged, as well as excruciatingly painful, but the second had taken effect on his head. His assailant had evidently gone away then, leaving him for dead; but, as a matter of fact, he was only stunned by the shock, and had, thanks to the adamantine thickness of the negro skull and the ill-direction of the chopper, only a very bad scalp-wound, the bone being no more than grazed. He had lain insensible for some time, and must have come to his senses soon after the housemaid had left the room. Terrified at the knowledge that his enemies had found him out, his only thought was to get away and hide himself. He hastily washed and tied up his head, enveloped himself in the biggest coat he could find, and let himself down into the basement by the coal-lift, for fear of observation. He waited in the basement of one of the adjoining buildings till dark and then got away in a cab, with the idea of hiding himself in the East End. He had had very little money with him on his flight, and it was by reason of this circumstance that Hewitt, when he found him, had prevailed on him to leave his hiding-place, since it would be impossible for him to touch any of the large sums of money in the keeping of his bank so long as he was supposed to be dead. With much difficulty, and the promise of ample police protection, he was at last convinced that it would be safe to declare himself and get his property, and then run away and hide wherever he pleased.

Nettings and Hewitt strolled off together for a few minutes and chatted, leaving the wretched Rameau to cower in a corner among several policemen.

"Well, Mr. Hewitt," Nettings said, "this case has certainly been a shocking beating for me. I must have been as blind as a bat when I started on it. And yet I don't see that you had a deal to go on, even now. What struck you first?"

"Well, in the beginning it seemed rather odd to me that the body should have been taken away, as I had been told it was, after the written paper had been pinned on it. Why should the murderer pin a label on the body of his victim if he meant carrying that body away? Who would read the label and learn of the nature of the revenge gratified? Plainly, that indicated that the person who had carried away the body was *not* the person who had committed the murder. But as soon as I began to examine the place I saw the probability that there was no murder, after all. There were any number of indications of this fact, and I can't understand your not observing them. First, although there was a good deal of blood on the floor just below where the housemaid had seen Rameau lying, there was none between that place and the door. Now, if the body had been dragged, or even carried, to the door, blood must have become smeared about the floor, or at least there would have been drops, but there were none, and this seemed to hint that the corpse might have come to itself, sat up on the sofa, stanched the wound, and walked out. I reflected at once that Rameau was a full-blooded negro, and that a negro's head is very nearly invulnerable to anything short of bullets. Then, if the body had been dragged out—as such a heavy body must have been—almost of necessity the carpet and rugs would show signs of the fact, but there were no such signs. But beyond these there was the fact that no long black overcoat was left with the other clothes, although the housekeeper distinctly remembered Rameau's possession of such a garment. I judged he would use some such thing to assist his disguise, which was why I asked her. *Why* he would want to disguise was plain, as you shall see presently. There were no towels left in the bath-room; inference, used for bandages. Everything seemed to show that the only person responsible for Rameau's removal was Rameau himself. Why, then, had he gone away secretly and hurriedly, without making complaint, and why had he stayed away? What reason would he have for doing this if it had been Goujon that had attacked him? None. Goujon was going to France. Clearly, Rameau was afraid of another attack from some implacable enemy whom he was anxious to avoid—one against whom he feared legal complaint or defense would be useless. This brought me at once to the paper found on the floor. If this were the work of Goujon and an open reference to his tortoise, why should he be at such pains to disguise his handwriting? He would have been already pointing himself out by the mere mention of the tortoise. And, if he could not avoid a shake in his natural, small handwriting, how could he have avoided it in a large, clumsy, slowly drawn, assumed hand? No, the paper was not Goujon's."

"As to the writing on the paper," Nettings interposed, "I've told you how I made that mistake. I took the readiest explanation of the words, since they seemed so pat, and I wouldn't let anything else outweigh that. As to the other things—the evidences of Rameau's having gone off by himself—well, I don't usually miss such obvious things; but I never thought of the possibility of the *victim* going away on the quiet and not coming back, as though *he'd* done something wrong. Comes of starting with a set of fixed notions."

"Well," answered Hewitt, "I fancy you must have been rather 'out of form,' as they say; everybody has his stupid days, and you can't keep up to concert pitch forever. To return to the case. The evidence of the chopper was very untrustworthy, especially when I had heard of Goujon's careless habits—losing shovels and leaving coal-scuttles on stairs. Nothing more likely than for the chopper to be left lying about, and a criminal who had calculated his chances would know the advantage to himself of using a weapon that belonged to the place, and leaving it behind to divert suspicion. It is quite possible, by the way, that the man who attacked Rameau got away down the coal-lift and out by an adjoining basement, just as did Rameau himself; this, however, is mere conjecture. The would-be murderer had plainly prepared for the crime: witness the previous preparation of the paper declaring his revenge, an indication of his pride at having run his enemy to earth at such a distant place as this—although I expect he was only in England by chance, for Haytians are not a persistently energetic race. In regard to the use of small instead of capital letters in the words 'La Tortue' on the paper, I observed, in the beginning, that the first letter of the whole sentence—the 'p' in 'puni'—was a small one. Clearly, the writer was an illiterate man, and it was at once plain that he may have made the same mistake with ensuing words.

"On the whole, it was plain that everybody had begun with a too ready disposition to assume that Goujon was guilty. Everybody insisted, too, that the body had been carried away—which was true, of course, although not in the sense intended—so I didn't trouble to contradict, or to say more than that I guessed who *had* carried the body off. And, to tell you the truth, I was a little piqued at Mr. Styles' manner, and indisposed, interested in the case as I was, to give away my theories too freely.

"The rest of the job was not very difficult. I found out the cabman who had taken Rameau away—you can always get readier help from cabbies if you go as one of themselves, especially if you are after a bilker—and from him got a sufficiently near East End direction to find Rameau after inquiries. I ventured, by the way, on a rather long shot. I described my man to the cabman as having an injured arm or wrist—and it turned out a correct guess. You see, a man making an attack with a chopper is pretty certain to make more than a single blow, and as there appeared to have been only a single wound on the head, it seemed probable that another had fallen somewhere else—almost certainly on the arm, as it would be raised to defend the head. At Limehouse I found he had had his head and wrist attended to at a local medico's, and a big nigger in a fright, with a long black coat, a broken head, and a lame hand, is not so difficult to find in a small area. How I persuaded him up here you know already; I think I frightened him a little, too, by explaining how easily I had tracked him, and giving him a hint that others might do the same. He is in a great funk. He seems to have quite lost faith in England as a safe asylum."

The police failed to catch Rameau's assailant—chiefly because Rameau could not be got to give a proper description of him, nor to do anything except get out of the country in a hurry. In truth, he was glad to be quit of the matter with nothing worse than his broken head. Little Goujon made a wild storm about his arrest, and before he did go to France managed to extract twenty pounds from Rameau by way of compensation, in spite of the absence of any strictly legal claim against his old tormentor. So that, on the whole, Goujon was about the only person who derived any particular profit from the tortoise mystery.

FINIS

ARTHUR MORRISON
A Biographical Note

ARTHUR MORRISON (1863–1945) was a journalist, author, and art collector. The bulk of his output falls into three categories: work depicting life in the poverty-stricken slums of London's East End; detective stories featuring the two different private investigators, Martin Hewitt and Horace Dorrington; and a highly regarded study of Japanese painting. Careful reading of the body of Morrison's work reveals overall the sensibility of a man who understood from personal observation both the ugliness to which poverty can drive a person and the beauty of high art.

A HERO TO REMEMBER

Morrison's eponymous hero of this collection, Martin Hewitt Investigator, also appears in three other collections: *Chronicles of Martin Hewitt* (1895), *Adventures of Martin Hewitt* (1896), and *The Red Triangle; Being Some Further Chronicles of Martin Hewitt* (1903). Like his contemporary Sir Arthur Conan Doyle (1859–1930), Morrison found publication for some of his detective fiction in the pages of *The Strand*. But while Doyle's awestruck narrator, Dr. John Watson, portrays his friend Sherlock Holmes as a mood-driven, egotistical genius, Hewitt's narrator, a down-to earth journalist called Brett, introduces Hewitt in this book's first story, 'The Lenton Croft Robberies,' as a man of 'cheery, chaffing good nature' who eschews egotism and understates his own cleverness. Brett adds that Hewitt 'always consistently maintains that he has no system beyond a judicious use of ordinary faculties.'

A former law clerk, Hewitt employs some knowledge of lower-class habits, pleasures, argot, and crime to his advantage. Overall, working firmly in the puzzle-centered tradition, Morrison uses to good effect Hewitt's relative modesty to let words of wisdom stand out more powerfully and add to the surprise of his conclusions, a method that no doubt helped to account for his popularity in his day – and wins the favor of readers discovering him today.

EARLY LIFE

Morrison's life and fortunes encompassed great contrasts, as he rose from poverty to become not just a respected author but an erudite art expert and collector whose acquisitions eventually found a home in the British Museum.

But while his most memorable work lies in his realistic depiction of life in London's slums, Morrison himself misled scholars to cloak the personal origins that made this achievement possible. While he was born in 1863 in Poplar, a Thames-side, East London slum teeming with poverty and crime, he identified his birthplace as Kent. He also misrepresented his father – who died when Morrison was just eight years old – as an engineer, when in fact the man held the working-class position of steamfitter.

After his father's death, Morrison lived with two siblings, his grandmother, and his mother above the latter's haberdashery shop in Grundy Street, Poplar. After Arthur Morrison's death in 1945, his wife burned the author's personal papers, literally creating another smokescreen that further obscured facts about his early life.

EDUCATION AND EARLY CAREER

Relatively recent scholarship has revealed that Morrison attended the Hale Street Wesleyan Day School until about the age of thirteen. Then he worked as clerk for the school board from 1879 to 1886, until he won the post of clerk for the Beaumont Trustees. This group administered funds for the People's Palace, a charitable institution with the mission to bring culture to the slums. Morrison became subeditor of their publication, *The Palace Journal*, in 1889; took chambers in the Strand in London's West End; and then left the subeditor post in 1890 to pursue his freelance work.

LOVE AND FRIENDSHIP

Through his work at the Peoples Palace, Morrison had met the woman he would marry – Eliza Adelaide Thatcher, who had also been born in Poplar. Meanwhile, his early work had appeared in a cycling magazine and *The Globe* newspaper. In 1888 and 1889 his 'Cockney Corners' pieces were published, providing observations about life in the East End. More observations were revealed in 'Whitechapel' in 1889.

In 1892, he married Eliza and also met William Ernest Henley (1849–1903), a celebrated editor and writer and enthusiast of Japanese art, who became his mentor and friend. Morrison's only child, Guy Arthur, born in 1893, would predecease him (owing to malaria) in 1921.

FROM SUPERNATURALISM TO
DETECTIVE TALES AND REALISM

In 1891 Morrison's first book, *The Shadows Around Us: Authentic Tales of the Supernatural*, was published. Meanwhile, the *National Observer* published many of Morrison's pieces about life in the slums. These and others that originally appeared in *Macmillan's Magazine* were collected in *Tales of the Mean Streets* published in 1894, the same year that his detective fiction featuring Martin Hewitt, which was first published in *The Strand* and *Windsor Magazine*, was collected in *Martin Hewitt Investigator*. Two more volumes of Hewitt stories came out in quick succession: *Chronicles of Martin Hewitt* (1895) and *Adventures of Martin Hewitt* (1896).

That year saw the publication of the novel for which Morrison was to become best known, *A Child of the Jago*. This classic of realism details the travails of life in London's slums and is dedicated to the Rev. Osborn Jay, a vicar and missionary working in the London slum known as Old Nichol, who asked Morrison to study conditions there. Morrison's earnest effort, involving months of interviews and participation in life there, profoundly informs the story of Dicky Perrott, the ill-fated boy who scrapes his way through life in a neighborhood called 'the Jago.' Here Morrison shows abject poverty as an ever-smoldering and frequently explosive propellant to crime and makes it brutally clear how inescapable such origins can be, while mocking the self-satisfied people who try to bring charity to the area. Next, in *To London Town* (1899), the orphaned protagonist, Johnny May, finds more possibility in adversity.

ANOTHER PROLIFIC DECADE

In 1900, Morrison produced *Canning Murrell*, which departs from the slums to a scene in Essex. Then, returning focus on London's East End, he turned out a classic of realism, *The Hole in the Wall* (1902). Here, Morrison makes characters and setting unforgettable in a coming-of-age story centered around a parentless boy called Stephen Kemp who lives with his grandfather in The Hole in the Wall, a public house that literally hangs over the foul waters of the Thames.

More works produced during this prolific decade include his collection *The Red Triangle; Being Some Further Chronicles of Martin Hewitt* (1903); and the novels *The Green Eye of Goona* (1904), also published as *The Green Diamond* (1904); *Diverse Vanities* (1905); and *Green Ginger* (1909). Two of Morrison's stories in *Tales of the Mean Streets* were adapted into the plays *That Brute Simmons* (1906) and *The Dumb-Cake* (1907). Later, *Selected Tales* appeared in 1929, and *Fiddle O' Dreams and More* in 1933.

FROM HIS OWN WITNESS

In 1911, Morrison published the highly regarded two-volume opus, *Painters of Japan*. He also turned out *An Exhibition of Japanese Prints* (1909) and *Guide to an Exhibition of Chinese and Japanese Paintings* (1914).

E.F. Bleiler, in his introduction to *The Best Martin Hewitt Detective Stories* (1976), was convinced that 'Morrison was writing about things he knew from his own witness.' More-recent scholarship underlines this. Cubitt agrees, 'Morrison knew, better than many of his contemporaries, the everyday of the East End, the "whole and real" truth of it.' And that includes the sense of wonder, portrayed in with the eye of a romantic rather than a realist. A place like the notorious Ratcliffe Highway could, for a small boy, provide 'the air and very breath of romance itself,' Morrison recalled in The Strand in 1912.

CRIME WRITING LEGACY

The popularity of Morrison's puzzle-centered fare has stood the test of time. As Bleiler opined in 1976, Martin Hewitt was 'probably the second-best detective from the period 1891–1905, or the Age of Sherlock Holmes.' While it can be argued that the scoundrel detective Horace Dorrington is Morrison's more groundbreaking and engaging creation, the Hewitt stories remained in demand and 'in print when his other novels did not,' as Cubitt notes.

Overall, if one considers not just both sleuths' familiarity with underclass argot, but Dorrington's giant strides over the borderline between the legal and illegal, Morrison's detective fiction sometimes echoes his realistic writing. And the criminal scheming in the Dorrington tales is as memorable as some in A Child of the Jago (1896).

TANTALIZING CLUES

More intriguingly, one can speculate that Morrison's whodunits may offer some tantalizing clues about how the author saw himself. Most obviously, in his story, 'The Case of Mr. Loftus Deacon' in The Dorrington Deed-Box, his knowledge of collecting priceless Asian art is significant to the clues and solution of the crime, and his first-hand experience of a collector's passion comes directly into play as he portrays a man 'whose whole life was given to his collection.' And perhaps, in 'The Case of Mr. Foggatt,' Martin Hewitt's query 'Why *will* you persist in assuming that the only way of escape by a window is downward?' may also serve to summarize the expectation-breaking trajectory of this remarkable author's own life.

A Glossary of Crime, Mystery & Literary Terms

A

abbess: nun in charge of a convent; female brothel keeper, a madame

abode: place where people live; period of living somewhere

accomplice: someone who helps a person commit a crime

acquittal: when someone is found not guilty of a crime

aeronaut: pilot of an aircraft or hot-air balloon

affidavit: written statement, used as evidence in court

afford: to provide, allow or supply something

affordability: inexpensiveness, often used in relation to automobiles

afterlife: existence after death; eternal life

alcove: small space or recess in a room

alderman: term for a half-Crown; senior local government official

ale: alcoholic drink made from hops and fermented malt, stronger and heavier than beer

alkaloid: plant-based chemical that contains nitrogen and affects people physiologically, such as poisons or drugs

apoplexy: a crippling cerebral stroke, sometimes fatal; a fit of anger

apothecary: pharmacist; one who prepares drugs and medicines and gives medical advice; lowest order of medical man

apple-polish: to flatter, curry favour or sweeten someone up

apprentice: someone who works under a skilled professional for a specific amount of time (usually seven years) in order to learn a trade. When one finished his apprenticeship, he became a journeyman and would get paid for work himself

apropos: with reference to something; appropriate

ardent: passionate or zealous feelings

area: servants' entrance in the front of many London townhouses, often below ground

area diving: sneaking down area steps to steal from the lower rooms of houses

arsenal: store of weapons

asphyxiate: kill or render someone unconscious by cutting off their air supply

asunder: divide or separate

audit: official inspection of accounts

automaton: someone who resembles a machine by going through motions repetitively, but without feeling or emotion

automobile: road vehicle, usually a car

B

badger game: a confidence trick or blackmail, in which a man (usually married) is seduced into a compromising position with another woman, then blackmailed by her male accomplice

baloney: nonsense, also known as bunkum or hooey

bank notes: paper currency; promissory notes of a bank to pay upon presentation of the note

bank teller: person who works in a bank

banns: announcement or notice of a forthcoming marriage in a parish church, proclaimed on three consecutive Sundays

bash: party, usually involving a lot of alcohol

beak: magistrate

bean shooter: gun

bearer up: thief with a female accomplice who would distract the victim so the crime could be performed

beating: repeatedly hitting someone; scaring birds from bushes out into the open for shooting parties

beat it: make yourself scarce; get lost

beat your gums: talking

Bedlam: nickname for the Hospital of St Mary of Bethlehem, a psychiatric hospital in London; place or situation full of noise, frenzy and confusion

beef: to have an issue with someone or something; to grumble

beg to: wish to

belladonna: poisonous deadly nightshade plant

big house: prison, also known as cold storage or gaol

big mitt: crooked poker game

bill of lading: official list of goods to be shipped

bindle-stiff: someone who died from a drug overdose; tramp

biplane: plane with two pairs of wings at different levels, often one on top of the other

blackleg: someone who works during a strike, often criticised by those who obey the strike (also known as a 'scab')

Blackshirt: member of a Fascist Italian party who wore black shirts

blag: to steal something, often by smash-and-grab; to trick or con someone

bleary: unfocused eyes, often caused by lack of sleep

bloodletting: reducing the volume of blood in the body by either opening a vein or by applying leeches as a way of restoring health, used from ancient times up to the nineteenth century

Bloomsbury Group: group of writers and artists who lived in Bloomsbury, London, in the first half of the twentieth century, known for their intellectual philosophies and eccentric activities

blow: leave or go

bludger: violent criminal who often uses a bludgeon or heavy, stout weapon

blue bottle: police officer, also known as cop, copper, crusher, escop, esclop, flatfoot, harness bull, pig or rozzers

blue nose: someone puritanical or prudish

blues: to be depressed or melancholy; musical genre originating in the Deep South of the US

bluff: to pretend one can or will do something, often used to describe acting confident during card games despite a poor hand

bluster: to talk indignantly or threateningly

boarder: person paying rent for a bed, a room and usually meals in a private home or boarding house

bob: cockney slang for a shilling or five-pence piece

body-snatching: the act of stealing corpses from graves, tombs or morgues, usually for dissection or scientific study

bonehead: unintelligent or stupid person

booby-hatch: mental institution

booster: shoplifter

bootlegger: person who makes and/or sells illegal goods

booze hound: alcoholic

bop: to punch someone

borough: town that had been given the right to self-govern by royal charter; in Victorian London, Southwark was referred to as 'the borough'

bow-legged: legs that curve out at the knee when the ankles are close together

Bow Street Runners: detective force in London who pre-dated the police, organized by novelist Henry Fielding and his brother John in 1750 up to 1829, when Robert Peel founded London's first police force

boycott: to refuse to use certain products or establishments in order to take a stand against them

bozo: stupid or uneducated person

bracelets: handcuffs

bread basket: stomach

broad: a woman, also known as a dame

broadcast: radio or television transmission

broke: to have no money

brown study: to be in a reverie; to be melancholy

brownstone: house built during the nineteenth century in the US and common to New York City, often made of reddish-brown stone

buck cabbie: dishonest cab driver

bucolic: relating to the countryside or pastoral places

bug hunting: stealing from or cheating drunks, especially at night in drinking dens

bull: cockney slang for five shillings; prison guard; nonsense

bulletin: official broadcast or statement of news

bullion: gold or silver valued by weight rather than value

bump off: to kill someone

bum's rush: to eject someone forcibly from a place

bum steer: false or misleading information

bunch of fives: fist

bunco: confidence trick or swindle

burly: strong, broad or heavily built person

bust a can: to open a safe

bust-up: fight

busybody: nosy or meddling person

busywork: work with little real value to keep people busy

buzzer: badge; form of identification

by Jove: mild oath, meaning 'by God'; Jove is also another term for the Roman god Jupiter

bygone: something from an earlier time; to let something go

by-pass: road passing around a town or city as an alternative route to passing through it

C

cabbage: money

cadaver: corpse

cagey: secretive

canned: to be fired

cant: present, often a free meal; language or vocabulary spoken by thieves or groups of people perceived to be common

caper: criminal act; dangerous activity

card sharp: excellent card player; card cheat

cargo: goods transported by vehicle

cash carrier: pimp or whore's minder, who would literally hold the money earned by soliciting

cathode: electrode with a negative charge

census: official list of the British population, including address and details of age, gender, occupation and birthplace, carried out every ten years since 1841

centuary: one hundred US dollars

certified cheque: a cheque that is guaranteed to be paid

cesspool: hole or pit in the ground for receiving waste matter or sewage from houses

chagrin: feeling humiliation or embarrassment

chandler: someone who deals in ship supplies

Charleston: vigorous, energetic dance originating in Charleston, US

charwoman: cleaning woman

chavy: child

cheaters: glasses

chesterfield: sofa with padded arms of the same height as its back; man's overcoat, with a straight cut, often with a velvet collar

chesty: someone with an over-inflated opinion of themselves

Chicago typewriter: machine gun

chilblains: red, itchy swelling to parts of face, fingers and toes caused by exposure to cold and damp

chink: money (from the noise coins make when they knock against each other)

chippy: young, promiscuous woman

chiseler: someone who steals or tries to cheat people

chiv/shiv: knife, razor or sharpened stick used as a weapon

choker: clergyman, referring to the clerical collar worn around the neck

cholera: disease of the small intestine, often fatal, marked by symptoms of thirst, cramps, vomiting and diarrhoea, caused by drinking water tainted with human waste. Victorians were hit with several cholera epidemics before sanitation conditions were improved

chopper: machine gun

choused: to have been cheated

christen: to remove identifying marks from; to use for the first time; to make something like new again

chump: someone easily deceived or tricked

clamp: to arrest someone; to clamp them in handcuffs

claustrophobia: abnormal dread of being imprisoned or confined in a close or narrow space

climbing the six-foot ladder: to die

clubhouse: police station

cly faking: to pick someone's pocket

coal scuttle: metal pail for carrying and pouring coal

come-hither: enticing or flirtatious behaviour

commencement: the beginning or start of something

complicit: involved in or aware of illegal activity

con: convict; someone with a criminal record

conjecture: an opinion based on insufficient or incomplete information

conspicuous: someone or something that stands out or looks unusual

constitutional: act that is in agreement with the constitution; the physical or mental condition of a person; taking a regular walk for one's health

cony catcher: cheat, also known as swindler, macer, leg or weasel

cooties: body lice

cordial: friendly or genial

costermonger: street peddler, usually selling fruits or vegetables

council of war: meeting of officials

covert: hidden or disguised

cozen: to cheat or trick someone, also known as double-cross or gyp

crackpot: person with crazy ideas

cracksman: safecracker, someone who cracks or breaks locks

crash out: escape or break out from prison

cravat: scarf or band of fabric worn around the neck and tied in a bow

cream puff: weak or soft person; pushover

crib: building, house or lodging; location of a prison

criminology: the scientific study of crime

croaker: nurse or doctor

crooner: singer

cross-bite: to cheat a cheater, to double-cross

croupier: person who runs a gaming table

crow: lookout during criminal activities; doctor

crowd-pleaser: shotgun

crown: to hit someone on the top of the head

crumpet: person, usually a woman, thought to be attractive or desirable

cryptic: having a mysterious or hidden meaning

cub reporter: inexperienced or young reporter

cuckoo: a person who is crazy or eccentric

cudgel: heavy stick used as a weapon

curare: poison derived from plants from South America

cursory: quick, superficial and not very thorough

curtains: the end; often used to describe someone about to be killed

cushy: easy or simple

cuspidor: bowl for spitting chewing tobacco into

customary: custom or practice of a particular time, place or society

D

daffy: small measure, usually spirits; medicine for children consisting of senna often mixed with gin

darb: person with money who often pays the bill; excellent or charming person

daresay: venture to say; think probable

deadlurk: empty premises

deadpan: tough guy; bodyguard; playing serious when you are joking

deaner: shilling

death warrant: official order for execution; often used as slang for someone who orders a killing

deference: to act with humility or respect

demimonde: term used for women of dubious social standing, sometimes because of promiscuity, that comes from nineteenth-century France

deprecate: disapprove of

despatch: send something; to send someone to carry out a task

deuce hog: two shillings

device: tuppence; an emblem or motto

Devil: the Devil, as depicted in Christianity and some other religions, stands as the enemy or opposite to God and tempts people to sin so that they go to Hell; the actual term 'Devil' comes from the Latin *diabolus*, meaning slanderous. Gothic characters are often tempted by agents of the Devil

dewskitch: giving someone a beating

dexterity: skilled with your hands; quick thinking

dibs: to have a claim on something

dick: private detective, also known as private dick, gumshoe, hawkshaw, private eye, sleuth, Shamus, Sherlock or peeper

dictograph: telephonic listening or recording device

diligence: public stagecoach; taking care or attention over something

ding: to throw something away; to take something that has been thrown away

dingy: drab or dreary

dip: pickpocket

diphtheria: infectious disease caused by germs in the throat, causing difficulty in breathing, fever and damage to the heart and nervous system

dip your bill: have a drink

disinformation: incorrect information given with the intent to deceive

dispatches: loaded dice; to send someone to carry out a task

divan: long, backless sofa

dive: disrespectable bar or restaurant

do down: to beat someone with fists, especially as a punishment

doing the book: serving a life sentence

doll up: to dress up or apply lots of make-up

dollyshop: unlicensed, often cheap, loan or pawn shop

don: eminent, professional or clever person; leader or head of a group

doozy: something outstanding or excellent

dope: information; drugs

Doppelgänger: literally translated from German as 'doublegoer'; the ghostly apparition of another, living person; double or alter ego

double-knock: applied to the door by a confident visitor, one who was known to the family and comfortable with the purpose of his visit (a single-knock signified a more timid caller, often of an inferior class)

dough: money

dovetail: joint in which two pieces interlock or join together; when two people work in harmony

dowager: widow with an inherited title or property from her deceased husband; distinguished, respected older woman

down: cause suspicion or doubt; to inform on a person, when used in the expression 'to put down on someone'

down-and-outer: person with no money, a sad case

drag: to draw on or smoke a cigarette

dragsman: someone who steals from carriages or coaches

draught: check or bill of exchange; a small quantity of liquid drunk in one mouthful

dreadnought: warm, thick, tightly woven woollen fabric

dressing: decorating something, such as a Christmas tree

drill: to shoot someone

drugstore: pharmacy that also sells other items, such as toiletries, stationery or cosmetics

dry-gulch: to ambush or attack from behind, often with the intent to kill

Dubliner: someone who hails from Dublin

duckett: street dealer or vendor's licence

duds: clothes

duffer: someone who sells allegedly stolen or worthless goods, also known as a 'hawker'

dwindle: diminish in size or amount

E

East India Company: private trading company established by the British government to trade with India, a country it effectively governed until the Indians fought back against the British in 1857

ecod: mild curse, most likely derived from 'My God'

economy: cheapness; giving better value

effrontery: shameless or insolent behaviour

egocentric: someone who thinks mainly of themselves; self-centred

electromagnet: metal made into a magnet by wrapping it in a coil of metal through which an electric current is passed

embezzle: steal or misappropriate funds belonging to someone else, often from the company a person works at

emetic: substance that causes vomiting

employ: to hire someone to work for you; if you were in the employ of or employed by someone, you worked for them

enigma: mysterious or puzzling person or event

entrapment: imprisoning someone; incarcerating or trapping someone, often in dark, strange or claustrophobic surroundings

E.O.: fairground gambling entertainment

epidemic: illness that spreads rapidly and extensively, affecting most of the people who come in contact with it

establishment: shop; place of business

ethnology: study of cultures and societies

evasive: avoiding a direct answer or action

exorcism: act of forcing the Devil, a demon or evil spirits from the body of someone who is possessed, done through religious prayer or rituals

expectations: chance of coming into an inheritance, property or money

extricate: to free oneself from a difficult situation

F

fadge: slang term for farthing

fakement: sham or trick, often used when begging

fall guy: someone who takes the blame for someone else; patsy

fallible: capable of making mistakes

fan: to feel surreptitiously under someone's clothing while they are wearing it, searching for objects to steal

faro: gambling game where people bet on the order of cards drawn

farthing: monetary unit worth a quarter of a penny; something almost worthless or of the lowest value

Fascism: far-right ideology

fastidious: highly concerned with detail and accuracy

fawney-dropping: trick where a criminal pretends to find a ring (which has no actual value) and sells it as an item of possible worth

fen: marsh or bog

ferret: to find information that has been well hidden

feverish: showing signs of having a fever; appearing over-excited or anxious

filibuster: legislative device that allows a senator to speak for as long as necessary to prevent new laws; to act in an obstructive manner

filing a beef: making a complaint

finesse: delicate or refined manner

finger: to inform on someone, usually to the police

fink: someone who informs to the police, also known as pigeon, rat or stoolie

finny: slang term for a five-pound note, also known as a five spot

fish: freshman in college

flam: lie or deception

flame-top: redheaded person, usually used to describe women

flash: to show off or try to impress; something special or expensive-looking

flash house: public house with criminals as clientele

flicks: movies

flimflam: trick or confidence scam

flimp: stealing or pickpocketing from a crowd

flivver: cheap or run-down car or airplane

floater: dead body found in water

floozy: cheap or disreputable woman; woman who brags about their partner, wants attention

flop house: cheap, often disreputable hotel

flue faker: chimney sweep, usually young boys

flunky: someone who works for someone else, often in a menial capacity

fly boy: man in the air force

fogill: handkerchief

foolhardy: rash or reckless

footman: servant in livery, usually in a mansion or palace; a servant who serves at table, tends the door or carriage, runs errands

forfeits: parlour games where each player needs to supply a correct answer and has a forfeit if the answer is not given

forgery: copied or counterfeited official document

four-stroke: type of internal combustion engine

foxed: discoloured by brown spots, often used to refer to books; to confuse or deceive

frame: to plant false evidence on someone

frisk: to search someone for contraband by running hands over their person or clothing

fruitless: unproductive; not achieving the desired results

furlong: unit of measurement equal to 201 m (660 ft), the length of the traditional furrow or plough trench on a farm

furrow: trench, groove or rut in the ground

furtherance: helping or advancing the progress of something

G

gaff: show or exhibition; cheap, smutty theatre; hoax or trick

gaiters: cloth or leather covering extending from the waist to the lower leg, usually buttoned up the side

gallows: structure on which criminals are hanged

gammon: misleading comment, meant to deceive

gammy: someone false who is not to be trusted

gander: to look at someone or something

garret: fob pocket in a waistcoat; room at the top of the house

gas station: establishment for refuelling motor cars, also known as a filling station

gattering: public house

gaudy: garish or brightly coloured

gee: guy

general post: mail that was sent from the London Post Office to the rest of England

ghost: phantom or spirit of somebody who has died and possibly not gone on to the afterlife. Often inspires fear or terror

gibbet: post with a projecting beam for hanging executed criminals, often done publicly as a warning to the public

gig: light, open, two-wheeled carriage drawn by a single horse

giggle-water: alcohol

gilded: covered in a thin layer of gold; person who wears a lot of jewellery

gill: unit of liquid equalling a quarter of a pint

gimlet: cocktail made with gin or vodka and lime juice

glim: light or fire; a source of light; begging by saying you are homeless due to fire; venereal disease

glob: lump or mass of a semi-liquid substance

glock: slow, half-witted person

glom: to steal something, also known as pinch

gold digger: someone after someone else's money, usually used to describe women who date or marry rich men

gonoph: petty, small-time criminal

good egg: a good person

goods: merchandise

goon: thug or heavy involved in criminal activities

goop: foolish person

goose-step: military parade step in which the leg is not bent

gothic: style of architecture, music, art or fiction generally associated with strange, frightening occurrences and mysterious or supernatural plots, characters or locations

gout: disease mainly affecting men, causing inflammation and swelling of the hands and feet, arthritis and deformity; caused by excess uric acid production

governess: woman employed to teach and care for children in a school or home

grabby: greedy; desiring something

grand: a thousand pounds or dollars

grease-monkey: mechanic

greatcoat: long, heavy overcoat worn outdoors, often with a short cape worn over the shoulders

grifter: small-time crook or swindler

grist: material used to support an argument

grog: mixture of alcohol, often rum, and water, named after an English admiral who diluted sailors' rum; rum-based cocktail

grotesque: misshapen or mutated character; something or someone unexpected, monstrous or bizarre

grouser: someone who complains a lot

guinea: gold coin, monetary value of twenty-one shillings or one pound and one shilling

gulpy: someone gullible or easy to fool

gussy: to dress up

gyroscope: device that spins freely around an axis in any direction, often used in automatic pilots or navigation systems

H

haberdasher: someone who sells personal items, often accessories such as thread or ribbons

hackie: hackney coach driver

hackney coach: carriage for hire, also known as hack

haggard: looking exhausted, gaunt or anxious

half inch: steal, rhyming slang for pinch

ham: actor, often not a good one

hammered for life: married

handcuff: engagement ring

hand in his checks: to die, usually by a planned killing

hanger-on: someone who attaches him- or herself to a group, not always wanted

hanky-panky: an easy woman; sexual activity

hansom cab: two-wheeled horse-drawn carriage where the driver sat on a high seat at the back so that the passengers had a clear view of the road

haunted: to be visited by a ghost or supernatural being

haybag: derogatory term for a woman

hayburner: a racehorse that never wins

haymaking: cutting and gathering hay to make haystacks

Haymarket Hector: pimp or whore's escort, especially those working in Haymarket and Leicester Square in London

heap: old or battered car

heap-clouter: car thief

heel: a creep or loser, usually a man

heist: hold-up or robbery

hell cat: wild woman; harpy

hen pen: women's prison

hepper: someone aware of the latest trends, especially in music

hick: unsophisticated person, often from the country; also known as rube or hillbilly

high roller: someone who places large, often reckless bets

hitch-hike: to travel for free by getting lifts in passing vehicles

hobo: tramp or homeless person

hock: to pawn something

hoisting: shoplifting; to lift something up

hooch: alcohol, usually inferior or illicit whisky, such as that made during Prohibition

Hooverville: shanty town built during the US Great Depression, named for the then-president, Herbert Hoover

hopping: picking hops used to make beer

horse's wishbone: something useless

hot shot: skilled, successful or daring person

hotsy-totsy: something pleasing or excellent

humbug: something insincere or nonsensical, meant to deceive or cheat people; used to express disbelief or disgust; a hoax or fraud

humdinger: someone or something outstanding or brilliant

hunch: feeling based on intuition; to bend the shoulders and neck forwards

hurly-burly: busy or noisy activity

hustle: to move someone by force; to cheat or swindle

hykey: pride, arrogance

hyperinflation: very rapid, out-of-control economic inflation

hysteria: uncontrolled or exaggerated emotion

I

ice: diamonds; also used as a verb to describe killing someone

incongruous: out of place or not suited to a situation

incubus: name for a male demon, thought to be a fallen angel, who forces himself sexually upon sleeping women, which often resulted in the birth of a demon or deformed, half-human child

influenza/flu: viral illness causing aching joints, fever, headaches, sore throat, cough and sneezing, even followed by death in Victorian times

injunction: official order or warning

in lavender: to hide from the police; to pawn something for money; to be dead

innuendo: oblique or suggestive hint or remark

inoculate: vaccinate to give immunity against disease

Inquisition: organization founded by the Catholic Church charged with the eradication of heresy or acting against God, by which those found guilty were often put to death

insinuate: to hint or imply something unpleasantly

insurrecto: insurgent or rebel

interred: buried

intrigue: secret plans; to interest or fascinate

ironmonger: someone who sells metal goods, tools and hardware

irons: guns, usually pistols or revolvers

J

jabber: talk quickly with excitement

Jack: detective; term sometimes used to address a stranger

Jack rabbit blood: what someone who habitually escapes prison is said to have

jalopy: broken-down car

java: coffee

Jazz Age: 1920s period in America in which jazz music and dance became very popular and where many people had more freedom and prosperity

jemmy: housebreaker's tool used on locks; someone smart or superior

jinx: something that brings bad luck

jitney: nickel

jive: fast jazz music and dance; to mislead someone; crazy talk

joey: slang term for a four-pence piece

joint: restaurant, bar or club of questionable reputation

jolly: disturbance or brawl; to be cheerful or happy

journeyman: skilled worker who has finished an apprenticeship and is qualified to hire himself out for work

jovial: cheerful or friendly

joyride: a reckless or enjoyable ride in a moving vehicle, usually a car

Judy: term for a woman, usually a prostitute

jump: ground-floor window, or a burglary committed by entering through the window

K

kecks: slang term for trousers

keen: attractive person

ken: house, lodging or public house

kept in lumber: to be kept in confinement

kick off: beginning of a violent event, to kill someone

kidsman: organizer of child thieves

killer: someone or something excellent

killjoy: someone who spoils other people's fun, often on purpose

kinetoscopic: early motion-picture device which allowed a single person to view film or images through a peephole

kitchenette: small kitchen, or a kitchen in one part of another room

kith: someone's friends, neighbours or relatives

Klondiking: prospecting for gold in the Klondike River

knapped: pregnant

knaves: jacks in a deck of cards

knee breeches: trousers that reach the knee

knock up: to bang loudly on someone's door to wake them up

know life, to: to be familiar in criminal ways; to be street-wise

kosher: fair or genuine

L

lackin/lakin: slang term for a wife

laconic: succinct or taciturn person

ladybird: slang term for a prostitute

lady-killer: very attractive man who is found irresistible by many women

lag: convict; someone sentenced to transportation or prison

larder: cool food-storage area

laudanum: solution of opium and alcohol used as pain relief or to aid sleep, highly addictive

lay off: to stop doing something; to fire someone

les vaches: French for cows, used to describe police officers

liberal: generous; tolerant or open-minded

lick: small amount

link boy: boy who carries a torch to light a person's way through the dark streets

live-wire: exciting or energetic person

loaded: rich

lodger: person paying rent to stay in a room (or bed) in somebody else's house

logged: to transport criminals

lollapalooza: attractive or impressive person

lollipop: weak or inexperienced person; to inform on someone

loogan: hoodlum or petty gangster; man with a gun

loony bin: mental asylum

louse: unpleasant or mean person

lowdown: underhand or mean trick; information or facts

lug: ear; bullet

luggers: earrings

lulu: attractive woman, a knockout

lumber: wood used for building or woodworking, often second-hand furniture; to pawn something; to go to prison

lurker: criminal; beggar or someone who dresses as a beggar for money

lush: alcoholic drink; someone who drinks too much alcohol; luxurious

M

Machiavellian: someone who cheats and schemes. Often used to describe unscrupulous politicians

mag: slang term for a ha'pence piece

magistrate: judge for trials of misdemeanours; civil officer who upholds the law

maid-of-all-work: a girl, usually young, hired as the only servant in the house and required to do any job asked of her

mail coach: carrier of the mail and a limited number of passengers. Replaced in the mid-nineteenth century by the railroad

malodorous: having an unpleasant odour

malt: grain, such as barley, that has been allowed to ferment. Used for brewing beer and sometimes whisky

mandrake: homosexual; type of plant

mark: the victim of a crime

market day: the regular day each week when country people would bring their livestock and goods to sell in town

market town: town that regularly held a market, usually the largest town of a farming area

masochism: psychosexual perversion whereby someone gains erotic pleasure by having pain, abuse or humiliation inflicted on them

materially reduced: having your circumstances and/or finances reduced or lessened

maudlin: overly emotional or self-pitying state, often brought on by alcohol

mead: fermented alcoholic drink made of water, honey, malt, yeast and sometimes spices

meat hooks: hands

meat wagon: ambulance or hearse

mecks: alcohol, usually wine or spirits

media: mass communication. Originally used to describe the advertising industry

mellow: relaxed or calm

mercenary: person who puts making money over scruples; professional hired soldier

mescal/mezcal: agave plant used to make an alcoholic drink, usually from Mexico or the southwest of the US

messrs: plural of Mr, used when referring to more than one man

metamorphosis: change or complete transformation in physical form, shape or structure, thought to be caused by supernatural powers

Michaelmas: Christian festival celebrating the archangel Michael, celebrated on 29 September, one of the four quarters of the year

Mickey: a drug, usually put into a drink. Also known as a Mickey Finn

Mickey-Mouse: unimportant or inferior

middle class: people who earn enough money to live comfortably, often in a skilled profession, such as doctors and lawyers

mill: fight or boxing match; machine gun

mist: cloud of water particles that condense in the atmosphere, often used in Gothic literature to obscure objects or to prelude something or someone terrifying

mizzle: steal or disappear; fine rain

mob: gang

mobsman: conman or pickpocket, usually smartly dressed

moll buzzer: someone who robs women

mollify: to placate or appease someone

mollisher: woman, often associated with a criminal. Also known as a moll

moniker/monniker: signature; first name

mortality: death rate; the number of deaths in a given time or given group

moucher/moocher: rural vagrant or beggar; someone who lives on the road

mourning clothes: black garments worn after a relative dies, the length of which depended on your relationship to the deceased

mouthpiece: lawyer

muck raker: someone who uncovers scandalous information about famous people and then publishes it

muck snipe: someone down on their luck

muffler: scarf

mug: face; fool

mug-hunter: street thief or pickpocket, from which the modern term 'mugger' comes

mutcher: pickpocket who usually steals from drunks

mutton: meat from a sheep, cheaper and less tender than lamb

myriad: a great number or amount

N

nail: steal; to catch someone who is guilty of a crime

narcissism: excessive interest in one's own appearance or self

necromancy: black art of conversing with the spirits of the dead, usually done to predict or influence the future, also for making the dead perform tasks for you; witchcraft or sorcery

nefarious: criminal or immoral activity

nethers: charges or rent for lodgings

netherskens: cheap, unsavoury lodging houses; flophouses

Nevada gas: cyanide, gas used in gas chamber

newshawk: reporter

newsreader: person who reads news stories that are being broadcast

nib: point of a pen, often a fountain pen

nibbed: arrested

nick: to steal or con

nickel-and-dime: of little importance; to eat away at someone, often through small but unfair charges

nickey: slow or simple-minded

nightmare: frightening or unsettling dream, often used in Gothic literature to heighten drama or fear; a malign spirit thought to haunt or suffocate people during sleep

nitro: nitroglycerine, an explosive substance

nobble: to inflict severe pain or bodily harm

noggin: head; also known as noodle

nonchalant: calm and relaxed in appearance

nose: informant or spy; to try to find something out

nosegay: small bunch of flowers

notions: small personal items, such as a handkerchief or snuffbox

numerous: many in number; frequent

nuts: expression of distaste or annoyance; used to describe someone crazy

O

oblivious: not concerned with what is happening

obsequious: excessively attentive or fawning

obstacle: something in the way or that blocks things from happening

occult: relating to the supernatural, witchcraft or magic; something not capable of being understood by ordinary people but known only by the initiated

occupation: job, means of earning a living

odour: smell

omnibus: single- or double-decker bus which was pulled by horses, capable of carrying lots of people

on fire: a wanted man

on the fly: while in motion, moving quickly; something done quickly or spontaneously

on the lam: on the run

on the outs: to have an argument or disagreement

on the square: truthful, honest

opium: drug extracted from the dried juice and seeds of the opium poppy which is highly addictive

orthodox: following established rules of religion or society; proper way of behaving

out-and-outer: a person who goes to extremes or excels at something

outdoor relief: charity for the poor which did not require them to enter the workhouse, eliminated in 1834 by the New Poor Law to stop people playing the system

out of twig: unrecognizable, in disguise

outsider: instrument used for opening a lock from the wrong side; stranger or interloper

P

pack: to carry a gun

paddingken: tramp's lodgings

page: boy or young man working as a servant or running errands

pall: detect; become dull or fade; gloomy atmosphere or mood

palmer: shoplifter; someone who 'palms' items to steal them

palooka: clumsy person; inexperienced boxer

palsy: medical condition producing uncontrollable shaking of the muscles

pansy: weak person or pushover

paper-hanger: someone who passes fake cheques

paraphernalia: belongings, equipment

parley: conference between two opposing sides

parlour: living room, usually for guests

paste: to punch someone

patent: official licence for the ownership and rights of an invention

patterer: someone who earns a living by recitation of a hawker's sales talk, convincing people to buy goods

peach: inform or give information against someone, often leading to imprisonment

pea-coat: short, heavy, double-breasted overcoat worn by seamen, usually dark blue or black

peelers: nickname for the new London police force, organized by Sir Robert Peel in 1829

penny-farthing bicycle: bicycle with a large front wheel, to which the pedals were attached, and a much smaller back wheel

pertaining to: concerning or to do with

peter man: safe cracker, also known as a box worker

phenomenon: fact or occurrence that is out of the ordinary or hard to believe, even though it can be seen

picnic: any informal social gathering for which each guest provides a share of the food; informal meal eaten outside

pie-eyed: very drunk

pigeon: victim; also known as a plant

pigeonhole: to label someone, often unfairly; small recess in a dovecote for a pigeon to nest in; compartment for letters

pill: unpleasant person

pinch: to steal or put someone under financial pressure; to arrest; a measurement of snuff

ping-pong: table tennis; rapid conversation

pinked: to be shot or stabbed

Pinkerton: detective who worked for the Pinkerton National Detective Agency, the first private detection agency in the US

pinochle: card game in which players use forty-eight cards to win tricks

pint-sized: holds sixteen ounces; small or diminutive

pleurisy: inflammation of the lungs producing a fever, hacking cough, sharp chest pain and difficulty in breathing

polygraph: machine that measures pulse, breathing rates and other physiological characteristics, used in lie-detector tests

poorhouse: place where poor, old or sick people lived, where anyone able was put to work; also known as the workhouse

portrait: likeness of an individual or group created through photography or in paintings

possession: being controlled by an evil, demonic or supernatural force

postboy: someone working at a post house or inn who helped to change the horses on coaches on long journeys

post chaise: enclosed, four-wheeled, horse-drawn carriage, used to transport mail and passengers

postern: small back entrance or gate

posting: travelling in a coach or carriage, stopping along the way in post houses or inns to change horses

prankster: someone who often plays pranks

prater: idle, foolish talk; bogus preacher

proctor: court officer who manages the affairs of others, answering to an attorney or solicitor

prodigious: great in amount or size; a lot

profane: vulgar or coarse; disrespect for religious or sacred topics

proprietor: owner of a commercial or business enterprise

prowler: person attempting to commit burglary

puckering: jabbering; speaking in an incomprehensible manner

pug: boxer

punch-drunk: groggy feeling acquired from too many punches to the head

punctilious: someone who acts in a very exact or particular way

punishers: men hired to give beatings or 'nobblings'

punk out: to back out of something, often from fear

purport: to claim something, sometimes falsely

pursuit: the act of chasing after someone, usually to attack or catch them, and often inspiring fear

push: slang term for money

pyramiding: building up stocks when the price is favourable

Q

quadrille: card game for four players using forty cards; dance

quagmire: difficult or embarrassing situation; waterlogged, boggy ground

quarter days: four days of the year when quarterly payments were made: Lady Day (25 March), Midsummer (24 June), Michaelmas (29 September) and Christmas (25 December)

quay: wharf or platform in a port or harbour where ships are loaded or unloaded

queen: male homosexual

queer bird: someone who has been in prison and returns to crime

quick-lime: white, corrosive alkaline substance consisting of calcium oxide, acquired by heating limestone

quid: slang term for pound

R

racket: illicit or dishonest occupation or activity; loud, unpleasant noise

radge: mad person

rag and bone shop: shop that bought and sold rags that were made into paper, and bones used for manure

ramshackle: run-down object, often a house or vehicle

rap sheet: record of arrests

rat: to inform on criminal activity

rattle: to disturb someone

rattler: a wanted man

reader: pocketbook or wallet

real McCoy: someone or something real or genuine

recession: period of economic decline

recherché: exotic, rare or unusual

recourse: help required in times of trouble

reefer: marijuana cigarette, also known as a joint

reflation: expanding economic output with the aim of preventing deflation

repeater: pocket watch that chimed on the hour or quarter past the hour, making it easier to tell the time in the dark

restorative: something taken to restore health or strength

resurrectionist: body snatcher; someone who steals corpses from graves, usually to sell to medical students. Legally, only the bodies of criminals could be used, but demand for corpses was so high that resurrectionists dug up the graves of the recently deceased

reticent: uncommunicative, not eager to reveal one's thoughts

revenant: dead person who has returned to terrorize or to avenge a score with someone living

revenge: act of avenging or repaying someone for a harm that the person has caused; to punish someone in retaliation for something done to them or to a loved one, carried out by humans or by spirits; a popular theme in Gothic literature

ribald: vulgar, lewd humour, often involving jokes about sex

ricin: poison derived from the seed of the castor oil plant

ringer: fake; a person or thing who passes off as someone or something else

rinky-dink: old-fashioned

ritzy: fancy or expensive

roller: thief who robs drunks; prostitute who steals from her (usually drunk) customers

Romanticism: arts and literature of the Romantic movement, characterized by the passion, emotion and often danger of love and associated feelings

rookery: urban slum or ghetto; nesting place for rooks

Rothschild, to come to the: to brag that you are rich

round heels: promiscuous or easy woman

rubbernecks: people who stand around to watch a crime or accident

ruffles: slang term for handcuffs

ruin: to go out of business; tom lose all your money or possessions

rummy: card game in which the aim is to match cards by rank or sequence

rum rigging: nice or expensive clothes

S

sabotage: deliberate disruption caused by disputes, often for political purposes

saddle: loaf; cut of meat

sadism: perversion where one person gains sexual gratification by causing physical or mental pain on others, first coined to describe the writings of the Marquis de Sade; delight in torment or excessive cruelty

saloon: bar or public house; type of car

salubrity: health or well-being

Salvation Army: worldwide religious organization founded by William Booth in 1865; it provided aid to the poor, helped those in need and sought to bring people back to God

sanatorium: medical facility, often for those with long-term conditions

sap: fool or fall guy, also known as a dope

Saturday-night special: cheap or home-made weapon

saveloy: highly seasoned, spicy, smoked pork sausage, sold as a snack ready to eat

scaldrum dodge: gaining sympathy, begging by means of fake or self-inflicted wounds

scalp-collector: attractive female whom men easily fall for

scandal-monger: someone who spreads scandal or gossip

scare-head: alarming or sensationalist newspaper headline

scarlet fever: infection usually suffered by children, causing a red rash and high fever; also called Scarlatina

science fiction: fiction based on futuristic or scientific advances, often including life on other planets or time travel

scran: slang term for food

scrap: to cancel something

screever: forger; writer of fake documents

scullery: area for dish-washing, preparing food and storing dishes

sealing wax: wax that is soft when heated, used to seal letters – red for business letters, black for mourning and other colours for general correspondence

sedan chair: covered chair to which two long poles were attached and on which a person was carried around by chairmen

seltzer: soda water

sepulchre: tomb or monument

servant's lurk: public house used primarily by crooked or dismissed servants

shake down: to search someone thoroughly; to cheat or defraud

shake lurk: begging under false pretences, usually those of being a shipwrecked, out-of-work seaman

sham: false or faked document; to cheat someone or pass money you know to be bad or false

shank: home-made knife, often used in prisons

sharp: conman, card swindler

shilling: unit of money equal to five pence in today's money

shine: bootleg alcohol, also known as moonshine

shirkster: layabout, work-shy

shofulman: someone who makes or passes bad money

shook a dummy: to pick someone's pocket

shoot the works: lay all gambling winnings on one more throw of the dice, spin of the roulette wheel or last hand of cards

sidekick: friend or associate of someone who is often a more well-known or successful person

simp: silly or stupid person

Sing Sing: a New York prison well known for its severe discipline

siphon: bottle used to dispense carbonated water

skein: length of wound-up thread

skid row: poor, run-down part of town, also known as skid road

skinful: a lot of or too much alcohol

slap-bang job: public house frequented by thieves where no credit is given

slay: to say something very funny

slick box: fixed dice game

slum: ghetto

smasher: someone who passes bad or false money

smelting: process of extracting metal from ore by applying heat

smoking bishop: drink made at Christmas from heated red wine or port flavoured with oranges, sugar and spices, so named because of its deep purple colour and traditionally heated with a red-hot poker

snakesman: small boy used for housebreaking, as they could enter a house through a small gap

snarky: to be annoyed or irritable

snatch: to kidnap someone

snoozer: someone who steals from sleeping guests in hotels

snowing: stealing clothes that have been hung out on a washing line to dry

society squib: someone well known in society for being dynamic

sock: punch; stocking

soiled dove: prostitute

somnambulism: sleepwalking, a dissociated mental state that occurs during deep sleep when, in Gothic literature, people would do things they would not normally do

son of a gun: piece of work, often used affectionately

sourpuss: sullen or unpleasant person

speakeasy: illicit bar, club or store that sells alcohol

spectre: ghost

speculate: invest in ventures or stocks to make money, with the risk of financial loss

speed cop: police officer who checks the speeds of passing motorists

speedo: speedometer on a car

spike: slang term for the workhouse

sponging-house: temporary prison for those who cannot pay their debts, prior to them being sent to a prison such as Marshalsea in London

spontaneous human combustion: combustion of a human (alive or dead), with no perceived ignition source

squalor: unpleasant state caused by dereliction, lack of money or neglect

square cove: honest person, someone who will not steal or commit a crime

srew: skeleton key, for use in burglaries

stampers: shoes

stand up: to not turn up for a date

steal a march: to get the better of someone

stenographer: someone who transcribes speech into shorthand. Often works in an office or the courts to record official proceedings

stiff: dead body

stir crazy: to become frustrated or restless from staying inside

stool-pigeon: informer, spy or plant

stranglehold: to have control over something; to choke someone using an illegal wrestling hold

stretch: to hang someone

stricken: affected by; suffering or struck by

strike: refusal to work due to a protest; to hit someone

sublime: to be awed, moved or transported by something, such as religion, beauty or emotions; used in Gothic literature as the thrill of being terrified, because fear inspires such strong emotions

subscription: collection of money paid over a period of time; fee to be paid; donation given to a charitable cause

subterfuge: deceit or trickery used to achieve a specific goal

subway: underground railway; tunnel for pedestrians to walk under a road

succubus: female demon, counterpart of the incubus (*q.v.*)

sucker: naïve person who might fall for a con

sumptuous: grand, expensive or splendid

supernatural: phenomena or events that seem unbelievable or cannot be explained by natural laws; occurrences relating to magic or the occult

superstition: deep-seated but often irrational belief in something, such as an action or ritual, that is thought to bring good or bad luck

swanky: fancy or luxurious

sweetmeat: sweet treat, such as candy or candied fruit, often served at the end of a meal

swell: elegantly or stylishly dressed gentleman; expensive dress

swifty: someone with quick reflexes

T

tail: someone who is following someone else

tallow: hard, fatty substance from sheep or oxen, used to make candles or soap

taper: small, slim wax candle, narrower at the top than at the bottom

taproom: bar room in a public house where working-class people ate and drank, as opposed to the parlour, which was used by the middle classes

tea leaf: rhyming slang for thief

tearjerker: sad story, book or movie

teetotaller: someone who completely abstains from alcohol, an activity which gained in popularity in the middle classes during Victorian times

temporize: to avoid confirming or deciding something in order to buy time

tenement: room or rooms forming a separate living space in a house

thermite: explosive substance

thick: to be close to someone; a confidant

thicker: slang for sovereign or pound

thicket: dense or overgrown trees or shrubs

thick 'un: slang term for sovereign

thriving: to be profitable or successful; flourishing

ticket: the licence of a private investigator

tight: feeling tipsy or slightly drunk, often pleasantly so

tip your dandle: to shake hands in order to seal an agreement or deal

toff: elegant or stylish gentleman; someone rich or upper class

toffken: house in which well-to-do, upper-class people lived

toke: slang term for bread

tomcat: gigolo; person who prowls for sexual activity

tooling: experienced pickpocket

topped: to be hung

torch: to commit arson; an arsonist

tradesman: man in a skilled trade, such as a carpenter or plumber; shopkeeper; someone who buys and sells goods

transportation: when exiled British criminals were sent to the colonies, usually Australia, as punishment

treasury: government or corporation's revenue or funds

tremulous: quavering or trembling

triggerman: hired killer, also known as a hatchetman or dropper

trolleybus: bus powered by electricity supplied through overhead cables

turnkey: jailor; keeper of keys

turnpike: toll road that people paid to travel on, the money from which was used to keep the road in good condition

tussle: fight or struggle

twirls: keys, usually skeleton keys

two-time loser: someone who has been convicted and/or incarcerated twice

typhoid: serious, often fatal illness caused by drinking polluted water (contaminated by sewage)

tyro: inexperienced person; beginner or apprentice

U

uncanny: something or someone too strange, weird or eerie to be natural or human; supernatural

under and over: fairground game, often used to swindle people

unfurnished upper storey: a person with not much intelligence

union workhouse: workhouse for the poor, which parishes were obligated to provide after the 1834 New Poor Law

unprovided for: left with no money or security

unsavoury: unpleasant or disagreeable

unsolicited: something not asked for or requested

upper class: people from rich, moneyed families, such as landowners or aristocracy

uptown: term most commonly used in New York City to describe Harlem

V

vag: vagrant, a down-and-out

vamp: to steal; to pawn something; to seduce or manipulate someone

vampire: supernatural being of a malignant nature, believed to suck the blood of the living for sustenance, from European folklore

vantage point: viewing point, often high up; perspective or way of thinking

vapour: steam

vendetta: feud caused by murder, whereby the family members seek vengeance

venture: risky trip or undertaking

verbiage: how something is expressed, often with too many words

veriest: emphasises a description; the most

verisimilitude: quality of being true or real

vespers: evening church service, prayers

vestibule: lobby or hall; antechamber

vestige: trace or sign of something no longer present

vexation: feeling annoyed or irritated

viands: tasty articles of food

vie with: compete with someone; strive for superiority

vintner: wine maker or merchant

voyeur: someone who watches others engaged in sexual activity

W

ward: child or youth under the care and control of a guardian

washhouse: building where clothes were washed, often shared

wassail: spiced ale or wine served at Christmas or other festive occasions

watch: men chosen to guard the streets at night, periodically calling out the time and ensuring that no crimes were being committed

weeping willow: rhyming slang for pillow

weeps: a person, usually a woman, with a tendency to cry

welcher: someone who owes money and does not pay it back

werewolf: someone who is human by day and turns into a wolf at night, living off humans, animals or even corpses, from European folklore

whimsical: playful or capricious behaviour

whist: popular card game

whistle and flute: rhyming slang for suit

wholesome: healthy, clean-living; decent

whoopee: a good time; sexual activity

whooping cough: infectious disease, often affecting children, that causes heavy coughing and makes it hard to breathe

whorl: pattern of circles or spirals; method by which fingerprints are identified

wino: an alcoholic, often homeless

wisecrack: joke or humorous remark

wisenheimer: smug or arrogant person

witchcraft: spells and magic performed by a witch; in Gothic fiction the witch is usually depicted as an old, hag-like crone or a beautiful, seductive young woman

without: outside, usually referring to outside the house in which someone is

work capitol: to commit a crime punishable by death

workhouses: place where the sick, poor, old and those in debt went or were sent for food and shelter. The New Poor Law (1834) made the workhouse almost a prison for the poor, who had to work hard in miserable conditions, often fed on gruel only and separated from their families

working class: those in heavy manual labour, usually for low, hourly wages, such as farm labourers, factory workers and builders

world-beater: someone who thinks he/she can take on the world; well-regarded person

worrit: worry; worry-wort

wrecking crew: gang, generally carrying out violence

Y

yack: slang term for a watch

yarn: a story, often exaggerated or unlikely

yegg: habitual criminal

yellow journalism: journalism based on little proven research; sensationalist journalism

yennap: slang term for a penny

youse: slang plural form of 'you'

Z

zipper: interlocking fastening used for clothes, bags and other items

COLLECTABLE CRIME CLASSICS
Complete & Unabridged

The new FLAME TREE COLLECTABLE CRIME
CLASSICS are chosen to create a delightful and
timeless home library. Each stunning edition
features deluxe cover treatments, ribbon
markers, luxury endpapers and gilded edges.
The unabridged text is accompanied by a
Glossary of Crime, Mystery and Literary Terms
produced for the modern reader.

See our expanding range at
flametreepublishing.com